FANGS AND FRONTPAGES

A RAVENS HOLLOW INVESTIGATION
BOOK ONE

ELLA STONE

PAPER CAT PUBLISHING

Also by Ella Stone

BY ELLA STONE & HEATHER G HARRIS

The Witchlight Magical Mysteries

Text copyright © 2025 Ella Stone

Paper Cat Publishing

ISBN: 978-1-915346-57-5

Edited by Dayna Hart
Cover by Christian Bentulan

ONE

L osing your luggage is never good. Losing your luggage when it contains a basilisk egg, only hours away from hatching, is a code-red disaster.

'There are only twelve of us on this flight,' I said. 'How can you have lost a piece of luggage? This package is the entire reason we had to make this stopover.'

It was taking all my control not to whip out my fangs. It had only been three weeks since I was turned into a vampire, and there'd been a pretty steep learning curve. One that led to an undeniable conclusion: I was so out of my depth, it was scary.

This damn egg and the fact that I'd agreed to *drop it off* as a favour to my best friend, Donna, was the final straw.

'This is a time-sensitive issue,' I added. 'Seriously time-sensitive. I need that bag.'

I had no idea how old a basilisk hatchling had to be before it had the ability to turn you to stone or whatever. Nor did I want to find out.

The pilot tilted his head to the side and scratched behind his ear as though he was trying to work out the answer to a cryptic crossword clue. Not that he gave the impression of someone who did crosswords. No, he seemed like the type of person who chose Password123 as the login for all his personal details, then still couldn't remember them. How the hell he had flown us here was a miracle.

'All right, all right, it'll be here somewhere,' he said. 'Don't get your knickers in a twist.'

Nothing like an old-fashioned sexist saying to stoke my dislike for someone, and that urge to flash my fangs was growing stronger by the second. Unfortunately, other than the people waiting on the plane, the island was in the middle of the Atlantic Ocean and entirely uninhabited. The last thing I wanted was for the pilot to decide that the world could do without one more recently turned vampire and leave me stranded here.

Then there was the added issue of not knowing what type of para he was. The last thing I needed was to arrive at my new home, cursed or covered in scales, and from what I had seen of the magical world so far, both felt like distinct possibilities. Meaning fake smiles and subtle hints of urgency were the tactic.

Brilliant.

A month ago, I would've been excited about this. Returning a basilisk egg that had been trafficked to the UK to its natural habitat would have been the biggest story of my life. Other than the one that ended up with me in this undead state. But just like this situation with the egg, that wasn't something I could write about. Not yet, anyway. Fingers crossed, my new job would change that.

Unfortunately, before I could restart my life and embrace all the possibilities waiting for me, I had to find this damn egg and get it to a suitable hatching ground.

'Are you sure you gave it to me?' the pilot asked as he scratched the other side of his head.

Was it lice? Or a skin condition? Or maybe a nervous twitch because he could see the way my hands were starting to flex?

'What did you say the bag looks like again?'

'It's a rucksack,' I said slowly. 'Red. About this high.' I held my hands about twenty inches apart. 'The one you said I shouldn't take to my seat because I told you it was extremely fragile. It was also the reason you were given a massive bonus to add this stop to the trip.'

The pilot's eyes widened.

'Oh, *that*. Shoulda just said. It's up front with me. Hang on a sec.'

While I stifled a hiss, the pilot disappeared into the small plane and returned minutes later with the bag. Relief flooded through me as I took it from him.

'You're waiting here, right?' I asked, enunciating every word clearly.

The last thing I needed was for him to misunderstand and leave me alone on this island with a newly hatched – and probably very hungry – basilisk. Even as a vampire, that wasn't something I fancied.

'Weather's not looking great,' he replied. 'Reckon I've got about twenty minutes before I'll need to leave. Can't risk staying down here if the storm hits. No shelter. What's in the bag, anyway? Was hoping to have a peek before you took it.'

Twenty minutes. I could work with that, couldn't I? Not that I had a choice.

'I'll be back,' I said, already running away from the thin strip of tarmac and into the undergrowth. 'Do not leave without me.'

'Donna is my best friend. I will not bite my best friend for this. Donna is my best friend. I will not bite my best friend.'

It was a short mantra, but I repeated it dozens of times as I stumbled through the grasses. Vampires had amazing speed. I learned that the night I was turned, but in order to pick up speed, I needed an unobstructed area to run over. Other than the small patch of tarmac where we'd landed, there was none of that on the island. Were there ravines? Yes. Vines, absolutely. Areas of swamp so dense that a normal human would have put one foot in them and been trapped for all eternity? You betcha.

And I've always said I'll do anything for a story, but there was no story here. At least, not one where I could put my name on the by-line. Donna had been very clear about that. This was a need-to-know mission. Even the people at my new paper at Ravens Hollow weren't to learn what I had done. No, I was doing this out of the goodness of my cold, unbeating heart.

'Just find some fresh water, away from the landing strip,' Donna had told me. 'Then put the egg somewhere near the water's edge. It should all be straightforward.'

Like heck it was. I was trudging through a swamp and had been bitten by at least a dozen leeches. Not that they got anything out of me. Was it wrong that I felt a smug sense of satisfaction watching them latch on in hope, only to shrivel up and fall off seconds later? No, I didn't think so.

Still, no matter how many leeches bit me, it still didn't erase the nervous churning in my gut. Donna had repeatedly stressed to me that the instant a basilisk hatched, it would begin searching for food. And if you were the nearest living thing to it when that happened, then you could pretty much guarantee that you were on the menu. Given that I technically wasn't living anymore, I wasn't sure if I still counted as basilisk food, but I wasn't about to take that risk.

Back in London, Donna had been my editor-in-chief, and one of her sources had dumped the egg at the office when they'd been worried about a potential raid by the magical police. Trafficked mythical animals were, apparently, a massive business, and Donna couldn't turn the item over without landing her source in deep trouble. Something she wasn't prepared to do. So, when the opportunity to get rid of it via me arose, she took it. And I couldn't complain, really. Not given everything she'd done for me. It was just hard to remember that while I was knee deep in sludge.

'I will not bite my best friend,' I hissed again as I tried to work out which direction I should go in.

More than once, I was tempted to leave the egg in the swamp and say I was done, but fresh water meant something like a stream or river. Running water, which moved and gurgled. That's what I was trying to listen for, but damn it, there were a lot of sounds. And trying to focus on them was a near impossibility.

There was only really one person to blame for my senses not being as honed as they should be. And annoyingly, that was me. Well, me and Andy, I supposed. Sure, the nerves over my newly turned state, combined with a massive to-do list that came from moving country, played some part in how little work I'd put into refining my skills, but it didn't help that anytime I was left on my own, I would think about the way Andy had dumped me, ending our engagement and breaking my heart. This, in turn, meant the one sound I heard most constantly was sobbing as I blew my nose into yet another tissue. It turned out that my personally-provided background noise of crying made it difficult for me to train my other senses.

As such, my hearing homed in wherever it wanted. Unable to focus on distances or directions, the way Donna assured me I should be able to do. Let alone pick out specific sounds or voices. Still, time was running out. If there was ever a time to master vampire hearing, it was now.

As another leech dropped from my leg, I figured that closing my eyes was probably the first step to focusing on my hearing. Taking a deep breath in, I tried to steady my thoughts, only for my arms to start tingling.

'Crap, not now.'

This was my third sunlight ward in as many weeks, but despite the witches telling me they would last a full month, none of them had even made the one-week mark yet. Tingling was the first sign that they were weakening, and while I probably still had a good few hours until it stopped working, that wasn't a risk I wanted to take. I needed to get this damn egg near a freshwater source now.

Finally, I picked up the sound of a slight gurgle. I turned my head, hoping that my ears would work like satellites, so I could pinpoint the direction. It was far from a perfect method, but I was eighty percent sure I knew where it was coming from. I picked up the pace and finally pulled myself out of the other side of the swamp.

'Thank god,' I said, spotting a stream a few hundred feet ahead. I had no idea how long it had been since I left the plane, but I knew I needed to get back. Thankfully, this stretch of land was clear enough that I managed to pick up some speed, and in a matter of moments, I had placed the egg in a patch of dense reeds. Then, after slinging the backpack over my shoulder, I turned straight back around the way I came.

The minute the plane came into view, I sprinted.

'I'm sorry! I'm sorry!' I yelled to the pilot, who stood at the top of the steps, a definite scowl on his face.

'Told you to be back 'ere five minutes ago,' he growled.

'I know. I know you did, but I'm here now,' I said, dropping my hands onto my knees.

Why I was panting, I have no idea. I was a vampire. I didn't need oxygen, but hey, I guess some habits die hard.

'I'm sorry,' I repeated. 'We can go now.'

I was more than ready to get on the plane away from the sunlight that was continuing to prickle my forearms, but as I moved towards the bottom step, the pilot jumped down to block me. The drop was at least ten feet, yet he landed on the step above me with perfect ease, which meant he was either a para too or seriously into parkour. I was willing to bet it was the former.

'You're not coming on my plane like that,' he said. 'I've got another job after this one. Very important clients. If I let you on here, things will need cleaning top to bottom first.'

'What are you—' I was about to continue my objection when I glanced down at myself and stopped. My jeans were caked in mud all the way up to my thighs, and my shoes looked as though they'd been forged from the swamp itself. There were also several shrivelled-up leeches encased in the sludge.

'Fine, yes,' I said in agreement. 'The rest of my clothes are in the hold. If I could just grab my bag—'

He shook his head. 'We're not opening the hold now. Didn't you 'ear me say we've gotta get going? Don't you 'ave something else to wear in that bag of yours? If not, you'll just 'ave to strip.'

'Strip?'

There was no chance of that happening. I didn't know what type of vampires this guy had met before, but I was the very professional type who kept all their clothes on in public. Still, I stood there, acutely aware of the rucksack's weight pushing down on my shoulder. I had taken the basilisk egg out of it, but it wasn't entirely empty.

'No,' I said, finally shaking my head. 'You have to open the hold. There's nothing in there I can wear.'

His eyes narrowed. 'You're lying.'

'I'm not—'

'Yes, you are. I can tell.'

I wasn't sure if he meant he could tell because I couldn't meet his eyes or because he was some supernatural lie detector. A knot formed in my stomach. If it was the latter, then the last thing I wanted was trouble with the magical community before I'd even properly integrated into it.

'It's not exactly... the type of thing you'd wear in public,' I said.

He arched an eyebrow. 'Is it the type of thing that's not covered in mud?'

'Well... yes.'

'Right then. Put it on. Go round the back of the plane where I won't see you. We're leaving in two minutes.'

I swallowed hard. There was no way around it. I had to comply.

Reluctantly, I opened the rucksack and stared at the garment I'd packed to cushion the basilisk egg. I'd only packed it because it was the softest thing I owned, and it was large enough to wrap around the entire basilisk egg. As I pulled out the corner of the fabric, the pilot's lips twisted into a smirk.

'Oh, this is going to be good,' he said, practically licking his lips in delight. 'Very, very good.'

I walked back onto the plane dressed in my lion onesie, complete with a mane-covered hood and fluffy-tipped tail. I had bought it for a World Book Day celebration we'd run at the paper. Donna had insisted all the staff dressed up for a photo, which was placed in the paper the following day, alongside other images from all across the city, schools, and libraries. Even a fire station sent in their photo. The double spread was amazing, and that's coming from someone who tended to frown at the more twee aspects of journalism. Was it news that someone had grown the largest turnip at their allotment? Not in my opinion. But I had loved The Lion, the Witch and the Wardrobe as a kid, so Aslan was a go-to costume for me. Also, it had been an uncharacteristically cold March that year, and the idea of being that comfortable at work, as opposed to shuffling around in my normal pencil skirts and heels, was an opportunity I couldn't pass up.

I'd admit, there were a couple of bitterly cold evenings in London where I'd worn the onesie at home, with a hot water bottle tucked down the front to keep warm. But my ex-fiancée was less than a fan of fancy dress and as such, the garment had only been worn in public that one time.

Until now.

There might have only been eleven other people on the flight, but it was still eleven strangers I would really rather hadn't seen me in this state. Sniggers erupted around me as I made my way down to my seat, feeling my cheeks get redder and redder by the second. Still, I held my head high and even gave my tail a little flick as I sat down. If I had to wear it, I might as well own it.

Until now, I hadn't paid much attention to the other passengers, having been too preoccupied with the basilisk egg. Not to mention thoughts of my new life in Ravens Hollow. But sitting there in my ridiculous costume, I realised some of these people might be part of my new life. In terms of first impressions, this wasn't one I'd planned on making.

As soon as Donna had secured the job for me, I'd tried to research the town. The weather was the first thing I'd got excited about. After a lifetime of living in the UK, where the sun might or might not make a two-week appearance somewhere between July and September, constant warmth was enough to have me buying shorts, booking in a last-minute wax and getting yet another sun-ward sorted. But beyond the fact it would be warm, I knew next to nothing about my new home.

No matter how many hours I spent trawling the internet, details of Ravens Hollow eluded me. I tried not to be disappointed. Donna had told me that magical communities were notoriously secretive, and that included using some of the best firewalls around. Still, I wished I could have known a little more.

On the plane, I didn't even know what direction I should look in. Was the town north or south? How big was the population? It had hollow in the name, so did that mean it was in a valley, or was there another reason it was called that? And what about the Raven aspect? I was well aware that in a matter of hours, I would likely have answers to all those questions, but as the type of person who likes to be prepared, the uncertainty didn't sit well with me.

The city lights grew larger and brighter beneath me. Hundreds and thousands of yellow and white lights, growing brighter by the second. LA. Los Angeles... It was a long way from London, that was for sure.

A pang of sadness struck me. I hadn't been able to tell my dad the entire truth about why I was leaving London and a job I loved, but I'd told him enough for the story to be believable. Andy and I were over, and I wanted a fresh start. That was the part I played up. The fact that I was dead and now had to drink human blood to survive were factors I ignored. When I'd broken the news, both he and my step-mum had tried to sound excited, but I'd seen the worry in his eyes. Not worry for me, necessarily, but for us. Our relationship.

'I will ring you every week, just the same as now,' I promised him. 'And I'll send you so many photos you'll get bored with them.'

'Just make sure you do.'

'I will, Dad. Promise.'

This wasn't the normal situation of a parent worrying they wouldn't hear from their child once they had fled the nest. Not that I'd lived with him for a very long time. Once I'd moved to London, I'd never looked back. But for over ten years, it had been Dad and me on our own. My mother, if she was justified to hold that title, had decided when I was nine that she was no longer cut out for family life, and while we were on holiday in Seychelles, she had written us a letter saying it would be better for everyone if we carried on our lives separately. No questions. No discussions. Just a letter.

My dad, understandably, had been devastated. He had

wanted to stay and hunt her down, but he'd known it would be futile. She could have got a ferry to any of the other islands and a plane off them to wherever she wanted.

For me, the emotions that came with her departure had been mixed. Yes, she was my mother, and I loved her, but Dad had always done the brunt of the parenting. My predominant memories were of her telling me she was *too tired*. Too tired to play with me. Too tired to take me to the park. Too tired to let me have play dates. Sure, now that I'm an adult, I see things differently. She was working. She was busy. And her health wasn't the greatest. I appreciate that now. But back then, it just felt like she didn't want to spend time with me, and the letter clarified that.

'Belts on, guys,' the pilot said from the front of the plane. 'We'll be landing in three, two—'

The tyres thudded against the ground, bouncing me up in my seat, causing my mane to flop across my eyes.

'Good landing, Robbie,' someone yelled. 'You nearly had us there.'

'You know I did,' the pilot called back.

It was my first experience of private jets, and I wasn't convinced, though maybe that was more to do with the man in the cockpit than anything else. Still, this was my introduction to living stateside, and I wanted to take it all in. Or as much as I could in the dark.

The thought hit me just as hard as the touchdown. As much as I was trying to approach this new state in my life – death – as positively as I could, I hadn't fully adjusted to being a vampire, and part of me wondered if I ever would. I loved the sun. Springtime walks, wildflowers, bluebells in the woods. When I was little, my mum called me her flower fairy because I'd spend all day outdoors and come home with daisy crowns. As an adult, walking my colleagues' dogs – Andy was seriously opposed to having one – through London parks and noting the changing seasons had been my favourite way to spend my lunch break. That, or simply sitting under a tree and having a sandwich as the sun beat down on my skin.

But that was over now.

Even if my new colleagues had dogs. Not that it mattered too much. Andy was now officially out of my life, which meant the lifelong goal of having my own dog was in.

As other passengers filed off the plane, I pulled out my phone, hoping to find a map of Ravens Hollow. I already had my new address and hoped that being closer might allow me to access some information about the town. But still, there was nothing.

'I guess you're just going to have to ask someone how to get there,' I said to myself.

Hurriedly gathering my things, I bundled myself down the steps and onto the tarmac. Darkness felt good against my skin and I was so busy drinking it in that I momentarily forgot I had hurried out of the plane for a reason.

Despite the city lights I had seen on the way in, we appeared to have landed on a small private airstrip with no immigration process, and definitely no taxi rank.

'Elodie Evergreen?'

I turned to find an astronomically large man with a grey beard, a wonky eye patch, and a baseball hat, staring directly at me.

'I'm Bobby Radcliffe, editor at The Oracle. Thought it'd be easier to come introduce myself and show you to your place. I see you dressed comfy for the flight.'

His voice was a low grumble as he extended his hand, though the twist on his lips told me his comment was meant as a good-natured ribbing. Something I more than expected from working at a paper.

'Thank you. I wasn't expecting you to do this. And there

was a little mishap during the stopover,' I explained, gesturing to the clothes. 'This was the only thing I had to change into.'

'Well, you might want to slip into something... less noticeable. Folks around here are used to all sorts, but a strange new vampire arriving in a lion suit probably isn't what they expected. Unless,' he added with a grin, 'you're the kind of girl who likes attention. In which case, be my guest.'

'No, definitely trying to avoid attention,' I said quickly. 'I'm here to work.'

Work and rebuild my life.

'In that case, there's a bathroom just there.' He pointed to a shack. 'Why don't you change and meet me out front in ten minutes?' He paused, then added with a smirk, 'Oh, and by the look of things, you've got a bit of chocolate in your mane.'

CHAPTER
THREE

Bobby picked me up in an old pickup truck. The bed was loaded with tools, ladders, and other bits of paraphernalia. It didn't look like a journalist's car – certainly not an editor-in-chief's – but what did I know about how things worked on this side of the pond?

'I really am grateful for this,' I said again as I strapped myself in.

'Ain't no trouble. Finding the island can be a pain when you ain't been here before, and para drivers ain't the most trustworthy folk. Always ready to rip off an easy mark.'

I wasn't sure I'd consider myself an easy mark. I'd got myself into and out of some pretty serious situations as a journalist. Then again, I'd been human back then, and I hadn't even known about the magical world. I was obviously more at risk than I'd realised. Otherwise, I wouldn't have been bitten by that vampire.

'Did I say something wrong?' Bobby said. 'You look a little peaky.'

I shook my head and flashed him a quick smile.

'No, I'm fine. I guess it's just the cloudless night. That half-moon is seriously bright. I guess that's what I'm feeling.'

It was a half-lie. I could definitely feel the moonlight prickling over my skin. But there were a lot of other contributing facts to the way I was feeling. Back in London, I had been the person at the office people would go to when they needed to know something about the job. People who weren't even in my department.

But now...now, I didn't even know how many departments this paper had. I didn't know how to get to my new home, and when it came to what I didn't know about the paranormal world... well, that list was longer than the list of foods that aggravated my ex's IBS.

Bobby frowned. 'Moonlight? Ain't you a vampire?'

'I am, but, you know, it's sunlight, right? Just reflected sunlight. The effects aren't quite as bad,' I added hurriedly, 'unless it's a full moon.'

He tilted his head to the side. 'Huh, how about that?'

The last thing I wanted was to have myself labelled as a freak, which, having arrived on a plane dressed in a lion onesie, was looking more and more likely. But thankfully, there were plenty of easy ways to steer the conversation in a different direction.

'So, have you always lived in Ravens Hollow?' I asked, keen to hear his answer while still looking out at the city lights as we sped past them.

'Born and raised,' he replied, flashing a smile.

It was definitely strange that he wore his eyepatch so far over on his head that it covered part of his other eye, too, but he obviously didn't have a problem seeing. Or at least, it didn't seem that way from his driving.

'And do your kids live nearby?' I asked, keen to keep the conversation going.

'Only one,' he said with a chuckle, though there was a

tinge of sadness in his voice. 'The other three couldn't wait to get out of here. Or away from me.' He crinkled his nose. 'Nah, they're good 'uns. All of them. Just big personalities who outgrew the place. Shame, but hey, they might come back.'

Yup, that was definitely a twinge of sadness in his voice, but something told me this was one of his favourite things to talk about. It wasn't just intuition. It was a skill I'd picked up over the years on the job, interviewing people for my varying investigations. If you actually took the time to watch and listen properly, it was fairly straightforward to see when people wanted to talk more but needed to be pressed a little. And when they just wanted a conversation to end ASAP.

Bobby liked talking about his kids.

'So, what do they do?' I asked. 'Your children, that is. I'd love to hear more about them.'

Bobby's visible eye lit up.

'Oh, they're highfliers and brainy, too. Not that they get that from me, mind. One works for a paper in New York,' he said. 'Another's with the Magical Council, travelling all over the world. She comes back when she can. The third's a vet. Specialises in mystical creatures. She moved to Greece. Good call, career-wise. She's patched up everything from gryphons to hydras.'

'Wow.' I hadn't even realised those creatures were real, but the way Bobby spoke told me he wasn't pulling my leg. And given that I'd just dropped a basilisk egg at a hatching ground, I didn't know why I was surprised.

'And what about the one who still lives here? What does she do?'

'Works at the police station. Deputy. You'll meet her at some point. I probably see her less than the others with how damn hard she works. June an' I keep busy, mind,' he continued. 'There's always somethin' goin' on on the island. Games night, karaoke... You a singer?'

'Not unless you want your eardrums shattered,' I said.

He laughed.

'Reckon just comin' along to one of the beach barbeques would be best for all of us.'

'The beach?'

A surprised laugh cracked from my throat when another thought struck.

'Bobby, did you say that Ravens Hollow is an island? Like, a surrounded-by-water, sandy-beaches type island?'

'That's right. You didn't know?'

'No.' I shook my head while feeling a grin rise on my lips. 'I had no idea. Does that mean we have to get another plane? Or do we take one of those ferryboat things?'

A flash of excitement tingled through me at the thought. As a decades-long fan of Grey's Anatomy, ferry boats had been a definite bucket list item for me, and now that I had been so unceremoniously dumped, I wouldn't mind finding my own McDreamy on one, either. Besides, unlike the beaches, I figured that ferryboats were something that I could still enjoy, even in my eternally dead state. As long as they still worked at night, of course.

'Neither,' Bobby said, breaking my stream of thoughts. 'We take a bridge.'

'A bridge?'

Well, there went that romantic notion. Still, bridges could be pretty, I supposed.

'Just up ahead,' Bobby said.

I gazed around. I could see we were near water. The land curved around, and in the distance, the pinpricks of light glimmered from the city skyline. The same colours as the buildings shimmered and blurred as they reflected on the rippling waves. It was an incredible view, but there was no bridge.

'Sorry, where did you say it was?' I said, scouring the view and seeing nothing.

Maybe it was just American slang, and 'up ahead' could be miles away. After all, the country was enormous.

And yet, Bobby was slowing the truck as he approached what appeared to be a derelict pier with nothing more than a hunched over fisherman on it. As if he was planning on stopping. Maybe he was going to turn around? After all, this was where the road ended. And yet, no sooner had the thought entered my head than he stopped the car entirely, cut the engine, and undid his belt. A frisson of fear fluttered in me. As an investigative journalist who prided themselves on always being aware of their surroundings, climbing into a truck with an eye-patch wearing giant just because he knew my name and told me he was my new boss hadn't been my most clearly thought-out plan. I hadn't even asked to see evidence. Who the hell was I with, and where was he taking me?

'Sorry, Bobby, where exactly are we?'

He stepped out of the truck.

'C'mon, I'll introduce you to Floyd. I've gotta season pass, so I don't normally have to mess with tickets unless there are tips hanging around and I have to wait.'

'Tips?'

'Typicals. Non-magical folks. They tend to stay away from the area. Lots of rip currents in the water, and this beach is notorious for accidents.'

Bobby didn't look back as he headed towards an old man sitting in the moonlight, fishing. Only when Bobby was about three feet away did the gentleman finally raise his head.

'Bobby,' he grunted.

A flicker of relief dampened my fear. At least Bobby hadn't been lying about his name. That was good, wasn't it? Unless he'd already decided it didn't matter if I knew it or not because he was planning on killing me, anyway.

'Hey, Floyd. Thought I'd introduce you. This here's Elodie Evergreen. She's going to be workin' with me at The Oracle.'

As I stepped forward, my fear subsided. All evidence pointed to Bobby being who he said he was, though that didn't explain where the hell this supposed bridge was.

Floyd grunted before finally standing and shuffling around to face us.

At a guess, Floyd was anywhere between eighty and one hundred and ten. Despite the humidity, he was wearing a battered fisherman's coat, with the hood up, revealing only a glimpse of his wispy white hair. And while his eyes were deeply sunken into the mass of wrinkles around them, I could feel how they scanned me.

'Working for you, you say?' he said, his gaze remaining on me.

'Yup, and she's a new para, too. So go easy on her.'

Floyd's lips twisted. 'I take it that means she was turned by someone or another. Don't tell me who. It's not my place to judge.' Finally, he turned away from me and looked back at Bobby. 'Just so you know, it's busy in there. Been letting folks in all evening.'

'Right, the art festival. I should be there, you know. The rest of the crew is working. So, if you don't mind...' He nodded out towards the water, at which point Floyd tutted in annoyance.

'Right,' he grumbled. 'Keep your hair on.'

From inside his coat, he pulled out a thin wand. I had only seen one wand before. Donna's. But while hers was crystal and seemed to emanate magic, Floyd's reminded me of the sticks my friend's dog Wilbur would pick up when I took him for a walk. Although I wasn't looking at the stick for long. Floyd had barely lifted his arm when the waves in front of us rumbled into life, doubling in height. As they crashed back down, a flash of lightning shot between the clouds, which opened with a torrential downpour of rain that poured over the road and sea.

'That should keep them away,' he said. 'You're good to cross.'

He looked at me with a slight twist of his lips.

'I'm sure I'll be seeing you again, Ms Evergreen,' he said.

Then, without waiting for either of us to thank him or say our farewells, he turned around and dropped back into his chair.

It was only when we reached the truck, and Bobby started the engine that I realised something. 'I'm dry,' I said, unable to hide my surprise. 'We're both dry? How?'

A small smirk twisted on Bobby's lips.

'Oh, if you liked that, you're gonna love this...' he said, and his smirk got even bigger.

CHAPTER
FOUR

The storm continued to rage, the wind whipping up the waves as we drove towards a rusty old pier that I didn't think would take my weight, let alone the damn big truck's, too. And yet we were about to drive onto it. And Bobby was next to me, looking calm as anything. He even flicked on the radio. He was going to drive us into the water, listening to country music.

I didn't even like country music yet. That was something I'd thought I'd get into when I moved here.

My thoughts moved from music to my impending fate. Could a vampire drown? I was already dead, so that didn't seem likely. So, what? I would just drop into the crazy, raging seas to be tossed around like a lone sock on spin cycle until I washed up somewhere?

'Sorry, Bobby, but is there any chance you can tell me what the hell's going on here?' I said, embarrassed by how nervous I was feeling.

I guessed fearlessness was another thing to add to the long list of mystic rumours about vampires.

'Deception veil,' he said as the front wheels rolled onto the pier. My stomach twisted into knots as the last of the sturdy road gave way to rickety planks. 'A real impressive glamour, you could say. Floyd's family put it in place back in the eighteen hundreds to keep the bridge outta sight. It ain't the only protection keeping the tips from wandering onto the island, but it's a pretty good one. I'm guessing if you ain't never seen one before, you ain't never gone through one before either?'

My nerves, which had barely dropped despite the words *deception veil*, shifted up another notch.

'No? Why?'

'Might feel a little... wobbly. The air kinda shifts. You'll get used to it.'

'The air kinda—'

I didn't get the last words out. Instead, it was like the air was stolen from my lungs as a cold rush whipped through my entire body. The effect couldn't have lasted more than a second, and yet it left my entire body feeling peculiarly hollow. It reminded me of the stomach drop sensation when you did a loop the loop on a fairground ride. Or took the summit of a hill a little too fast. And I had never been a fan of either of those.

'Does that happen every time you go in and out?' I said, pressing a hand against my stomach and letting out a long blow of air.

'Happens both ways. It's a warning to the kids, really, not to go wandering out. The younger you are, the more it hurts. 'Fraid as a young-ish vamp, you're gonna get a little woozy every time.'

'Great.'

I'd thought that being eternally in my late twenties was going to be a slight upside of this damn vampirisation issue. Even that came with a drawback.

'Is Ravens Hollow the only town on the island?' I asked

while trying to use my vampire sight skills to see as far as I could, but it was hard. Cat's eyes glimmered down the centre of the road, and the truck's headlights were pretty strong, but there wasn't much sign of life.

'Is that forest?' I added, staring at the dark that stretched out on either side of us.

'Aye, it is. Island's still about eighty percent vegetation. And yes, answerin' your other question. Ravens Hollow's the only town, though there's a few other communities. Lots of the rich folk live over by Peppers Bay, and all the wolf packs have their own little communities. Guess you could think of some of those as villages. Now, just need to get up this hill, and you should get a good view of it.'

Anticipation tingled through me as we climbed higher and higher through the constantly undulating terrain. Now and then, I would get a glimpse of the water and the shimmering waves or catch snatches of light between the trees that I suspected were these steadings he'd mentioned, but still, no sign of the town. How high were we climbing exactly? Bobby had definitely said hill, yet this felt close to mountainous.

'Is it okay if I wind down the window?' I asked.

'Be my guest.'

The minute the glass shifted down, a crisp, salty sea aroma filled the air. I closed my eyes, wanting to capture the scent and the feeling of the warm wind on my skin, yet I had barely had a moment to appreciate it before Bobby spoke again.

'There you go. That's home.'

I opened my eyes, stifling a gasp at the light that shone out from beneath me. A town. From what I could see, Ravens Hollow started inland and spread out across at least three bays, the central of which appeared to be the city centre, with the brightest array of lights gleaming up from it. There were dozens of small pockets of light on the hillside too. Sometimes in clusters big enough to be villages. Others were just pinpricks in the darkness.

As we turned a corner, the view disappeared and reappeared again in a heartbeat. For the rest of the journey, my eyes remained locked on the lights which grew closer and closer, until we finally started passing buildings. Sparsely at first, then more and more dense until we hit the large white sign.

Welcome to Ravens Hollow.

Rather than just white and yellow lights, there was a full spectrum of colours stretching out in front of me. It almost looked as if the entire place was a fairground.

'Ridiculously over the top,' Bobby grumbled as he drove beneath an archway of red and purple lanterns above which was written. "Ravens Hollow Art Festival."

That was the reason for the fairground feel, then.

'This town. Every year, it gets more over the top. I remember when this used to be held in a barn over by Crim's farm. But that ain't good enough anymore. It's gotta be all marquees and tents and countless food stands. Not that I'm complainin' 'bout the doughnuts, mind you.'

'So what's it all about? Art, as in paintings? Or music, drama, *The Arts* type thing?' I tried to spot any signs on the side of the road that could explain in a little more detail what exactly this festival was, but I was struggling to see anything beyond the crazy lighting that had now switched to blue and yellow.

'The first one,' Bobby replied. 'Paintings. Sculptures. Gotta lot of creative folk in Ravens Hollow, so a few years ago, someone decided it would be nice to showcase it. Now we've got three nights of folk queuing to see some old dear's tapestry that she's made out of werewolf fur.'

'That's a thing?' I replied, only for Bobby to let out a slight laugh.

'Some of the team's there,' he continued, thankfully ignoring my ridiculous comment. 'Small paper like ours, you've gotta double up desks. Chloe does sports and features. Diego's our photographer, but he's got his own finance column and runs the business desk—' He stopped and shook his head. 'Heck, listen to me ramblin' on. You've just got off the plane. You probably want the night off. I'll take you to your place to get settled in ...'

He caught me looking at him with a distinct look of disapproval. 'I'll start work tonight,' I told him. 'I had plenty of rest on the plane.'

If you ignored the fact that I was clambering over rocks and swamps midway through the journey, that is. And that no matter how soft or fluffy a onesie might be, it was surprisingly hard to sleep in when the tail was determined to wedge itself into parts of my body where things really shouldn't be wedged. But hey, what's that saying? You can sleep when you're dead, right?

Or not, in my case.

'Town's not going anywhere,' Bobby assured me. 'And if it's art that you're interested in, you can cover it tomorrow night when you're rested.'

'No, I'm fine,' I said, looking out at the kaleidoscope of colours. Not being able to work back in London had stung, even if it was only for a couple of weeks. I needed to feel like I was digging up stories. Art had never been my thing. But being out there, hunting stories, was. Besides, I needed to know my new environment and what better time to start than the present?

'What about the investigative things?' I asked, keen to get back to talking about the paper. 'Who handles that?'

Bobby's visible eye narrowed slightly as he turned and looked at me.

'That'd be me,' he said. 'If anything looks even the

slightest bit suspicious, that's where I come in. You need to tread careful here, what with all the sect politics and things going on. It's safer that way. Plus, I have connections with the police.'

People were filling the sidewalks in front of us. Families, young couples holding hands, couples standing and talking. Old and young, conservatively and eccentrically dressed, Ravens Hollow seemed to have them all.

I stared at the scene for a moment before I turned back to Bobby.

'Well, I guess that means you and I'll be working together,' I said. 'If the story needs both of us, anyway. I can handle smaller ones on my own. Investigative is my thing. That's what I do, that's what I've always done.'

His frown deepened. 'Investigative *was* your thing,' he said pointedly. 'I don't mean it cruelly. Like I said, I need to keep you guys safe. That's what matters to me. Maybe when you know the place a bit better, we can talk about it again.'

There was no way I would accept that easily, but rather than responding immediately, I got distracted by the sight of a small group of people. Unlike everybody else, they didn't seem to be out enjoying the evening. Instead, they were holding placards, chanting as they blocked a pathway. A protest.

'Well, that wasn't here when I left,' Bobby said.

A glint shimmered in his eye. The exact type of glint I would get every time I knew there was a story to be told. He slowed the car and pulled it to a stop at the side of the road.

'You stay here, I'll go check it out.'

While even someone with human hearing, let alone a vampire, would have had no difficulty hearing what Bobby had said, there was a distinct difference between hearing and listening. A protest in my new town on my first night there may not have been investigative journalism as such, but at least it was a story. Something to sink my newly pointed teeth into while I learned about the place.

'Hey, did you hear me?' Bobby said as I followed him out of the truck. 'You need to keep out of trouble.'

'I heard, but there's one thing you probably should've been aware of before you offered me this job. I'm an investigative journalist, and there's no chance of that changing. Ever. Now, are we doing this together or not?'

FIVE

'Just let me do the talking for now,' Bobby said. 'Please.'

Thankfully, my new boss had realised there was no point in telling me to get back in the truck, but he didn't look terribly pleased at having me tag along. His grouchiness felt surprisingly paternal. Like I was a little kid refusing to do what was asked of them. Only I wasn't a little kid. Then again, I was probably similar in age to his daughters, maybe even younger than some of them, but that didn't change how I was a full-grown adult. In human years, anyway. I was going to ignore the vampire side of things for now.

'You've got all sorts in there. Shifters, werewolves....' he continued, his voice low. 'The ones that I know are more bark than bite, but there are a couple of faces I don't recognise. Out-of-towners.'

Shifters. Werewolves.

My heart made a quick, skipping motion in my chest. Until now, the only paras I had come across were vampires and witches. Given that the witch was my best friend, and the vampires used me as a test subject to practise their ability to turn, I may have already formed a couple of biased opinions there, but I was going to do my best to ignore those. After all, I was a vampire now, too.

Besides, I had yet to form any thoughts about shifters. So, while talking to people in what seemed to be a very tame, very respectful protest might have been dull as far as a journalistic story went, in terms of my new life, my excitement was palpable. Still, I did as Bobby said, stepped back and let him take the lead.

'Ines Ortega,' Bobby said as he approached a woman in the centre of the protest. She was dressed in jeans and a well-worn plaid shirt, but it was her eyes that held my attention the most. Flaming orange eyes. Orange or amber, perhaps? Yes, amber seemed more fitting.

She inhaled slowly before she responded to the greeting.

'Bobby,' she said.

'So what's going on here?' He continued. 'A protest. 'Bout paintings? Don't seem like your normal type of thing to get riled up about.'

'The protest isn't about the art,' Ines snapped back. 'It's about the people behind it. Or one of them.'

'Really?' Bobby's brow twitched in interest. 'Who's that then? And how come I didn't know you'd be here? You normally let the paper know when you're pulling one of these stunts.'

Ines's expression tightened. 'Raising awareness of the environment isn't a stunt,' she said. 'And as for not letting the paper know, we only heard a couple of hours ago that they'd brought in Wren Belkin last minute and are allowing her to exhibit her new work at the art festival.'

Wren Belkin? The name meant nothing to me, but Bobby's bushy unibrow rose a good inch up his forehead.

'Is that right?' he said. 'You're sure? She wasn't on the list of exhibitors the paper published this week.'

'No, of course she wasn't,' Ines replied. 'Because the

council knew half the island would be up in arms. Trust me. I saw all her lackeys carrying her things a couple of hours ago. You know her ex-husband is linked to the mermaid mafia, right?'

I struggled against a snort. Mermaid mafia?

Bobby let out a sigh. 'So that's why you're protestin'? 'Cause of her husband? You know he's locked up already.'

A young woman came up behind Ines. She looked remarkably similar, with the same red hair, narrow nose, and glowing eyes, just younger. A sister, most likely.

'He's not the reason we're protesting. She is,' the young woman said, her hands gripping a placard. 'The planet would be better off without that woman in it. And we're not afraid to tell people that.'

'I've got this, Sofia,' Ines glared at the woman.

'You need to make them—'

'I said I've got this,' Ines repeated.

Sofia scowled. Yup, there were a hundred percent sibling vibes going on there. She stepped back, though she didn't look happy about it.

With her attention back on us, Ines picked up her placard and held it out in front of us. Unlike many of the haphazardly painted slogans her comrades carried, Ines was holding a picture of a woman in her mid-fifties standing in front of a tree. I really didn't see how it fitted into the theme at all, but I had a feeling she was going to tell me.

'This is where she posed for her article in The Quill when they ranked her in the top 1000 influential paras. She chose to be photographed in the Lonesome Forest.'

From the way she spoke, it was clear she expected us to know what she was talking about, but I was still absolutely none the wiser. This time, though, considering the blank look on Bobby's face, I wasn't the only one.

'Sorry, the Lonesome Forest?' I said. Her head snapped

around to me. 'Elodie Evergreen. London—' I caught myself short. 'Ravens Hollow Oracle. I've just arrived in town. Lots to learn, apparently. Could you tell me what's so wrong with this Wren person having her photo shoot done there? It's not somewhere I've ever heard of.'

Ines's jaw twitched. 'Well, it's the only known breeding ground for the linen-winged snow moths,' she said.

'Linen-winged snow moths?'

From behind Ines, Sofia let out a scoff.

'Honestly? And we expect these people to actually understand.'

Ignoring her sister's remark, Ines offered a far more subdued sniff.

'They are the only breed of moths that can live in below-zero temperatures. They're unknown by tips and completely endangered, and their habitat is shrinking at such a rate some scientists reckon we have less than a decade before they're entirely extinct. And yet, Wren was there holding a goddamn modelling shoot because the trees matched the colour of her hair?'

'Her hair is freaking dyed!' Sophia cut in. 'And that's only half the issue. Don't get me started on the fact that her being here is completely unethical, and I'm not talking about the fact that her husband is the scum of the earth. This is the Ravens Hollow Art Festival. She hasn't lived in Ravens Hollow for over a decade, and yet, suddenly, all these other artists had to pack up and move to smaller exhibition spaces because we've got a big international star who wants us to roll out the red carpet.'

'Really?' I asked, looking at Ines as I spoke.

While the sisters seemed to share their values, one of them was clearly more skilled at controlling their emotions.

Ines dipped her chin and nodded.

'Several exhibitors have been told there's no space for

them at all now. She also insisted on having her own people do the wards on her tent because her works are so expensive. Witches were already hired to do that, who were expecting to get paid, and they don't know if they're going to or not. It's not right. This was meant to be a community event.'

'No, it's not.'

If all this was true, then I was very much siding with Ines. Sure, if Ravens Hollow was a big city, I wouldn't be surprised to hear about things like this happening, little people being pushed aside for those with more money. But that wasn't the impression this new town was giving. Not from how she was speaking.

'So, you're telling me that exhibitors already in place had to move or were no longer allowed to exhibit?'

'That's exactly what I'm saying,' Ines replied. 'Which is why we're here. We're not trying to stop people from going to the festival. We're just trying to stop them from seeing her work while they're there, that's all. And if they're planning on buying anything, then we want to convince them to buy locally from people who would really appreciate it. Not that I expect many of us can afford a Wren Belkin.' She paused for a moment and looked between Bobby and me. 'It would be great if you could get a piece out supporting the cause. Though knowing Wren, she'd probably just pay you off with a big donation to the paper.'

Bobby let out a low growl. His single visible eye narrowed on Ines.

'We don't take bribes at our paper,' he said. 'We tell the truth. But we don't write things without evidence, either. We'll talk to some of the exhibitors. And if the festival committee were paid off so that she could have that prime spot, we'll find out about it.'

'You will,' Ines replied. 'Well, I guess I should let you get on.' She turned to look at me. 'Nice to meet you, Elodie. We'll be here for the next three days if you fancy doing something to protect the planet.'

As she finished talking, she lifted her banner back into the air and restarted her chanting.

I had covered protests, yes, but never been part of one, and in terms of my journalistic non-bias, it seemed like a good thing to stick to. Especially when I was still learning about the place. Yet before I could get out an inoffensive response, Bobby let out a huff.

'I think you might find yourself moving along sooner than you expect,' he said.

I turned to follow Bobby's line of sight, only for every muscle in my body to tighten.

There was only one person in the direction Bobby was looking, and all six-foot-four of him was walking towards us. His black, tousled hair shimmered; even from a distance, I could see the glinting flecks of green in his eyes.

I am not an ogler. I do not objectify men. Or at least, I thought I didn't. But maybe I'd just never seen a man who could so easily be objectified before. At the same time as I couldn't draw my eyes away, everything about him screamed *don't mess with me*.

'No,' Ines said, her chanting stopped suddenly as her voice cut through my internal monologue. Her tone was close to furious. 'I don't care what he says. We're not moving. We have the right to peaceful protest. We're not going to move from this spot. I don't care what he says. We're not going.'

Bobby's lips twisted ever so slightly.

'Oh, I'm sure you're right,' he said, looking at me with a twinkle in his eye.

Something was going to happen. I could feel it in my journalistic bones. And all I could do was wait and watch.

SIX

If I had thought that the man's physical attractiveness would diminish when he spoke, I was very, very wrong. Just like Bobby had done, he strode straight towards the woman at the centre of the protest, offering her his full attention and flashing her a smile.

'Ines,' he said, with a voice so deep it caused a physical rumbling in my abdomen. 'I'm guessing this is about Wren Belkin?'

'You shouldn't have ever let her on the island, Whip,' Ines growled. 'You know who her husband is.'

Whip.

Had I heard his name right? Where did that name come from? Did he have a thing for whips? And if that was the case, was he on the receiving end or the giving?

No, Elodie. That is not *what we are thinking. This is your first possible story in Ravens Hollow, and you're not going to get distracted. Especially not when you promised yourself men were off the table for at least a year, if not a decade.*

'Of course I know who he is,' Whip said, answering Ines with that beautiful, deep drawl of his. 'Though, I think you mean *ex*-husband. Who is safely behind bars, as I'm sure you're aware. And the magical courts fully cleared Wren of doing anything wrong.'

Another guttural roll rose from Ines' throat. If I had to take a bet, I would place her as one of the werewolves Bobby had mentioned.

'Wren might not be a criminal in the eyes of the law,' Ines replied, 'but the things she does in the name of art are unacceptable.'

'Hmm. Well, I don't know about that,' he said. 'What I *do* know is that I've had complaints about people disturbing the peace here. It's meant to be a family event. Rightly or wrongly, people don't feel particularly at ease walking past your group here. Intimidating is the word they used.'

Ines's jaw locked hard, and Sofia let out a growl. Not a growl-like sound. But an actual growl.

Part of me wanted to get my phone out and snap a photo of the scene. If this came to blows, it could make front-page news in a sleepy small-town paper. Not that it was very sleepy at this precise moment. Still, Bobby was just watching, and he was my boss. It seemed sensible to follow his lead. Besides, I didn't want to do anything that might affect the outcome of the situation, so instead, I held my breath and waited. Ines had made it very clear she wasn't going to go anywhere. So what did that mean? Arrest. It felt like the only option. But there were twenty protestors and one police officer. That hardly felt like a fair fight.

And yet Whip didn't bat an eyelid. Part of me wished he would. I could only imagine how good those eyelashes would look when they fluttered. *Jesus Elodie, get your thoughts under control.* This was not the moment to be thinking like that. I needed to focus on the protest. Get quotes and names and details from the story. And if all hell did break loose here, I needed to get out of there. Safely. I looked at Bobby, ready to react when needed, but if anything, he looked amused by the matter. Did he have a vendetta against the police officer, perhaps? Did he want to see the protest turn on him, twenty to one?

'Look, Ines, I get you need to make a point here. And you're completely right in what you're doing,' Whip said. 'Which is why Bobby's going to write a piece on it, aren't you?'

'You know me,' Bobby said lightly. 'Always there for a story.'

'Right,' Whip continued. 'But here's the thing. I might even give you a quote. Law enforcement agreed that how the committee handled Wren's appearance was disappointing. No forewarning, questioning actions in the past, that kind of thing.'

'You would?' Ines seemed surprised.

'I *could*,' he said. 'But then I could also say how protesters unnecessarily tried to ruin our wonderful art festival. You know, dampen the spirits, even though we have the honour of an international artist gracing our little town. An international artist who people have travelled hours across the mainland to see. Two very different pictures, wouldn't you say?'

Sofia looked between Bobby and her sister, emitting another of those guttural growls.

'You're not really going to let him control the press like that, are you?'

'No,' Bobby said, but he let out a long sigh. 'You're right. I'm not. But you know he has a valid point, too. There are two sides to this. From what Floyd said, we got a lot of traffic coming in today, probably because of this new addition. It's bringing money to Ravens Hollow. And even if the committee took a bribe so that Wren could have centre stage at this thing, then that's as much on the committee as it is her. Your sister knows that. Right, Ines?'

Ines exhaled slowly. She had been incredibly resolved

before Whip had arrived. The type of resolve I would have bet wholeheartedly would get her arrested, yet now it appeared to be wavering. After just a couple of words from a polite police officer. I couldn't believe I'd judged her that wrongly.

As I awaited her response, her attention went back to Whip.

'You promise you'll give us a quote supporting us?'

'You have my word,' Whip said. 'And you know I won't break it. Come on, Ines. You don't want to make this any more difficult, do you? Ravens Hollow festivals are meant to be nights when the communities get together. I know some of your pack has got exhibitions on. Surely you'd rather be there, supporting them, than here arguing the toss with me?'

I watched as a muscle in her jaw twitched, certain she was about to tell the officer exactly where to stick it. Yet her expression softened. She was actually giving in to him. I turned my attention to Sofia. If one of them was going to start a fight, then maybe I should have had my money on the feisty younger sister to start with? Her eyes were locked on Whip, but her hands were no longer clenched. Was she giving in too?

'Come on, guys,' Ines said, turning back towards the group. 'We might as well go and give the others all the support we can, considering they've just had their work derailed. But remember, no one goes near Wren Belkin's tent. You got that?'

A grumble rippled through the protestors, though not one of them put up any objection. It made no sense. Surely they couldn't have all just changed their minds and decided to give up, just like that?

'Nice to meet you, anyway, Elodie,' she added, glancing at me. 'If you ever want to write a story about how the council really values the residents of Ravens Hollow, then seek me out.'

With that, she turned around and walked away.

That was it. No fight. No glass bottles thrown. No swearing

or arguments, and definitely no arrests. As they dispersed, I wasn't sure if I was pleased or frustrated. Sure, there was a story to write up here, but maybe they could have pushed back *a little* more. I mean, the whole point of having principles is that you stand up for them, isn't it? Maybe I was just annoyed at myself for buying into Ines' story so easily when she was so quick to drop the issue. Maybe I needed to find out more about this Wren Belkin myself.

I moved to speak to Bobby, to ask if he was all right with me writing this one up, only to feel a prickle along the back of my neck, and somehow, even without turning around, I knew exactly what it was.

It was one thing being able to sense when someone was looking at you when you were human. But as a vampire, that sensation was amplified tenfold. That awareness, that feeling of someone boring into the back of my skull, came with an actual heat that travelled all the way down my spine in a long, rippling tingle.

A corkscrew of knots took hold in my stomach. I turned around, completely unsurprised to see those green eyes looking straight at me.

'Elodie Evergreen.'

The way he said my name was like a song lyric. Slow. Deliberate. Every consonant so clearly enunciated it caused the hairs to rise on my arms. His lips lifted into a smile, and good god, what a smile it was. Sure, Americans were known for having far better dental hygiene than the Brits, and pearly whites were something I expected. But these? Wow. Vampire or not, he could sink those teeth into me any time.

'Elodie.' Bobby's voice was sharp and pulled me out of my totally inappropriate daydream. *What the hell was wrong with me?* That was the second time in five minutes that I had lost myself, internally anyway. With a sharp swallow, I refocused. I was there to do a job.

I was not drooling over the first attractive man I had encountered since my breakup. That was just ridiculous.

'Yes, Elodie Evergreen,' I said, stretching out my hand to shake his.

His smile broadened into something that had the ability to melt my very insides.

'Well, isn't that something? I've been looking forward to meeting you.'

CHAPTER
SEVEN

en are bad news, men are bad news.

Men are bad news, men are bad news.

I wasn't sure when repeating things over and over in my head had become a habit – maybe it was something all vampires did – but that was the only thought I allowed into my mind right now. Because if I didn't... if I let myself think anything else, it would be: *Oh my God, how hot is he? Oh my God, how hot is he?* And yes. He was *absolutely* freaking beautiful.

His jaw wasn't just chiselled, it was sharp enough to give a papercut. Assuming I could ever get close enough to find out. And those damn eyes... Yet he had said he was looking forward to meeting me? Why the hell would that be? I cleared my throat and tried to sound as casual as possible. 'So, you like whips?'

Crap! Where the hell had that come from?

'You're Detective Whip. Sergeant Whip?'

Ugh, god, I was making things worse, but fingers crossed my faux pas in getting his rank wrong had meant he'd not properly heard my first comment, though judging from the smirk on his lips, he had heard me perfectly. It was a smile skewed to one side slightly, creating a dimple. An incredibly cute dimple.

'Chief Inspector Whip,' he said, that dimple still in place. 'And you're the vamp who staked one of those trafficking arse-holes. Can't tell you the number of people who would like to have done the same. But I guess they have different rules for what you vamps can do on that other side of the pond.'

The conversation had started. I needed to continue it. This was good. Conversation was one of the swiftest methods of making a previously attractive man utterly undatable.

Now, what was he talking about?

Yes, me killing the vampire.

I could talk about that. Although was I meant to? The vampire I had killed was part of a potential trafficking ring, and Donna had made it very clear that I was to keep my mouth shut about what I'd done. The last thing I wanted was the Guardians – as I believed they called themselves – getting wind of where I'd gone and deciding they needed to pay me a visit to even the score for killing one of theirs. And yet here I was on the first night being asked about them.

I cleared my throat.

'Um... I...I...'

Normally, I had no problem in steering a conversation. Twisting it back away from me in whatever direction I wanted, but it was like I had lost control of my tongue. Was it because the question had caught me so by surprise, or just that he had? I couldn't be sure.

'It's my job,' Whip said, interrupting my jumbling stream of thoughts. 'Me knowing who's coming in and out of the island. Visas, that type of thing.'

'Right... Right.'

I should have figured out that keeping what I'd done from everyone wouldn't be quite as straightforward as I hoped. Donna had already told me that vampires had to register who their sires were on all sorts of registration documents, and that had already caused her a few issues back in the UK, given that I'd accidentally killed mine without having any idea who they were.

'Right. Yes, that was me.' There was no point pretending when Whip already knew who I was. 'Though I wasn't a vampire when I killed them, so maybe that made a difference. I'm not exactly sure how para politics work. It's all new to me.'

He tilted his head slightly to the side as if he wasn't sure he understood me. Had I babbled? It was a distinct possibility. And the fact I couldn't remember what I'd said thirty seconds ago probably wasn't a good sign.

'Sorry, you're saying you were still a tip when you staked it?' he said.

Tip. Typical. Non-magical.

'That's right. I was on a story. Following a lead.'

His eyes widened as he let out a low whistle.

'And you killed one of those arseholes. Wow. That's impressive.'

As impressive as the broadness of his chest that I was desperate to run my hands over?

No, now I was just being ridiculous. It was the jetlag doing this to me. Jetlag and the wards and the fact that I had solemnly sworn off men since Andy ended things with me. That was all this was. A physical and mental response to my self-inflicted abstinence. I needed to get control.

'Can I ask how?' he said.

'How what?' I replied, aware that I was unable to form a single thread of thought that didn't involve one or another part of this man's body.

'How did you stake a trafficker as a human? I don't think I've ever heard of a tip managing that before.'

How did I kill the trafficker? That actual answer was that I'd channelled my years of throwing javelins at sports contests and used a stick covered in dog drool as a stake. But that didn't sound like the cool, attractive answer Whip would be impressed by. So, I went for vague elusiveness, hoping to sound at least a little enigmatic.

'I just followed my instincts,' I said

His eyes glimmered. 'You must have some hell of an instinct.'

'Yes, I do.' My eyes locked on his. 'I have excellent instincts.'

The moment the words left my lips. I felt the flood of heat colour my cheeks. Why the hell had I responded like that? At best, I sounded utterly arrogant. At worst, I sounded like the most terrible flirt in history.

And why the hell would I flirt with this guy? Sure, he was the very picture of an Adonis, causing an unnecessary flush of feral thoughts loose in my head. He was also the chief of police in this small town I had just moved to, and I was a professional journalist who would never get involved with someone who could be an invaluable source for my work.

'Anyway,' I said as I stood there, praying that paranormal communities might have the luxury of spaces where the world genuinely opened up to swallow you whole. 'Hopefully, I'll get some leads on them while I'm here. See if I can track down whoever's leading this. According to my friend, it's a world-wide problem.'

'You're planning on bringing down an entire ring of vampire traffickers?' he said.

For a second, I assumed he was being sarcastic and mocking me, but his tone was genuine.

'Yes, I am,' I replied. 'You could always help me if you want? I'm sure I could use a man with your expertise. Though it'll probably mean lots of late nights together if you're up for that.'

My jaw dropped. What the hell? That was definitely flirting. One hundred percent. But how? Why? I had definitely not planned on saying that, so where the heck had the words come from? Was I simply that much in need of a little TLC that my brain had hijacked my mouth because it didn't think I could get the job done otherwise? It sure as hell felt like that.

And it was safe to say that Chief Inspector Whip looked less than impressed by the suggestion. His eyes narrowed as cheeks pinched inwards.

'My colleague is the person you want to talk to about the trafficking rings. He's been following them closely for a few years now. I'm sure he'll be keen to talk to you too.'

'I'd rather talk to him too,' I spat out. 'You're clearly not the type of person I should spend alone time with.'

What the actual fudge?

'I'm sorry,' I said. 'I have no idea where that came from. I... I...'

'It's fine,' Chief Inspector Whip said, though from the scowl on his face, it was anything but.

I stood there, my lips clamped together in fear of what else I might say and offered only a quick nod in response. A dark shadow crossed Whip's expression.

I must have looked like a complete idiot.

Bobby cleared his throat. 'We should go find the others,' he said.

'Others?' I said. 'Yes. Others. That sounds good.'

'I'm sure we'll be seeing you. Cheers, Inspector,' he added.

Whip nodded. 'Always a pleasure, Bobby,' he said before his gaze shifted to me, something unreadable glinting behind his eyes. 'Elodie, it's been... enlightening.'

Terrified of what I might say if I opened my mouth again, I offered him one quick nod, turned on my heel, and strode away next to Bobby. Well, one thing was for sure: I was not ready to start dating again.

We were several steps away from Whip when I spoke.

'I would appreciate it if you never mentioned whatever just happened then ever. To anyone.'

A smirk rose on Bobby's lips.

'You talking about you staking the vamp? That might be difficult. News travels fast in a place like this. If the mayor's office knows, then half the island probably does too.'

My stomach twisted into a deep knot. That wasn't ideal. Not ideal at all. Sure, I was a vampire now, but so were they. Still, as worried as I should probably have been, that wasn't the part of the conversation with Whip I'd been asking Bobby to stay quiet about.

'And the other bit?' I said, knowing there was no need to clarify what I was talking about as Bobby's smirk rose higher.

'I'll try,' Bobby grinned. 'But I ain't making any promises.'

EIGHT

'So, is Chief Inspector Whip your person on the inside, so to speak?' I asked Bobby as we walked away from Whip.

I could still feel that prickle on my neck telling me that the dashing detective - or whatever he was - was still watching me, and I didn't know if I was excited or terrified. Or just plain confused. If that was my flirting game, alternating between gushing and being outright rude, then I was screwed. Still, I tried to sound casual as I mentioned the police chief's name.

'No.' Bobby flashed me a smile that was so broad his eyes near enough disappeared. 'My daughter is. The one who's still on the island, remember?'

'Of course.' I felt like an idiot. He'd already told me that. So much for trying to act cool. 'So your daughter and the chief work together?' I said, only to realise that once again, I'd mentioned Whip. I hurriedly tried to redirect. 'How long has she been on the job?'

''Bout three years, she's been at the station,' Bobby said. 'She's a gem. Takes after her ma, in more ways than one. But you'll meet her. She'll like you. Probably wanna know all about life in London. Itchin' to spread her wings, that one. I'm makin' the most of the time I've got with her before she up and leaves like the others. She's workin' tonight. I'll introduce you, if I see her, o' course.'

I could practically feel the love billowing from his body as he spoke and how much it saddened him that his other daughters lived away. I felt a flicker of guilt that I hadn't seen more of my father in the months before my turning, though I wasn't entirely to blame. Over the last couple of years, he and my step-mum had discovered cruises and spent as much time as they could on luxury liners, sunning themselves on the top deck or learning to make towel animals, and dressing up as everything from pirates to primates as part of the fancy dress buffets. Come to think of it, maybe I should send the lion onesie to them.

'Now, I know you don't want some old guy poking his nose into your business,' Bobby said, reinforcing that fatherly impression. 'You're a grown woman an' all, but when it comes to Chief Inspector Whip, he's real good at what he does. Best this town's had. And probably a good thing he knows about the traffickers, too. I know Donna wanted to keep that under wraps, but in my opinion, there's a lotta good folk on the island, and having it out there means more people know to look out for you.' Warmth began to bloom within me, until I realised Bobby wasn't done. 'That said, on a personal level, you might want to steer clear.'

I wouldn't have thought it possible, but my embarrass-ment hit an even higher level. Having your boss tell you to steer clear of a guy before you've even started work has to be a record.

'Well, you really don't need to worry. Staying clear of men is something I intend on doing.'

Even ones that looked like he could take on the Greek Gods and win.

Now that I was away from Officer Whip, I couldn't believe what an idiot I'd made of myself. Yes, he was the most picture-perfect specimen of a human male I'd ever seen, but I needed to be honest with myself. I didn't even know if he *was* human. Maybe that was the reason I had acted the way I did. Maybe he put some spell on me that turned me into a horrendous, babbling flirt. If that was the case, he and I would have serious words. Whether I'd actually be able to get any of them out was another matter.

'Chloe just sent a message,' Bobby said, interrupting my stream of thoughts. 'Said she and Diego are over by the doughnut tent, waitin' to meet you there.'

'Doughnuts?' I said.

'*Good* doughnuts,' Bobby stressed. 'But if you meet my wife, June, you gotta tell her I didn't have any. Promised her I'd cut back. But really, what does she expect? Best thing 'bout these festivals is the food.'

Now that Bobby had drawn my attention to them, it was hard to ignore all the aromas floating through the air. Maybe it was just the fact that he'd said *doughnuts*, but I was sure I could detect the scent of sugar somewhere in the deep amal-gamation of fragrances, but just like sounds, they seemed to get muddled in my mind. Barbecuing cocktails, meat shishka. Sugary seawater. None of the scents made sense together, but it took more than a bit of focus to separate them out. Hope-fully, along with pinpointing where sounds were coming from, I would work it out with time.

'You all right there?' Bobby asked, giving me a look.

'No...yes, fine,' I said quickly. 'Just taking in all the sights and smells.'

He chuckled. 'I forget vampires do that a lot. Been a while since I've worked with one of you.'

'What are the others at the paper?' I said, keen to move the topic of conversation away from me. 'You said we're meeting

Diego and Chloe, right? Can I know what they are, or is it not polite of me to ask?'

'Oh, you can ask,' Bobby said. 'But I wouldn't. These two might be okay, but everyone's different. Easier if you figure it out for yourself. The werewolves tend to hang around in their packs, so it's fairly obvious who they are. Not to mention the eye thing.'

'Eye thing?'

'Uh-huh. You can tell what pack a wolf is by the colour of their eyes. Onyx wolves have black eyes, peridot have green. That kinda thing. Thing is, you have to know they're a wolf first.'

'So, Ines and her sister,' I said, recalling their identically hued irises.

'Yup, they're amber wolves. But I mean, don't take the eye colour thing as a rule of thumb. Just 'cause you see a pair of blue eyes, don't mean you're looking at Lapiz wolf. Could be a fairy, or a vamp, or hell, a tip, for that matter. And people can be funny if you get it wrong. I spent a decade thinkin' the guy who ran Weirdoughs was a troll. Turned out he was a hummingbird shifter.'

'Weirdoughs?' I question, although there was a lot about Bobby's sentence I wanted to unpick.

'One of the bakeries in town. Best croissants for miles,' he said. 'Vamps love it, too. They'll toss a shot of AB in the shak-shuka or cappuccino, so you can get your fix that way. Unless you prefer the taste of the stuff neat, that is.'

'Oh no. I like my blood well and truly disguised.'

I still hadn't got use to the vicious iron tang of the liquid despite having had it daily since I turned. Donna had used magic to make it taste like different cocktails. Piña coladas, cosmopolitans, old-fashioneds. The one she did best was a mojito.

But there was going to be none of that anymore. No, I was

just going to have to pull on my big-girl boots and drink it as it was. Or regularly eat at this Weirdoughs place. Weirdoughs. I liked it.

'It's a sign of trust,' Bobby explained, returning to our earlier topic of conversation. 'Letting folk know what you are. It's a personal thing. Some people let you know straight away. I expect these two'll tell you by the end o' the week. Others at the office are a little more private. You might never know.'

Okay, so don't ask. Fair enough. Bobby had already mentioned being wary of sect politics, and though I couldn't imagine any reaction would be worse than the one Andy had when I'd told him what I was, I had no intention of causing an incident.

'What about you?' I asked, treading lightly. 'Are you the type of person who lets others know what they are?'

Bobby's grin twisted a little tighter, his single, bushy eyebrow drawing down.

'What do you think?'

'Really? Am I supposed to guess?'

'It'll help if you can at least figure out what sect people are,' he said. 'You know, if you find yourself in tricky situations. The last thing you want is to think you're up against a Selkie, only to discover you've got a dragon shifter standing in front of you.'

'There are dragon shifters?' I asked, feeling the blood drain from my face.

'Not in Ravens Hollow,' he said. 'Course, they can fly, so who knows...'

Well, that wasn't all that comforting. Pushing the thought of getting on the wrong side of a dragon shifter aside, for the first time since he had picked me up from the plane, I looked at Bobby a little more closely. He was a massive man. Half a head taller than Whip, but his body was built differently. There was something about his solidity. I couldn't imagine him ever being a stakeout guy, not with his size. And yet, at the same time, there was something about him that was incredibly earthly. If he had disappeared into the background, I wouldn't even notice him.

What kind of paras had those abilities?

I didn't have a freaking clue. I focused on him a little more, seeing if I could pick out any giveaway details, though what I was expecting to see, I didn't have a clue. A large shifter perhaps. An elephant shifter? That could work. But then there was that eyepatch. It was still in that wonky position. Was that because he didn't care that it was blocking a fraction of his good eye too, or was it a clue?

But before I could think of anything else, a shriek of delight rang out from behind me.

'*Elodie!*'

Whether it was the high pitch of the tone or the fact that it was my name being shouted while I was in a totally unknown situation, I wasn't sure, but either way, the moment I was touched from behind, my fangs came out, and the screaming started.

'I am so sorry,' I said for what felt like the hundredth time. 'They just come out when I get startled. I wasn't expecting that.'

'You have no need to apologise,' Chloe assured me. Again.

'It's being new, you know, and the whole jetlag thing. Though I'm not sure vampires actually suffer from jetlag.'

I didn't know if babbling was helping my case, but I really was sorry. In terms of meeting colleagues, it went even worse than when a new copy editor back in London ordered a massive charcuterie board at the end of the week, having forgotten that over half the office was doing Veganuary.

'Really, it's fine,' Chloe said. 'I shouldn't have startled you like that.'

'Chloe is a hugger,' Diego said. 'She don't seem to grasp that other people ain't.'

As well as a hugger, Chloe looked to be in her early twenties, with pink and purple ombre hair, light lavender eyes and pointed ears that led me to believe she was some kind of fae. Although, given that my only experience of fae folk had been watching and reading The Borrowers when I was a kid, I was in no position to start guessing which type. Diego, on the other hand, was stocky and gruff, and it looked like his face might crack in half if he was forced to smile. Though the pair of them had been nothing but polite to me so far, despite the fact I'd probably broken a hundred rules of etiquette with the whole fangs thing.

'How was the flight over?' Chloe asked. 'Was the food okay? The food can be hit-and-miss on the small planes, right? And I've heard they can be bumpier, too. Not that I've ever been on one. Have you done many long-haul flights? I really want to go to New Zealand, but it's so far away, you know. One day, though. Have you got any bucket list places you want to visit?'

As she paused for breath, I debated which of her questions I was supposed to answer first or whether it was even going to be possible before she started up again. Although, as it turned out, neither Chloe nor I were the next to speak.

'It's like the hugging,' Diego said as he took a bite out of the hotdog he was holding. 'She hugs, and she asks a lotta questions. But you can ignore them. I normally do.'

Chloe shot him a glare, which he reciprocated with his bright blue eyes. What was the wolf pack Bobby said had blue eyes? Lapiz. I wasn't going to presume he was a werewolf, of course. Not without more evidence. But the way they glowed definitely reminded me of Ines and Sophia.

'So, how are the pieces coming together?' Bobby said as he looked at Diego. 'Got some good photos?'

'Yeah,' Diego said. 'Normal stuff. Pretty lights. Paintings.'

'What about the protest?' I asked. 'Did you get a photo of that?'

His gaze flicked to me. 'Wren Belkin, I'm guessing?'

'Yeah.' Bobby nodded. 'Whip came and broke 'em up, but they were less than happy about having her here.'

'Not surprised,' Diego said. 'The stunts her husband

pulled...' A low, rumbling growl rose from his throat. 'You know, they say he's killed over a dozen alphas in his time. That guy's mermaid venom is crazy. 'Bout four times as toxic as normal. It's why he rose up the ranks so fast.'

I felt my jaw drop. So, the mermaid mafia really was a thing. And the way Diego was talking about packs made me think I was definitely right to suspect him of being a wolf.

'We ain't writing another piece on Macoy Belkin,' Bobby said. 'Not now he's behind bars. We're sticking to the small-town angle. That said, could be worth speakin' to the other exhibitors. See if they really were pushed out to make room for Wren.'

'That's what Ines seems to think happened,' I added.

Chloe nodded. 'Well, it's not the kind of piece I normally do, but I'll make sure to ask people while I'm chatting.' She clapped her hands together. 'Now, are we going to stand here chatting, or are we going to order some of these doughnuts?'

Half an hour later, my brown bag of doughnuts was empty, and I had wandered through just a fraction of Ravens Hollow's annual art festival. It was incredible. Not just the number of people exhibiting, or the number of people who had come to support them, but the feel of the place. The community. People constantly stopping to say hello, to greet one another, to catch up on life.

I lost count of the number of times I heard people stop Bobby and the others to ask how their families were doing. And it wasn't like Bobby knew who half of them were. Every time I asked him who they were to pocket the information away for the future, he would shrug and reply that it was probably some friend of June's.

'It's such a shame that Dylan and Theodora aren't here for you to meet,' Chloe said as she continued to mingle when Bobby was drawn into a longer conversation. 'You'll love them both. Dylan's such a star. He's one of my oldest friends. You can trust him with anything. Well, you can trust any of them, really.'

It was easy to see why people were drawn to that small-town environment. Although, as a new vampire, it was also a minefield for my senses.

Maybe it really was the jetlag, but I was struggling to differentiate the different sounds even more than ever. One minute, I would be talking to Chloe, and the next, I would be distracted by a sound miles in the distance. Like the horn of a massive cruise liner leaving the mainland, or a baby crying somewhere on the other side of the festival. Once, it was a chipmunk that caused the reaction. A very noisy chipmunk, admittedly. But still, a chipmunk.

And in between it all, I was trying to cope with people introducing themselves to me.

'Welcome to Ravens Hollow. Love the outfit!'

'Elodie Evergreen, right? The paper's so lucky to have someone like you.' That was followed by a hushed, 'My sister-in-law's aunt works at the mayor's office. I heard all about what you did.'

But some were a fair bit stranger.

'Show us your teeth, Elodie Evergreen!' someone said to me.

'Prefer the other outfit!' someone else said.

Another person roared in my face.

I wondered if perhaps they were a lion shifter and that was the normal manner of greeting people, but from the way Chloe moved them away from me, I wasn't so sure.

'Chloe,' I said quietly. 'Do people know about my outfit on the plane?'

'Outfit on the plane? What do you mean?' She smiled broadly, not even blinking while holding my gaze as she spoke.

Holding gazes wasn't a sign of lying, was it? I thought it

was looking away. My stomach tightened slightly, but with a sigh, I let the feeling go. Sure, there was a chance that one or two people who had been on the plane also lived in Ravens Hollow, but it getting all around the island in a matter of hours was just me being paranoid. Right?

I was about to apologise to Chloe for my strange question when another sound caught my attention.

It wasn't particularly loud, like the cruise liner or the baby had been. In fact, it was a whisper.

'We are not having this conversation here,' a female voice said. 'We know what has to be done. And you will do it. Or you will find yourself a new job.'

'What about if I go to the police?' a male voice responded.

'You'd be dead before you could open your mouth. And that's not a threat. That's a promise.'

My stomach tightened, though the sensation was quickly joined by a flurry of excitement. Whatever was going on between the pair, it sounded illegal, and illegal goings-on made for great investigative journalism. The only problem was, I didn't know who was speaking.

I spun around on the spot, trying to work out which of the hundreds of people I had been unintentionally eavesdropping on. A man and a woman. Middle-aged? I thought so, though it would help to hear them again to know for sure. But there were too many people. If they would just talk once more.

'Elodie, did you hear what I said?' Chloe said next to me, concern clouding her expression.

In one last-ditch attempt, I tried to pick out the voice, but there was nothing.

'Sorry,' I said. 'Just thought I heard something.'

'Ahh, new vampire hearing. I heard from my cousin's wife it's a nightmare. She was older than you when she was turned, but she said that the best thing you can do is...' Whatever the best thing was, I didn't get to find out, as Chloe didn't finish the sentence. Instead, she lowered her voice to a hushed whisper. 'Okay, don't look now, but we need to subtly turn around.'

'Turn around,' I responded. 'Why?'

Only one person was walking towards us, a woman, similar in age to me, with bright red, curly hair and a sparkling white smile. I could almost picture her fifteen years earlier in a school cheerleading outfit. She gave off that vibe.

'Elodie Evergreen,' she said, leaning in and kissing me on the cheek like we were old buddies. 'I'm so glad to meet you in person,' she said, stressing her last words like we'd met some other way before now.

'I'm ever so sorry, Prue,' Chloe said. 'We're on a very tight schedule. You know, doing actual journalism.'

Prue's smile tightened.

'Oh, Chloe,' she said. 'I thought you'd have the night off. I'm not sure what there is for you to work on here. I haven't seen any people throwing balls or doing handstands. That *is* what you refer to as reporting, isn't it?'

'What I refer to as reporting is a lot better than what you do,' Chloe said.

Yeah, there was no denying it. Chloe did not like this woman at all.

'Oh, I don't know,' Prue said. 'My latest post has gone down magnificently.'

'Remind me again, Prue, are you a sea witch, or just a sea bitch? I struggle to remember sometimes.'

Prue's lips twisted a fraction, but her smile didn't falter.

'Same old taunts, CloClo. Doesn't say much about your writing skills, does it?' she said. 'Then again. I've read your articles, so I shouldn't be surprised.'

I could feel Chloe tense beside me, and while I was eager to have a story to dig into, I didn't want her to be part of it when this ended up in a brawl. As gently as I could, I tugged Chloe by the arm.

'Nice to meet you, Prue,' I said over my shoulder as I started marching the other way.

I waited until we were a good ten feet away before I spoke again.

'What was that about?' I said.

Chloe let out a sigh and rolled her eyes.

'Prue Parsons. Don't worry, I'll fill you in on more about her later, but right now is probably not the time. I'll just get too angry.'

She let out a long breath, and a little more of the tension ebbed from her body. Finally, she managed to smile. It was weak, but it was still a smile.

'Now, is there anything else you want to know before I take you back to Bobby? I should probably go in a minute. I promised Mick that I'd meet up with him.'

'Your boyfriend?' I asked.

'Fiancé,' she corrected, flashing a sparkling ring on her finger.

It was beautiful. Bold and far bigger than the one I had been wearing on my finger for several years. But it still reminded me of that empty place on my hand.

'Are you okay?' Chloe asked. 'Did I say something?'

'No. Nothing. Nothing at all.'

'You go. Find Mick. I'm sure I'll manage to find Bobby.'

'Are you sure?'

'Absolutely.'

She turned to face me, arms wide, then hesitated.

'It's fine. You can hug me now,' I told her. 'I'm prepared.'

After releasing me from our second and substantially less dramatic hug, Chloe disappeared in the direction of the main tent, though I stayed exactly where I was. Despite what I had said to Chloe about finding Bobby, I had another task I wanted to do first. Namely, finding the people who had been talking nefariously earlier on.

Given that I had no idea which way to head, I figured that from the middle of the crowd, I might be able pick out one of the voices again. Yet, as I started to walk, I felt a tap on my shoulder.

'Elodie?'

I struggled not to start as I turned around to find myself looking at... at a what? An elf?

The woman appeared to be in her mid-thirties, and like Chloe she had pointed ears, but unlike Chloe, these weren't subtle small points that you could easily cover with your hair, assuming you wanted to. These left the woman's head at a forty-five-degree angle and protruded at least four inches from her emerald green hair. Though, unlike many of the paras I had been introduced to, her eyes were incredibly normal. No glowing. No lilac tones.

'Sorry,' she said, shaking her head. 'It is you, isn't it? Elodie Evergreen.'

'Yes,' I said. 'That's me.'

I wondered how she had found out about me. Maybe her gardener was also the gardener at the mayor's office. Or maybe she did the nails of the mayor's under-secretary. Not that I was sure that was even a job.

'Right,' she said, her jaw slack as she continued to stare at me. 'And now you're in Ravens Hollow?'

'Yes.'

The reply felt somewhat unnecessary, considering I was there standing in front of her. Unless some paras were holographic and could project themselves to other places.

Nothing felt impossible.

Whether it was an elven thing or not, this woman seemed to struggle to hold a conversation. Not that I wanted one. What I wanted was to find the owners of those voices.

'Well, I should get going,' I said, trying not to seem rude whilst also not wanting to waste my time standing here in silence with a random elf woman. 'It was nice to meet you...?'

'Amira,' she confirmed.

'I'm sure I'll see you about. I hope I will.'

'Great,' I replied.

There was something about the intensity of the woman's stare that prickled me almost as deeply as Whip's had. But not in a good way. As the silence swelled again, I offered a small little wave before walking away.

Having lost time in another random conversation, I was desperate to start working on my hearing and see if I could home in on those voices, but before I'd gathered my bearings and worked out which direction to head in, my new editor was strolling towards me.

'So,' Bobby said, another bag of fresh doughnuts in his hand. 'Everything okay?'

'Yes. I can't believe what a tight-knit community everybody is,' I said.

'Well, it has its bonuses. And its problems,' he grunted. 'You'll learn that soon enough. Anyway, Wren Belkin is about to open her exhibition. Thought you might wanna go and see.'

There it was; that journalist's twinkle in his eye again. I had a feeling he'd already seen it in mine as well, in which case, maybe he wouldn't be so reluctant to let me in on some of his stories while I was finding my feet. And if we were going to write up a piece on this woman, we absolutely needed to know what was so special about her that the other exhibitors had been pushed aside.

'There's quite a queue,' I said, noting the line snaking its way from the door of the marquee.

'We don't have to waste time queueing.' Bobby pulled out two lanyards with the words PRESS PASS written boldly on the bottom and handed it to me. I slipped it over my neck and turned towards the entrance when a scream shot out into the night. A scream that seemed to come from inside the main marquee.

'That doesn't sound good,' I said quietly to Bobby.

'No,' he agreed. 'It doesn't.'

Together, we quickened our pace towards the fabric doors when a woman ran out of them, her arms in the air.

'She's dead,' she cried, turning in a circle like she had lost the ability to move in a single direction. 'Wren Belkin is dead.'

CHAPTER
TEN

I had been to plenty of murder scenes before. Sure, they weren't the only thing I covered at the paper. My title of investigative journalist kind of gave that away. I would look into anything that required investigating: corrupt cops, misuse of funds, bribery, and scams, not to mention missing people. That was the last thing I had investigated, and it had ended with me being eternally pulseless. Still, I had investigated murders too, and that meant visiting the scenes of the crime.

But never like this. Never at the moment of discovery.

'What shall we do?' I said to Bobby. 'Do we need to start taking names of people? Potential witness, that sort of thing?'

It sounded more like a police task than a reporter's, but standing around and just taking photos didn't seem like doing enough. Still, I took my phone out and got a few snaps, anyway. Diego would undoubtedly get some much better quality ones, but it wouldn't hurt to have the moment of discovery caught on film. Particularly if I captured the assailant fleeing in one of the shots. Although at the moment, everyone seemed to be fleeing.

'I'll ring Raquel,' Bobby replied. 'She's here somewhere.'

'And Whip?' I said, hoping Bobby realised this was me being professional, not just wanting to see the inspector again. However, as it happened, there was no need for him to respond to that.

Whip was already marching through the crowd. Did his type of para have extra-sensitive hearing that actually worked? I didn't have any evidence, but I was inclined to think so, given how quickly he'd appeared out of nowhere. Or maybe he was just attracted to crowds, like the protest.

'Exhibition's over, people,' Whip called out. 'Go home. Time to get home.' He turned to look at me. 'This is not the time for the press, Miss Evergreen.'

I was about to disagree, but he'd already turned away from me, getting his own phone out, though rather than taking photos, he held it to his ear. Thankfully, he was close enough that I didn't have any difficulty hearing what he was saying.

'Floyd, no one goes in or out of the island. We've got a murder here. Yup, up the ward to stun. Anyone tries to cross, you ring me.'

My stomach lurched. They could set the ward to stun people?

Holy hell, that was terrifying, but at least it explained why he had told people to get lost rather than trying to keep all the potential witnesses and suspects at the scene. I was included in the people he wanted to scram, but this story had just taken on a whole new angle. Not only had people not wanted Wren Belkin here, but now she was dead. If that wasn't my investigative bread and butter, I didn't know what was.

It was time to show Chief Inspector Whip that the press could be useful when we were on their side. 'You heard the chief, people,' I called out. 'Time to get going, please! Parents, find your children! Exhibitors, you need to close up now! It is time to leave.' I strode to a group clustered together and lifted my hands. 'This is a crime scene, people. Get moving.'

I glanced over my shoulder as I spoke, catching Whip still looking at me. Whether he was impressed or annoyed, I didn't know. But I wasn't going to give him a chance to stop me. He could hate it all he wanted, but he would be hard pushed to convince me I wasn't helping. Which meant he owed me a favour, and there was nothing an investigative journalist liked more than a cop owing them a favour.

The area around the tent was quickly cleared, and I was about to ask Bobby what our next move should be.

'Evergreen?'

I turned to find Whip looking at me.

'There's crime scene tape in my truck,' he said, throwing me a bunch of keys as he nodded towards a car park a little way off the park. 'Go fast. Fast fast.'

There was something about the stress on his second repeat of the word that made me realise exactly what he was talking about. I needed to vamp-speed it.

I didn't wait to second-guess myself. I pushed off the ground and ran towards the car park. Yup, this was way easier than the hearing thing. Or separating smells. Feeling the salty sea air whip against my skin was a rush in itself, and I was surprisingly disappointed when, a second later, I was standing in the carpark.

It was fairly full, but there were surprisingly few cars. Most of it was motorbikes or pedal bikes, but the police truck was there in front of me, black and gleaming. With a push of a button, I unlocked the vehicle and opened the back door. It was immaculate. Not a scrap of dust in sight. The tape was exactly where Whip had said it would be.

I took hold of it, but my attention was suddenly stolen by two hushed whispers. And even though my distance perception was crap, they sounded close.

'This is what's best,' a man said. 'You just have to hold your nerve. We agreed.'

'I know we did.' The second voice was also male, but I could hear the quiver of nerves trembling in his throat. 'But I think we should tell someone. Just so they know where to look.'

'That'll get us in trouble. This is the best option. Someone'll find it, do what needs to be done, and no one will be able to point a finger at us. That's what we agreed, and we're doing it.'

The hairs on the back of my neck rose. The only reason people argued like that and talked about hiding things was if they'd done something wrong. Like maybe, oh, I don't know... murdered someone? The murder weapon. Was that what they were hiding? If that was the case, I needed to act fast before they could get away. Tension coiled through my body. As quietly as I could, I eased myself out of the car. I didn't even bother closing the door. Instead, I looked around me and tried to work out where the voices had been coming from. Nothing. I took another step, wishing I'd spent more effort honing my skills, yet when I turned to look a hand grabbed me from behind.

'I thought I asked you to be fast,' Whip said, taking the tape out of my hand.

'There were voices,' I said. 'People talking.'

'People talking?' he said incredulously.

'These people were doing something... something wrong,' I said.

He frowned. 'They're probably just kids. Who need to get out of here. Just like you do.'

Like hell I did. I had just heard people admit to doing something they shouldn't have. There was a good chance they were the people we needed to find.

Whip's eyes locked onto mine. 'Do you understand?' he said. 'I said you need to leave. Find Bobby and go. Now.'

I clenched my jaw.

This wasn't how it was supposed to go. Investigative journalists and law enforcement worked on mutual respect, and he wasn't showing me any of that right now. I opened my mouth, ready to refuse, but then... maybe he was right. I didn't know anything about the island. Anything about how the paper or the police worked here. Maybe leaving would be a good idea.

'Fine.' I nodded my head as I spoke. 'Yes. I understand you. You're right. I should go.'

'Good,' he said, a deep crease between his eyes. But before I could pay it any mind, he was gone.

I stood there next to the police car, feeling my jaw hanging slack.

What the hell had just happened?

ELEVEN

I found Bobby away from the main exhibition tent, his single visible brow furrowed. 'Raquel's here,' he said. 'They've stopped anyone going in or out of the island.'

I wasn't sure whether to say I'd eavesdropped on Whip's conversation with Floyd and already knew that, but there didn't seem to be anything to gain by telling Bobby. Other than ensuring he didn't have important phone calls when I was in earshot.

'So, whoever's responsible is still on the island,' I said instead.

I didn't know if that made me feel relieved or terrified.

'Right. Well, Raquel's said she'll get us the official police report and any photos when she can, but she's already warned me it ain't pretty, so we likely won't be able to use any of the images. And Whip'll want to have crossed all the t's and dotted the i's before he lets us see anythin'. We'll probably have to go to print with a holdin' piece. No point speculatin'.' He looked at me, as if waiting for me to agree, only I didn't respond. 'Are you all right? You look... tense.'

'Yes,' I said, momentarily debating how much I should tell

Bobby. This time, though, I went for the truth. 'I just heard something over in the carpark. Whip sent me to get the crime scene tape from his truck, and when I was there, there were people whispering. Saying they wanted to tell someone. Sounded like they'd done something wrong. I wanted to stay, but Whip persuaded me to go and find you. I'm still not exactly sure how that happened.'

'He can be very persuasive,' Bobby said, looking at me with a new intensity. 'What do you mean, they sounded like they'd done something wrong? Like murdered someone?'

'Possibly,' I admitted.

He nodded, glancing back at the exhibition tent, letting out a slight sigh before turning back to me.

'Well, there's no gettin' in there anytime soon. Why don't we go back to where you were? See if we can't find any clues.'

I couldn't help but feel a smile rise on my lips.

'I thought you said I wasn't to have anything to do with investigations until I knew more about para life and Ravens Hollow.'

'I did say that.' Bobby groaned. 'But you ain't gonna let this go, are you?'

'No.'

'Exactly, which means we can go together, and I can try to keep you safe. Or you can go runnin' off on your own, thinkin' you know what you're doin', and I'll have to clean up the mess at the end. I don't think Donna and my friendship'll survive me getting her best friend killed on her first day on the island.'

I narrowed my gaze on him.

'So what you're saying is that, for now, we're a team?'

'What I'm saying is I don't trust you on your own,' he replied.

Still, he flashed me a slight smile as he spoke, like it wasn't the worst thing in the world.

'What about Chloe and Diego?' I asked as we walked back to the car park. This time at normal speed. 'Are they still here?'

Bobby shook his head. 'Nope. This definitely ain't Chloe's wheelhouse. As for Diego, they won't let him in for photos now, and he's got enough of the outside of the tent. I told them to go home. Now, where did you say these people were talkin'?'

'I was just up here, by the police truck, when I heard them. But my hearing's a little haywire at the moment.'

He nodded as if he understood. Maybe like Chloe, he had known newly turned vampires in his life, too.

'And you couldn't see no one? Any chance they could've been in a car and driven off?'

'I didn't hear any other cars,' I told him. 'And if they were in the car park, then they disappeared the moment I looked for them.' My stomach lurched. 'Is there some type of power that can do that? That can just... disappear?'

He shrugged. 'Honestly? Dunno. Maybe some of the fae. I'm not too sure. Folk are private 'bout the powers that can get them in or out of trouble. For obvious reasons.'

'So, somebody invisible could have gone into the tent, murdered Wren Belkin, then snuck out here?'

'Right now, we have no idea. There were guards posted outside. And heavy wards, too. She's pretty strict about that. Her stuff's expensive. Like I said, Raquel'll fill us in on things, but 'til then, I'm not sure. Where'd you say you heard those whispers? Maybe you can hear something with that vamp hearing of yours now. No pressure, mind.'

No pressure. I wondered if anyone in the history of forever-ness felt less pressure just because someone said that. I sure as hell didn't. Still, I did as Bobby said, trying to focus my hearing again. I assumed the reason he hadn't listened in himself was because he didn't have that skillset. So what type of paras did that rule out? I needed to get a book or something to learn the features a little more, but I was pretty sure it meant Bobby being a werewolf was out of the question. What about other shifters?

I was still turning the thought over in my mind when a sound caught my attention. Rustling. In the grass. And it sounded like it was coming from the same direction as the men's voices had.

'Down there,' I said, pointing ahead. 'I think there's something in the bush.'

My adrenaline surged. Was Wren Belkin's murderer hiding in the bush, waiting for the moment they could leave the island? It didn't seem like the most sensible decision. But then, murdering someone at a crowded festival didn't seem like a great idea either. Slowly, I inched in the direction of the sound, feeling a rush of excitement as it got louder. Did that mean I was getting better? Maybe. Or maybe it was pure luck, but with two steps, I was certain there was something there. And my ears weren't the only reason I knew. Another one of my senses kicked in.

The smell. It was revolting. After one inhale, I felt it burning at the back of my throat, causing my eyes to water. Some kind of poison, perhaps? Is that what was used to kill Wren Belkin? If that was the case, then we had just found the murder weapon.

I quickly saw the flaw in that idea. No sensible person would hide with the poison they used, and the rustling implied something or someone was moving. Yet what the hell could smell that bad?

Unless Ravens Hollow's sewage plants backed onto their main park, that aroma was one hundred percent unnatural. And definitely had the ability to stun, if not worse. I was about to use my fingers to block my nose when another noise joined the rustling. It was quiet, barely a whimper, and yet it caused my heart to lurch.

This was what the men were talking about, I was sure of it, but now I knew exactly what had been left in the bushes. And despite the smell that was making it near impossible to breathe, I couldn't have been happier.

'I consider myself a pretty lenient boss, but there ain't no chance you're bringing that into the office until it's had a bloody big bath. Or three,' Bobby said, pinching his nose as he scowled at my newest friend in Ravens hollow.

'*That,*' I emphasised the word. 'Is a he.'

Back when I worked in London, I had been desperate to get a dog. But as Andy had been allergic to anything remotely resembling fur - he even stopped me buying fluffy cushions once because he thought there could have been a risk of contamination - a dog had been out of the question. But the moment he had decided to end the relationship – in a less than empathetic state considering the trauma I had already been through that night – getting a dog had gone straight to the top of my to-do list. And now, on my first day in a new country, there was this little one, who needed a home. It seemed like fate to me.

As I picked him up out of the grass, I stared into his big blue eyes. He had to be young for them still to be that colour, didn't they? I would need to read up on puppy training straight away. Especially if he was going to be coming to work with me like I planned.

'Come on, Bobby, look at him. He's...he's...' I cut my words short, not sure how I was planning to end the sentence.

Adorable was not the right word. Not currently, anyway. Maybe he was adorable underneath all that matted fur, but it was pretty hard to see. Dark brown and potentially fluffy was all I could determine. And along with the smell, he undoubtedly had fleas, mites, and goodness knows what else. He was a mess. A thin, trembling, terrified mess. And it was love at first sight. For me, anyway. He was mine. I could feel it in the very marrow of my bones. If I even still had that now that I was dead. Either way, it didn't matter.

'Bobby, the place you've found for me has a garden, right?'

'Yeah, a small one. Come on, I was gonna suggest I drive you there now, but it's going to be walkin', I'm afraid. June'd never forgive me if the car ended up stinkin' like this one.'

Even with the stench, I was hardly going to complain. Walking meant I got to cuddle this one longer. It also meant I got to see a little more of the town, and it allowed us to take a detour past the supermarket, where Bobby went in and picked me up a bag of dog food and some medicated dog shampoo.

'I'm sure they've got a couple o' things in the police station,' he said when he came out. 'Collars and like, from when they had dogs. I'll ask Raquel. Or maybe Josephina. She'll know. She's been there the longest.'

'Josephina?' I said. I'd seen a couple of other officers cordoning off the marquee. A young woman, I'd assumed from her height alone, was Raquel and two young men. 'Is she another of the officers?'

Bobby let out a deep chuckle. 'Josephina's the ghost that works down the station. Though we use the term work kinda loosely. She can't do anything but remember messages when folk come in, but she'd been haunting the place for a good few decades before Whip took over. He decided that if she was going to be hangin' around anyway, she might as well be useful. And she's real good at remembering where stuff's stored. Guess it helps if you can walk into wardrobes and cupboards without openin' the door. She'll know if there's anything left from when they had dogs. Like I said, she's been there since back in the 1900s.'

'The nineteen hundreds?' I don't know why I'd assumed Ravens Hollow was more modern than that, given that I'd hardly seen anything of it.

'So,' I said, unable to keep the question in my head any longer, 'do you have any suspects for who might be behind Wren's murder?' I asked.

The puppy had been a great distraction, but I could only switch off the journalist side of my brain for so long, and I was sure Bobby was the same. He had to have been pondering it just as long as I had. Still, he was far too professional to answer immediately. Instead, a swell of silence rolled around us before he let out a long sigh.

'Her family ain't the most popular around here. You already know that.'

'Right,' I said, aware there was an unspoken question hanging in the air. Was Bobby going to mention it? Surely he had to? But it didn't look like he was. I hesitated for a moment before I couldn't hold it in any longer. 'What about Ines?' I said. 'She seemed pretty damn angry that Wren'd been allowed to come in and push other exhibitors out of their space.'

'We ain't had confirmation it was a murder yet,' he said. 'Could be a tragic accident.'

'Of course,' I replied. 'And even if it is—'

'We need to look at all angles.'

And my mind was already starting to do just that.

Wren had been given the biggest tent in the entire festival.

That had to have been earmarked for someone else. Someone who had to pack up all their things last minute and move to a less prestigious spot. I could imagine that would make anyone mad. And then there was the ex-husband with the mermaid mafia connections. Even if I still found the idea of a mermaid mafia absurd.

Along with Ines and her sister, those were the suspects that immediately sprang to my mind. Though, I knew next to nothing about Wren, meaning there was a good chance that there were other people to add to the mix. I was fairly sure a little digging would throw up more. It always did. And then there were the other voices I heard talking. Where one person had literally been threatening murder. Had I unknowingly been listening to Wren Belkin? And if that was the case, had the man she'd been talking to got in there and done the deed first?

I was about to mention my first overheard conversation of the night to Bobby when he slowed his pace and cleared his throat.

'Well, this is your street,' he said. 'Magnolia Drive.'

I took the time to properly look around.

'It's so pretty,' I said, needing to stop and take in the number of trees and bushes surrounding me.

Andy had written to the council several times, whining about the singular cherry tree that blossomed outside the house because of his allergies. There was no way he would cope here. The thought was surprisingly pleasing.

'Wow, frangipanis,' I said, looking at the pink and white blooms on one tree before shifting my attention to the next. 'And are those... mangos?'

I might have been a vampire, but I couldn't imagine anything that would make it easier to glug down my next pint of AB positive than knowing I could devour a piece of tropical fruit from my very own tree the second I finished it.

'Think you've got a couple of those in your yard,' Bobby told me. 'And you've got Chloe to thank for how everything looks inside. As for the outside gift, well, Donna paid for it. The boys sourced it.'

'Sourced it?'

What the heck would Donna have bought that she couldn't have given to me before I got on the plane?

As Bobby pointed ahead to a small two-storey house, I quickened my pace, only to stop when I reached the driveway. My jaw dropped, and not because of my new home that was more beautiful than I could have ever hoped for, but because of what was in front of it.

'That's my new car?' I questioned.

'Guess people thought you might want a little taste of home,' Bobby said, his eye glinting as he grinned from ear to ear. 'And this way, they'll definitely see you coming.'

CHAPTER

THIRTEEN

An actual vintage Mini was sitting on my driveway. They had found me an actual vintage Mini.

Not a modern one with all the legroom and standard height, but one where anyone who sat in the back would have their knees up under their chin, and the only people you'd be able to see over were children on tricycles. Safe? Probably not. Stylish. Absolutely.

'It's perfect,' I said, running a hand over the bright yellow paintwork.

I knew next to nothing when it came to cars, but surely something like this would have cost a pretty penny. Either that, or it didn't run. As I struggled to know what to say, the puppy in my arms reached out, ready to place his muddy paws on the glistening door. I jumped back with vamp speed, moving him out of the way.

'Not yet, buddy. Let's get you a bath first, okay? And that little front seat in there, that's gonna be yours.' The bundle of grubbiness looked up at me... dizzily. 'Crap, sorry, buddy,' I said. 'Lesson learned. Vamp speed while holding small living things is not a good idea.'

'Donna wanted to make sure you settled in quick,' Bobby said, as I carried on walking around the car.

A warmth spread from my chest. Even on the other side of the world, my best friend was doing everything she could to look after me. I knew there was a reason I loved her so much. And as soon as I'd got this one cleaned up, I'd ring her and tell her as much.

'I'll let you get settled,' Bobby said, handing me a bundle of keys. 'I'll probably head to the office 'round eight tomorrow. Check in with Raquel. Hopefully, she'll fill us in on the Wren Belkin case by then. Up to you if you wanna come in. Didn't you mention needing another light ward? If you can't come in until after sunset, it's no big deal. We can always catch up over the phone.'

I remembered the prickling on my skin that had started when I was trying to get back to the bloody plane. It was definitely a sign of a weakening ward, but there was no way I wanted to be getting information about the story second-hand. Besides, a weakening ward still worked. Just not as well as a full one.

'I'll see you at the office at eight,' I said to Bobby.

Though it was only when he turned to leave that I remembered something else.

'Bobby?'

'Yes, Elodie?' he said, turning back to look at me.

'Where is the office?'

AFTER HEADING into the house to find a piece of paper, Bobby drew me a quick map of the town, indicating where the key points were, which, in his mind, meant the office and Weirdoughs. He also tried to put some sort of scale on it, but considering my house was drawn at double the size of the only supermarket, I didn't think it was very reliable.

As he walked away, I looked at my new housemate, who had now recovered from his dizziness and was busy sniffing my top.

'You need a name.' I walked toward the side gate that led into the yard. 'Stinky would be a bit cruel, wouldn't it?'

The dog whined, and I didn't think it was a coincidence. This entire walk, he had not made a sound. Even when I put him on the ground, he had trotted at my heel, as if he'd known exactly what was expected of him. Now, though, at the mention of the name Stinky, he seemed less than impressed. As I held him back against my chest, I noticed how large his paws were, considering his height. It was almost comical. Could I think of a name to do with that? Hobbit perhaps. No, I didn't even mention that one to him.

'Well, I think we need to give you a name that's indicative of your current state,' I said. 'So if it's not Stinky, we need to come up with something better.' I wanted something to commemorate the moment of finding him. My first day here in Ravens Hollow. 'Raven?' No, that was ridiculous. Not quite as ridiculous as Stinky, but still bad, considering he was very definitely brown and not black. 'Pongo?' I said as the name flashed into my mind. 'Do you like Pongo?' The dog tipped his head to the side as if he was considering my suggestion. 'You know, like Pongo from *101 Dalmatians,* but also Pongo because, you know, you're not the freshest there is. At the moment, of course.' I continued to stare at the dog – my dog – unable to stop the warmth flooding through me as he beat his tail firmly against my arm.

'Pongo it is,' I said.

'I'M REALLY SORRY, buddy, we're going to have to start this outside,' I told Pongo, opening the side gate to find that the small yard Bobby had mentioned was in fact a decent-sized garden with several mature trees, a patio dining area, and, thankfully, a drain.

I noted the outdoor tap, then decided against it. Sure, the night in Ravens Hollow was far, far warmer than England right now, but Pongo was only a little pup. The last thing I wanted to do was freeze him.

'Just wait out here for me, okay?' I said. 'While I go and get some warm water from inside. Can you do that? Can you wait here? Can you sit for me? Can you sit, Pongo?'

The dog tilted its head, lifted his paw, and barked loudly twice before wagging his tail enthusiastically,

'Good try, buddy,' I said, before rifling through the bundle of keys Bobby had given me and opening the back door.

As I stepped into the house, I found myself standing in the kitchen-diner, which was larger than the entire living area of my flat in London. Immediately, my mind flicked forward to thoughts of dinner parties. Given my ex and his food intolerances, IBS, and general inability to push himself even a nanometre out of his comfort zone, our food situation had been bland, and our social lives had existed in a fairly similar state. But there was no need for it to be like that anymore.

No, maybe I would have a little *Welcome to Ravens Hollow* party. A housewarming for the people from the office. It would give me a chance to get to know them a bit better. Not to mention, it might help me settle in.

I had to do a doubletake at my own thoughts. I'd had a few firm friendships at *The Sentinel*, with Donna and a couple of others, but Donna was the only one I actually socialised with outside of work. Part of that was the job – it didn't leave much time for socialising – but part of it was also professionalism. Boundaries.

Ravens Hollow felt different.

Two of my colleagues had sorted out my car. Another –
who happened to be my boss – had picked me up from the
airport and walked me home, and a third had sorted my
house. Maybe I didn't need to be so cautious. But maybe I'd
spend a little time in the office before I started inviting people
over. That was assuming they wanted to socialise with me.
They already had their own friends – they didn't need an extra
addition. Then there was the whole Guardians thing to think
of too. The way the people had mentioned it to me tonight,
with a sense of quiet awe and gratitude made me wonder if
perhaps Donna didn't need to have been so fearful about
knowing what I'd done back in the U.K. Maybe the more
people who knew, the more there would be to help if the
Guardians did come for me.

Pushing aside the nervous churning that came to mind
with thought of the Guardians, I refocussed my attention back
on the present. And on Pongo.

Three minutes later, I had one bucket and one washing-up
bowl filled with warm water, a bottle of dog shampoo at the
ready, and Pongo's big blue eyes looking up at me expectantly.

'Okay then, little guy,' I said. 'Let's try to make this as painless as possible.'

The experience seemed to be painless – if not enjoyable –
for Pongo. Unfortunately, I couldn't say the same for myself.

Six times in total, he decided to shake, coating me in
water. While my vampire senses were less than pleased at this,
at least the sprays gave me a good indication of how much
cleaner he was getting. By the third shake, I was no longer
gagging from the smell when it hit me, and by the sixth, the
water was clear.

'You need a bit of a dry before you come in, buddy,' I said,
nipping back into the house and grabbing a towel from the
bathroom. 'Come on, let's do this.' With his tail wagging,

Pongo buried himself into the towel – only to roll onto his back and show me his belly. 'Oh, I take it you like this, do you?' I said, feeling the grin stretch my cheeks as his tail beat the ground with such ferocity it made a smacking sound. When I tried to stop, he nipped at me, offering a playful puppy bite. 'Oh no, no biting, thank you. Now come on, let's get you inside.'

I stepped back and removed the towel from around him, only to let out a laugh at the sight in front of me.

'Oh, that is a *look*, Pongo...'

All his fur had fluffed up so that he appeared four times bigger than he had when he was wet. It looked like he had been standing with his paws resting on a Van de Graaff generator. But it did give me a better chance to see his colouring. Especially now that they were no longer darkened with grime.

'You look a little bit like an Alsatian.' I said, feeling my lips pout as I studied him. 'A kind of a round Alsatian. With rounder ears too.' And with paws as big as his, I reasoned he was likely to be a mid-sized dog. Not that it mattered. He could be a hundred different breeds mingled in one, and I would love him just the same. After stripping off so that I could leave my stinking clothes outside, I tapped my thigh and looked at him.

'Alright, Pongo,' I said as he trotted to my side. 'I guess it's time we go and have a look at the rest of the house together.'

FOURTEEN

Despite my urge to explore my new home, it turned out there were only two places in the house that Pongo wanted to see: the food bowl and my bed.

Bobby had driven back with my suitcases while I was out back cleaning Pongo and had left them on the front doorstep, along with a note that he'd slid under the door to tell me they were out there. I had got as far as shifting them indoors, but that was as much as I was going to manage. I was not in the mood for unpacking now.

'Maybe you should sleep on the sofa.' He clambered up onto the dark blue duvet cover, curling his head under his legs.

Chloe had done an amazing job of making the place feel homey, and had even put up several touches to remind me of my old life – including black and white photos of Tower Bridge and Big Ben in London, and several packs of Yorkshire tea in the cupboards. She had even picked out some books to place on the nightstand for me – a thriller I'd read, and a romantasy I had intended on reading for months, but had struggled to find time for. But now, without Andy to make bland meals for, my free time was going to be mine to enjoy as I wished.

Reading and walking Pongo. And making friends with Chloe, too. After all this effort she had gone to, I definitely needed to take her out for a drink.

I could already see it now. Life – or death, I supposed – was going to be good.

'Pongo, did you hear what I said about the sofa?' I walked into the bedroom, yet before I even reached him, I could hear the soft snores reverberating from his body. I sat down and gently stroked his soft, clean fur.

From the way he had eaten, the people who'd had him before hadn't bothered to feed him, and I'd felt more than one or two ribs protruding beneath his wet fur when I'd washed him. Well, I would fix that soon enough. And as for the sofa, well, one night on the bed wouldn't hurt, would it?

'Okay, just tonight,' I said, looking at him. 'We're not gonna make a habit of this. You understand?' His ear twitched slightly, but I was pretty sure that was just because I was disturbing him, rather than because he was actually listening to what I was saying. As Pongo let his dreams take hold, my own yawn escaped.

There was so much I didn't know about being a vampire. When I had first been turned, I'd naïvely thought I would have unlimited energy – or at least endless energy during nighttime hours – but I had never imagined I would feel like this.

My bones were so heavy. It was like they had been replaced with an alloy of solid tiredness. Heavier than anything else known to man. As such, I was tempted to crawl straight in next to Pongo, but I had to shower first. The water pressure was good, Chloe's choice of shower gels amazing, and the towels so soft I would have happily worn one as a dressing gown. But instead, I opened one of the suitcases, unpacked my pyjamas, and slipped into bed next to Pongo. I was asleep before my head had even hit the pillow.

I had expected to sleep all the way through the night.

I was hoping to wake up refreshed and ready for work.

Therefore, I was both surprised and annoyed to open my eyes and notice the pitch blackness beyond the blinds.

'Vampirism meets jetlag,' I muttered to myself. 'Perfect.'

JETLAG IS A BITCH.

It had been my first and only long-haul flight – my first flight ever as a vampire – and I'd come to that very solid conclusion. Whether I needed sleep or not was irrelevant. It was 3 a.m., and my brain was absolutely wired. For a while I toyed with the idea of unpacking. If not the books and photos, then at least get some of my work clothes out, but Pongo was fast asleep, and the last thing I wanted was to disturb him.

I didn't think I'd ever seen a puppy sleep more soundly than my new roommate. He'd somehow wriggled himself up the bed so his head was on one of the pillows, like he knew that was what it was for, while his little belly went up and down and occasional soft whimpers rose from his lips.

I'd always heard a house wasn't a home without a dog, and I hadn't wanted to believe it, since I'd feared it would never happen, but having him here with me I could fully understand. Of course, it was night one, and I knew that feeling could shift when he started chewing through my shoes and leaving messes on the carpet, but I didn't think so.

As I stared at the puppy, I tried to figure out what to do with myself. I had toyed with reading, but I've never been one of those people who can read a couple of pages before bed to help them drift off to sleep. No, reading was something I got absorbed in, to the point that I lost all awareness of time. If I started now, I'd be lucky to get a single hour's kip before work. What I needed was to get rid of some of my excess energy. I needed to stretch my legs. After a fair bit of deliberation, my mind was made up.

'I'll be half an hour at most,' I said, giving Pongo one last look as I closed the bedroom door. 'Sleep well.'

I didn't know exactly where I was heading, but I figured if I moved in more or less a straight line, then turned around and did the same on the way back, it should stop me getting lost. Although, after five or ten minutes of walking, I had a destination in mind; the park that only hours ago had been set up for the art festival. More specifically, Wren Belkin's murder.

The park was a very different place now that all the people had gone. It gave me a chance to see the area properly. We were inland, but not too far, because I could hear the waves crashing against the shore somewhere in the near distance. I could also hear the rumbling of cars, rolling in and out of focus. Or was it thunder? Crap, I really needed to get this hearing of mine sorted.

The night was warm, but it still made me shudder to think of Pongo left out there. If I hadn't found him... no, I wasn't going to think about that. He was safe, warm in bed. And I wanted to get back to him fairly quickly, just in case he woke up. Yet, as I turned around to head back, raised voices caught my attention.

'This is absolutely unacceptable.'

Whip.

My heart did an unexpected stutter as I glanced at my watch. It had been nearly eight hours since the incident with the protest, and I was guessing the chief hadn't stopped work at all since then, meaning he'd had a very long shift. Again, my mind flickered to Pongo, but the likelihood of him waking up seemed low, and the last thing I wanted was to miss out on another opportunity to talk to Whip. From a professional point of view, obviously. There was nothing like being able to get the information first-hand as it was happening.

Making no attempt to quieten my footsteps, I reached the main exhibition tent. Yellow tape had been stretched around the outside, with the words 'do not cross' very clearly written in black at least a dozen times. But when it came to my job I often took the ask for forgiveness, rather than seek permission approach. Of course, that was how I ended up in this state, but given that I was already technically dead, I wasn't worried about that happening again. And if Whip wanted to chuck me out, fine, but hopefully I'd get a quick glimpse at what the actual crime scene looked like before that.

Realising there was no need to hold my breath – since I didn't actually have to breathe anyway – I pulled open the tarpaulin door and stepped inside. It was a mess.

'God,' I whispered as I looked around me.

The body had gone, but a large pool of blood remained on the plain wooden floor spread out and smeared in a multitude of directions. More than one of the floorboards had been broken, along with two of the large light fittings, while several of the sculptures had been smashed. The smell was over-whelming. Enough to have my fangs tingling. Trying to block the aroma out, I looked at the scene.

Standing on the other side of the tent, with his back to me, was Chief Inspector Whip, talking to a thin, angular woman, who was wearing both an impressive scowl, and very dark sunglasses that hid a large portion of her face. Sunglasses. In the middle of the night. Inside a tent. It was an interesting choice.

'Mayor,' Whip spoke. 'This is a murder scene, you don't—'

'You don't seem to understand the significance of this work,' the mayor cut in. 'Before, when Wren was alive, these pieces of art were considered masterpieces. Now, posthumously, they are relics. Irreplaceable. You can't just ship them, put them into boxes and store them. The material these sculptures are made of is incredibly susceptible to damage. They need to be properly handled. Properly packaged. I've had her people on me all evening demanding we don't touch things. And you and I both know Wren was friends with very powerful people. Those are connections we do not want to upset.'

'I am well aware of Ms Belkin's connections, Hilary,' Whip said. 'But this is a crime scene. I'm not going to have a horde of antique dealers or art critics traipsing in here until we've got this sorted. But... if you can get the team in tomorrow – today – then I will personally supervise them as they box everything up.'

The deal sounded fair enough to me, but the mayor pursed her lips. 'They were told the exhibition was going to be here for three days. Several people left the island after setting up, and they're the only ones qualified to move the objects. They were quite insistent about that. And as you've insisted on keeping the barrier up at stun strength, with no one going in or out...'

Whip scratched his head, and I couldn't say I blamed him. He was trying to be helpful, and a murder had to come above a couple of pieces of artwork, didn't it? Still, there was good news story fodder in here, that I was sure of... even if it was just that the police were having to bow down to the mayor's request.

'What do you propose I do instead, then Mayor?' Whip said. 'What is the solution you want? You obviously have one.'

'It's not just what I want, it's what needs to happen, Whip, and that is this place needs to be guarded. Around the clock police patrol, until they can work out how to ship the items safely. This is going to bring a lot of attention to Ravens Hollow, Chief. Good and bad. We need to try to limit that bad. Hopefully, protecting this work will go some way to doing that.'

Whip pressed his lips together. 'That will have to come out of your budget. I don't have enough for it.'

'The council will foot any bill.'

Whip let out a sigh and dug his hand in his pocket. Was he going to agree to her? If I had to take a bet on it, then I'd say yes, he was. But rather than responding to the mayor he twisted around and locked his eyes on me.

'Miss Evergreen, what do you think?' he said, those perfect eyes looking straight at me. 'Do you care to weigh in on this conversation, or is your normal style of reporting simply to eavesdrop?'

CHAPTER
FIFTEEN

Yes, I had been busted. He may have been on the other side of the marquee, but my vampire sight had no issues seeing those green-flecked eyes staring straight at me. In fact, Whip held my gaze for so long I was half wondering if we'd slipped into some blinking contest without knowing. Finally, he cleared his throat and turned back to the other woman.

'Mayor Hillard,' he said. 'I assume we are done here. I'll put together a security team, and you'll foot the bill. Now, I need to walk Miss Evergreen home, as she seems to have forgotten where she lives.'

A lump filled my throat. I was desperate to respond, and for a split second, I considered walking out with Mayor Hillard to see if I could get a quote for the paper from her instead – but she was already scurrying past me and out through the doors, eyes down, as if she was deliberately avoiding looking at me. Maybe because the leaks about what I had done back in England had come from her office. The marquee door fluttered shut leaving Chief Inspector Whip and me inside alone.

And he didn't look happy about it.

'You're going to hang around here for ten minutes or so,' he said. 'I need to get the wards put back before I can go anywhere. Not to mention the security team. I doubt Mayor Hillard would be impressed if the first thing I did after our conversation was leave all this unguarded. Now, can I trust you not to take any photographs while I make these calls, or do I need to take your phone off you?'

Damn it. I should've taken the shots before I first came in, but then again, he'd have spotted that.

'It's fine. I'm not going to take any photos,' I said. 'But I can wait outside if you don't trust me.'

'Trust a journalist?' His smile glittered. Shit. It actually glittered. How was that possible? On any normal person, I'd have said the facial expression was closer to a smirk than a smile, but the word smirk has unattractive implications, and there was nothing unattractive about Chief Inspector Whip. Even when he was clearly furious with me.

'Fine. Just stay where I can see you,' he said, pulling out his phone, tapping the screen, then lifting it to his ear.

'Alex? Sorry, buddy. Got a bit of a thing here. I'm going to need you to cover me at the scene. Yeah, now. That a problem?' He paused. 'Thanks, buddy. Can you message Nyrah too? She needs to get here ASAP. Yeah, I know she'll be pissed, but tell her the mayor's footing the bill. Yeah, sure. Thank you.'

He hung up and turned back to look at me.

'You don't have to walk me home,' I said. 'I'm pretty sure I know where I live.'

'Hmm, remember that conversation about trusting a journalist? Besides, I've been wanting to talk to you. Find out more about that issue with the trafficker. Not to mention your choice of attire on the plane journey over here.'

Now that was definitely a smirk. And that damn dimple was back in place, too. My cheeks burned.

'How did you hear about that?' I said. 'Bobby?'

He crinkled his nose. 'You should know better than to ask someone for their sources, Ms Evergreen. But no, despite his line of work, your boss isn't one for gossip.'

Annoyingly, that didn't make me feel any better. It meant someone else on the plane had obviously spread the news. As long as it was just a rumour, and there was no photographic evidence of it... because that would be mortifying.

Whip grinned. 'If it makes you feel better, I thought it was funny. I like a woman who's confident enough not to be defined by her clothes.'

My non-existent heart skittered. That sounded remarkably like flirting, didn't it? Or did it? I'd spent years with Andy, and I was completely out of the loop on what flirting was actually like. It was probably just a normal compliment. Plain and simple. But if it wasn't, then flirting back would be a good thing to do, wouldn't it? From an educational point of view. Just to make sure I knew how to flirt, if the opportunity ever arose again. Obviously with someone far more dateable than Whip. Because no journalist in their right mind would get together with the Chief Inspector of the new town they had just moved to, unless they wanted to add a whole new list of complications to their life. Would they?

I cleared my throat, wishing my mind would think of something witty or funny or just anything at all to say. But it was blank. Completely and utterly empty. Finally, a line took hold. Something about uniform. I should say something about his uniform, I thought. But before I could work out what, the tent door opened again. As my head turned to the sound, my eyes bugged.

Did they put something in the water at the police station here?

The man standing in front of me was dressed in uniform, though. His white shirt unbuttoned and his mane of blonde hair wild around his shoulders. Though I could easily imagine him topless in jeans, standing in a forest as he chopped wood with an axe for millions of online followers. For once, I had no difficultly isolating the smell of fresh grass and honeysuckle which rose from him. Was that the first time I had ever smelt a man like that? Yes, I was pretty sure it was, and it was a good smell.

His eyes were a glinting gold, and for a second they looked at me in confusion before his gaze shifted to his boss and a slanted grin rose on his face.

'Not interrupting anything, am I, boss?' he said. His voice lilted with an Irish accent. He had the type of voice and looks that could make someone's knees go weak, and by someone's, I meant mine. *You are steering clear of men. You are steering clear of men.* I repeated it silently in my head. Yup, internal mantras were definitely my new thing, and they seemed to be working. Sure, he was good looking and everything, but was that really my type? All brawn and no brain? Then again, how did I know he had no brain? And what was wrong with a bit of brawn now and then? But really, it felt like he'd come on very strong. Too strong to be attractive, but how could that even be when he'd not even said hello to me? I didn't know if it was jetlag or pure insanity, but my mind was struggling to form a cohesive thought as it yo-yoed back and forth as if I was no longer in control of it.

'Elodie Evergreen, this is Inspector Alex Yardley,' Whip's voice brought me back to the moment, bringing a halt to the back-and-forth thoughts. 'Elodie is going to be working at The Oracle.'

His eyes widened.

'You're the one who staked the trafficker, right? Respect.'

'Right,' I said, not sure how else to respond. 'I'm starting to think that everyone knows about that.'

Alex shrugged. 'It's a small town. You get used to it eventually. But seriously, I was working in Paris for a bit, and we had new vamps turning up all the time. One of them was only seventeen. These traffickers are the scum of the world.'

'You're the one Whip said was looking into them?' My voice hitched in excitement. 'Do you have any leads? I would be happy to help. Maybe you could put me in touch with a couple of the people that you were talking about. It would be great to get some first-hand accounts. We could get together and discuss it at some point.' I could already feel that journalistic itch rising under my skin, desperate to be scratched.

Wren Belkin's murder, leads on the traffickers, and an apparent plethora of attractive men. Ravens Hollow was certainly ticking a lot of boxes already. But at the same time, there was another tugging in my mind. Had the way I'd spoken sounded like I wanted to be alone with Alex in a date type manner? No, surely not, so why did I feel the need to clarify that? But then, if I wanted to go on a date with Alex, then that was okay, too. He was a nice guy. Or was he? I didn't even know him.

Crap, what the hell was wrong with me? I was incomprehensible, even to myself.

Alex's amber eyes continued to look at me for a moment longer before he turned to Whip.

'Why do I get the feeling that this one's going to cause us a whole heap of trouble?' he said, flashing me a quick grin.

'Because you're probably right. Which is why I'm going to walk her home.'

Whip walked towards me and, once again, I was torn. Did I want him to walk me home? Well, it depended on the situation. Being escorted wasn't exactly the same as being walked. And there were several things I wanted to talk to Alex about. Like how much he knew about traffickers. And whether he had to have his uniform custom made so that it could fit all the way around his chest. Not to mention how the hell he smelt so good.

But then there was one man in my life I wanted to be with more than either of them. Pongo. Which was why I turned and looked at Alex.

'Nice to meet you, Alex,' I said, before turning back to Whip. 'You really can trust me to walk back by myself,' I said. 'But I suspect you're not going to. So with that in mind, I guess you can walk me back.'

Alex chuckled beside us. 'Wow,' he said, throwing his boss a look. 'The way she said that sounded like she almost believed she had a choice. I like this one.'

SIXTEEN

Had I not already been certain that Whip was escorting me home, rather than just walking with me, the fact that he didn't talk for the first three minutes of the trip was a pretty clear confirmation of it. For a while, I wondered if we were going to make it the entire way without saying a single word – but I couldn't do it.

It's not that I'm one of those people who can't deal with silence. I can. But there was something about silence next to Whip that was so much harder.

'So, did the crime scene throw up any evidence?' I said, as we continued up the road. 'Any suspects? Off the record, obviously.'

'Obviously,' he said, shooting me another of those smiles that brought out his dimple. 'How about we talk about something that can't get you into trouble?'

'Like why you cowed to the mayor's request?' I replied. 'And is her name really Hillary Hillard? Did I hear that right? Because if that's the case, her parents must hate her.'

He let out a low chuckle, that resonant sound melting right through me. Yup. Being around Whip was going to be a problem if I was sticking to my rule of steering clear of men. Not that this was my fault, of course. No, this was all on him.

'I want to know more about you,' he said, his eyes meeting mine for the first time. 'I have to say, I'm desperate to hear how you staked that trafficker when you were still human. Other than using your instinct, that is.' He threw my own words back at me with a glint in his eyes – but before I had time to feel embarrassed, he was already speaking again. 'I take it they hadn't turned anybody by that point?'

'Oh no. They'd already turned one person. But then... well, let's just say they didn't make it either.'

Whip stopped in his tracks and turned to look at me. 'You killed a second one?'

My lips pressed together in a tight line. It wasn't that I didn't want to respond, I just wasn't sure how to.

'Indirectly,' I said.

'Indirectly. You're going to have to explain what that means. What happened? You didn't stake him then?'

'No, he just died. Like—poof.' I waved my hands in the air. 'After biting me. After turning me.'

'He died from turning you?' Whip repeated slowly, as if he hadn't heard me properly. Although I was pretty sure he had.

'I kind of thought it was just because he was new, maybe. That he did something wrong. Or there was a one-in, one-out rule about vampires that I didn't know about.'

Whip's eyes were still trained on me. 'Vampires can turn as soon as their fangs come through.'

'So that wasn't normal then,' I replied.

It was Whip's turn to press his lips tightly together. 'No. Definitely not.'

I'd mentioned this happening to Donna too, after the incident, and she had looked at me with the same confused expression. But I'd kind of brushed it off. After all, Donna was a witch. A powerful witch, yes, but a witch, nonetheless. I was sure there was plenty about being a vampire she didn't know.

But Whip. Whip was chief of police in this town. He had to know vampires, hell he could even be one for all I knew. He began walking again, silence filling the space between us. It was a different silence to the one before though. I could practically hear the cogs turning in his brain as he tried to work out what to say next. I, however, had a whole ton of questions though by some miracle I managed to keep them inside until we finally turned onto my street.

'What about the whole moonlight thing?' I blurted out. It was wrong to ask questions about Whip and other paras. I got that. But I had to be able to ask questions about my own type, didn't I?

'The moonlight thing?' Whip frowned.

'Struggling to be outside when it's a full moon if there's no cloud coverage. That's a normal vampire thing, right?'

His lips were slightly parted, as if he was trying to hide his surprise, but given how well we could both read facial expressions, he had to know just how bad a job he was doing.

'No. I think you and I need to get together and have a proper chat about things. Although now, you should get inside. This is you, right?' For the first time since I had mentioned the vampire who had turned me, the slightest hint of a smile twisted on his lips. 'Nice wheels.'

'Whip,' I started, but he shook his head.

'We will talk about this Elodie, I promise. But we've both had a very long night.'

And even though I wanted to object, I didn't. Instead, I just nodded my head. Alex wasn't joking. Whip was a very hard man to say no to. And I was starting to think there was a reason for that.

SEVENTEEN

W hen I climbed back into bed, my mind was just as full as it had been before, though somehow I managed to fall asleep, only for my alarm to wake me up after what felt like seconds.

'Well, somebody seems happy today,' I said to Pongo, as he wagged his tail again. 'You liked sleeping on the bed, I take it? Well, don't get too comfy. I'm going to see if I can get you a dog bed today. If this Josephina doesn't have one at the station, we'll just have to find out where to get one. Now, do you want some breakfast?'

He tilted his head to the ground, lifted his paw, and barked twice. At some point, I was going to have to teach this dog that the word for *paw* was *paw*. But then again, if that was the only command he could actually follow, what did it matter?

'Oh god, why is this so horrible?' I said, coughing as I swallowed my first mouthful of blood. 'I think I'd prefer what you've got,' I added, pouring Pongo a bowl of dog food, which he hastily tucked into. Once we were both fed and I was dressed, it was time to get going, though I was torn.

What I wanted was to take my car to the office. I loved my

new car. But it was a ten-minute walk. Could I really justify the money or environmental expense of gas just because I wanted a quick ride in my new toy? And it didn't help that a large swarm of butterflies, or some other winged insects, had taken my abdomen hostage. This was my first time at a new job for almost a decade. I wanted to make a good impression. What did turning up in a car tell them about me? That I was lazy? That I didn't want to walk the short distance? And Pongo was only a puppy, he still needed some short walks. It appeared my mind was made up.

I slipped the opal bracelet around my wrist and stared at the stone. I was certain the ward was waning, which meant it wasn't ideal to be walking outside, but I didn't need that much power, did I? It was morning, not midday, and I just needed enough to get to the newspaper.

'Come on boy, let's do this.'

Prepared for the onslaught of light, and armed with a wardrobe that was still suited to British winters, I slipped a hoodie over my T-shirt and followed it with gloves, and a beanie hat, then sunglasses. Anything I could do to stop the sunlight reaching me. It wasn't like I could overheat the way a normal human body did. Or at least I didn't think I could.

'You're gonna have to stay by my heel again, okay, boy?' I said, even though I knew he didn't understand. 'But if it gets too fast for you, if you get tired, you just give me a bark and I'll pick you up and carry you, okay?'

As I could've predicted, Pongo lifted his paw into the air.

'I'm just going to take that as a sign of agreement,' I said. 'Alright. Let's just check that map again.'

I kind of hoped that an eidetic memory would have come with my vampire powers, but that hadn't been my luck. Apparently, my sense of direction – and memory blindness when it came to reading maps – was still in place. So I checked Bobby's rough sketch several times before I left the house.

'Here we go,' I said. A few minutes later, we were jogging down the street. 'Okay, this isn't too bad,' I said. Dappled sunlight broke through the canopy of leaves and trees, showing only hints of the blue sky above us. 'This isn't too bad, boy, is it?' I said. 'Okay, now we're gonna go right here. Yep, that's it. Stay by my side right here. The sun might hit—'

I had spoken too soon. Without the shade, the prickling started a full assault, stepping up to near singeing. My throat dried as I glanced over my shoulder. If I'd judged the distances right, I was about halfway between home and the office, which meant it would be just as sensible to keep going forwards as it would to turn back. I just needed to go fast.

'Okay, Pongo, change of plan,' I said. 'Gonna pick you up. Ready?'

I scooped the dog into my arms, momentarily wondering if I was doing the right thing. He hadn't coped too well with vampire speed last time. Not to mention, if I suddenly dissolved into a mass of dust, poor little Pongo would drop to the ground. But fingers crossed, I'd have a heartbeat's notice before that happened.

'Okay, just up here,' I said, picking up my pace slowly at first, until I was finally running. I kept my eyes forward, ignoring all the sights and smells that I desperately wanted to take in.

'There,' I said, pointing to a small horseshoe-shaped shopping area with various shops and offices. Was it a strip mall? I wasn't sure if that was the right term or not, but to say it looked tired would've been generous. The paint was peeling, and the concrete had seen better days. It was a world away from the floor-to-ceiling, gleaming glass windows that had made up the building we worked from in London. I didn't have time to think about that. The tingle in my skin was becoming distinctly heated and from the way Pongo was wriggling in my arms, he was feeling something too.

With a flood of relief rushing through me, I pushed opened the door, and let out a gasp.

'Okay boy, maybe that wasn't my most sensible idea.' I stripped off my hat and unzipped my hoodie. 'That is not something we should do. Although,' I glanced down at my watch to see it was only seven thirty-four. 'It looks like we're here early.' It was only as I took the narrow stairs up to the office that I realised, despite my earliness, Bobby, or one of the others, had to already be in, given that the front door was unlocked. I had only been in Ravens Hollow one day, but I had already learned it was not the type of place that was safe enough to leave your doors unlocked. Not if Wren Belkin was anything to go by.

Wishing I'd brought something for the new team, I pushed open the door, ready to thank Chloe or Diego for everything they'd done. But it wasn't a member of the team standing in the office at all. No, it was the one person in this town that I didn't seem to be able to disagree with. And he also happened to send my stomach into flips.

EIGHTEEN

Eyes up, Elodie.

E It hadn't been my imagination. Chief Inspector Whip really was as attractive as I remembered. Those deep eyes. That jaw.

Goddamn it.

'So, it didn't take you very long to make friends,' he said, a smile twisted on his lips, revealing that single, irresistible dimple.

'I didn't?' I said, before realising he was talking about Pongo. Somehow, despite me only just opening the door, the puppy was now asleep in my arms. 'Bobby and I found him last night,' I tell him. 'Someone left him near the festival.'

'And you just took him?'

Maybe it was just the walk out in the sun, or the fact I had to swallow un-spelled blood that morning, but I swore I heard judgement in his voice. And I was not in the mood for judgement.

'Yes, I took him. He was starving and dirty and clearly needed someone to give him a loving home. I also overheard the people leaving him, and trust me, they had no intention of coming back. So yes, I took him.'

Whip tilted his head to the side as if he was trying to see parts of me that weren't visible. Was that another paranormal ability? I wondered. To sense what people were, or read thoughts? It would be a hell of a lot easier settling into this life if I knew what all the different powers were. Maybe I would see if there was a library, and someone to fill up my serious lack of knowledge.

'We have some dog things at the station,' he said matter-of-factly. 'I'll get Josephina to find them for you. I'm sure there's a bed and a couple of different harnesses. They probably won't fit him when he's fully grown, but they should do for a couple of months.'

'Oh,' I responded, not sure how else to reply. I had expected a lecture on picking up strays, or maybe a spiel about how he could just be a runaway from a very loving family. Instead, I'd just got niceness. I hadn't been prepared for that. 'Thank you,' I said. A smile flittered on his lips, but it was gone before it had fully formed, and instead, his expression fell into a deep frown.

'The hat,' he said, pointing to the beanie in my hand. 'Did you walk over here without a sunlight ward? You know you can't go out in sunlight, right? It's a sure-fire way of killing a vampire.'

That time, there was definitely judgement in his voice.

'No, I did not walk here without a ward,' I said. 'It's just the one I've got seems to be running a little low.'

'A little low?' He held out his hand. 'Can I see it?'

Despite his wording, he wasn't asking, and I was struck with an overwhelming urge to tell him to do one. What did it matter to him what type of wards I was using or whether they were weak? It didn't. And yet, another part of me wanted to show him. It would be the sensible thing to do. I knew that. Maybe he'd tell me there was a simple fix to how quickly I was draining these things. Like I was wearing them wrongly. Or that I was meant to leave them out in the moonlight to recharge.

Once again, Whip was going to get his way.

Wordlessly, I slipped the bracelet off and held it out to him. His eyes narrowed as he turned the item over in his fingers.

'This is black opal and moldavite,' he said.

'That sounds right,' I replied.

'Something like this should hold on to its power for years. Months, at least. How long have you had it?'

'Um, a fortnight, I think.'

'And it was freshly warded when you got it?'

'Umm, I think so.'

'Did the witch you used specialise in wards?'

What was this? Twenty questions? I had no idea. But Donna hadn't done it herself because she was worried she wouldn't be able to do a good enough job, so she'd got another witch she trusted instead. Which made me assume the answer to his question was yes. And as irritating as it was, I didn't feel the need to keep any of this back from Whip.

'I think so,' I said again. 'I'm sure it was. But maybe they just put enough magic in it so I could manage the flight over here. They knew I was moving to a magical community. They could have assumed I'd just get it sorted there.'

Put enough magic in it? What was I saying? Did I even know if that was something people did? My God, I sounded like a babbling idiot. That wasn't what I did. Ever.

It didn't help that Whip was continuing to look at me with his brows knitted together. If he would just say something that wasn't a question, or more than three words, that would be helpful.

'I'm going to send someone to see you,' he said. 'A witch

who will do your ward here. Don't go anywhere until you've had it.'

Wow. He really did think he could tell people to do whatever he wanted. Was it because he was chief inspector, or was it something to do with those eyes? I should just tell him I could sort my own wards out if I wanted. But why the hell would I say that when I didn't know the first thing about getting jobs like that done? And why were my thoughts doing that damn yo-yoing thing again? Like I wasn't sure if I wanted to kiss him or kick him in the balls, simply for existing? Was this how normal attraction went for vampires?

'Did you hear what I said?' he repeated.

'Yes, yes.'

'Good.' He pushed a manila envelope towards me. 'This is the coroner's report and some of the photos from the crime scene. So you don't have to go sneaking around in the middle of the night. Now that I've given you that, I hope you'll stay out of the way of the investigation. I'd hate for us to have a reason not to get along.' Was that flirting again, or was it a threat?

Shit, you've been out of the game way too long when you can't tell the difference.

Apparently done, Whip turned around and walked towards the door before he stopped and looked back. 'I forgot to ask,' he said. 'What's his name?'

'His name?' I looked down at the bundle in my arms. 'Pongo.'

'Pongo, as in *101 Dalmatians*? Cute. Although I would have thought you'd have gone for something more like Simba?'

'Simba?' I said, in confusion. Sure, Pongo was furry and I could see how in time it could grow to look a mane-like but he was a little dark to be a lion. Only when I looked back at Whip and saw the smirk twisting on his lips, I realised it wasn't Pongo he was talking about.

'I need to know where you saw my outfit,' I said, as my stomach plummeted at the humiliation and yet Whip's smile only grew.

'I have eyes everywhere,' he said. 'Although everyone who reads The Scoop saw your outfit. And as I already told you, I thought it showed an impressive degree of confidence.' He turned around before twisting his head over his shoulder. 'Don't go anywhere until Nyrah's warded you,' he said. 'That's not a request. And be careful what you do with that information,' he nodded to the envelope. 'I'm *trusting* you.'

The words settled in me, and I felt a shiver down my spine. I wouldn't leave until I got the wards done. It would be stupid to even think about doing that. This time, when Whip turned around, he walked out the door and didn't look back. Not that I minded. The view from that angle was perfectly pleasing.

CHAPTER
NINETEEN

Fifteen minutes later, Bobby and Chloe walked through the door together, along with a tall man in shorts and a T-shirt I assumed was Dylan.

'It's great to meet you,' I said, stretching out my hand and shaking his. 'Chloe's told me all about you.'

'I hope that's not true,' he said, elbowing Chloe and offering her a flirty wink, to which she grinned back.

'You know I'd only ever tell her good things, because there's only good things to tell,' she said, before turning back to me and Pongo. 'So, this is the little bundle of fluff I heard all about. Aren't you just adorable.'

Pongo's tail wagged hard as she crouched down and I knew he was looking forward to another person to show him fuss and attention. Yet before Chloe could get to him, I stepped between them.

'What's The Scoop?' I said.

'The Scoop?' her voice was the epitome of innocence, but she and Bobby exchanged a look. Even if I hadn't had my vampire senses, I would've been able to tell.

'The Scoop ain't no concern of yours,' Bobby replied. 'But

it's good to see you in so early. You got some rest, I take it? And the pup slept okay?'

It was a diversion tactic, pure and simple, and I wasn't having it.

'Chloe,' I said, homing in the one I figured would break most easily.

'Bobby's right,' she insisted. 'It's nothing, just an online blog thing. It's not even proper journalism. I promise. It's just, well, a gossip site, that's all.'

'And was I on that gossip site?' I said. 'Was I on that gossip site wearing a lion onesie?'

Again, the pair exchanged a look. Chloe's lips pressed tightly together, her brow wrinkled apologetically, though she continued to look at me, unblinking, while Bobby fiddled with the strap of his eyepatch.

'Nobody cares about anything on there. Honestly, there will have been a dozen photos of people doing ridiculous things on it since then,' Dylan said eventually.

So I was on it then. Indignation flooded through me.

'Do you know how they got it? Who took the photo? And who runs this blog thing?'

'It's run by Prue Parsons,' Chloe said, both her voice and head dipping slightly. 'You met her last night. She's a sea witch.'

'Prue Parsons.' It took a moment for the image to form in my mind. Bright red hair that was more Ariel than Ursula. But really, a sea witch who stirs up trouble? Talk about being a cliché.

'I need to see the site,' I said, just wondering exactly how horrific the photos were. Maybe if I was standing at the bottom of the steps, meeting Bobby with a smile on my face, that would be one thing. But if I was fast asleep in the seat with a spool of drool rolling from my chin? That would be another.

'Okay, we'll get to The Scoop at some point, but first, I need to give you this.' Chloe reached into her bag and pulled out a large tome, which she promptly plonked down on the desk.

'What's this?' I was annoyed at myself for being distracted, but books were a sure-fire way of grabbing my attention. I swear, that internet meme where they talk about the escape room idea of taking someone to a bookstore and seeing if they can find their way out was made for me. Unable to resist temptation, I flicked it open to a page to find myself looking at some seriously detailed images.

'This book has all the para creatures currently known,' she said. 'Or at least the ones that were known when this was printed, twenty years ago. My cousin bought it for his wife when they met. She'd only been with vamps before then and didn't know about all the other types of paras, so I thought it might be useful for you, too.'

'Wow,' I said.

'There's a good index in the back, and it's well ordered,' Chloe continued. 'All the fae are in one section. All the water shifters in the next.'

'That's amazing, thank you, Chloe,' I said, wishing again that I'd brought some sort of welcome gift with me. 'And you're sure you're okay if I borrow it?'

'Absolutely.'

I had just flicked to another page on birds and their fledglings when Bobby spoke.

'What's that?' he said, picking up the manilla folder.

'That? Oh! Whip dropped them round,' I said. 'Photos and coroner's report.'

'And you just thought to say that now?' he said.

A flash of embarrassment rolled through me. He was right. I had been too obsessed with thinking about myself. I'd forgotten that there was an actual story here.

'Whip dropped them round?' Chloe said.

'Is his name actually Whip?' I said, aware that I was once again asking questions about the Inspector. But I figured Chloe might know the answer. 'I didn't see his name on his badge. So, is it his surname? Or just a nickname?'

Chloe shrugged. 'I don't know. I've never heard him referred to as anything else. No first name or surname either. Just Whip. Like Madonna.'

'But Madonna has a surname,' I replied. 'She just doesn't use it.'

'You'll have to ask him then,' Chloe smirked. 'Though he's not exactly the most personable person. And he doesn't normally make house calls to the paper.'

I shrugged, trying to act as though this piece of information didn't intrigue me. Not personable? I thought of Ines. She had done what he'd asked without a second's thought. She wouldn't have done that if she didn't respect him, would she? 'Well, I'm quite pleased he did,' I added. 'He's arranging for some witch to come and help me with a daylight ward.'

Chloe and Dylan exchanged a look. 'I wonder who he's got,' Dylan said. 'There's no way he could've booked Nyrah that quickly. I thought she was the only person he used, but she books up months in advance.'

'Nyrah, I've heard that name before.'

'You'll hear it again, that's for sure,' Chloe said. There's no one in Ravens Hollow that hasn't seen Nyrah for something at one point or another. Not that they'll always admit to it.'

'Are we gossiping, or are we looking at this?' Bobby said.

'Right. Yes. Absolutely.' I gave Chloe an apologetic look. It wasn't so much that I wanted to be in on the office gossip, more that I needed to know everything that was going on in this small town to do my job properly. At least, that was what I told myself.

'Well, I've got a soccer match to write up,' she said. 'Or

football, as you guys call it. And then my cleaning column. Which is amusing once you find out just how messy I am, but hey, that's the job. I'll let you get on with your investigation.'

Despite saying she was going, Chloe crouched down and finally gave Pongo the strokes she'd wanted to do since she arrived. 'If they get too boring,' she said to him, 'you just come and sit with me, okay?'

I smiled. Yes, I had definitely judged Chloe right. She was great.

Bobby nudged his office door open.

'I guess this is the type of thing we want to look at in private,' I said.

'Sounds good.'

Ten minutes later, we had both read the coroner's report, sitting side by side in silence, and then we had looked through the photos. Once or twice, I'd covered my mouth out of instinct, but a couple more times, I had needed to pick the pictures up and angle them around to work out what it was I was seeing.

'Is this normal?' I said to Bobby. 'I mean, this kind of death?'

'No,' he replied. 'Nothing about this is normal.'

'Those bite marks....They are bite marks, right? Is there something that could've made those? A bear shifter? A werewolf?'

Bobby shook his head. His single eyebrow had been pinched down since he started reading, and it didn't look like it was going to go back to a relaxed position anytime soon. 'Like you said, I'm not even sure if they're bite marks. That type of force... But there were no weapons found on the scene.'

Wren Belkin had not had a pleasant death.

Something had crashed into her with such force it had crushed the entirety of her rib cage. Although, according to the report, there had been more than one impact. Several small impacts at the same time, that had somehow managed to crack her rib cage.

And then there was the fact her heart was missing.

Added to that, there were cuts on her hands, which seemed to have been made from several of her sculptures, which were smashed around the space.

It was an absolute mess.

'So where do we start with this?' I said. 'I mean, I don't know what time the witch is coming to do the ward, but I guess I can start with an online search first. Then maybe we should go and talk to Ines.'

'I can't imagine Ines would be able to do something like that,' Bobby replied, almost absentmindedly.

'Ines on her own, maybe not. But if there was a whole group of them...'

Bobby let out a sigh. 'Right, well, so much for hopin' you'd have a slow start,' he said. 'Let's sort out your desk. It's time you start earnin' that salary of yours.'

This town's first impression of me had been in a onesie lion suit. Not exactly the professional impression I had planned on giving them.

Now, it was time to show them what I was really made of.

CHAPTER
TWENTY

By the time I'd finished my research, I was confident that I at least knew who Wren Belkin was and what she did in terms of art. She was a sculptor, creating large pieces out of plaster. Her palettes varied. Some were visual cacophonies of colour, while others focused on single muted tones. According to the articles I read, the shapes were inspired by the past, present, and future, with the 'devolution of the soul' at the centre of all her work. In my mind, that was the artist speak for saying she would do whatever she wanted, but what did I know?

As well as the variation in colours, the size of Wren Belkin's work was equally diverse. While some of her sculptures were over ten feet high, others were barely the size of a hen's egg. But whatever the creation, she could really bring in a crowd. Several images showed queues forming around the outside of buildings, including a gallery in London, where she had been only two months before. It was insane to think that a paper as big as *The Sentinel* hadn't run at least a small piece covering the event. But that was the thing about the paranormal world – you didn't know anything about it until you were in it. And even then, I felt like I was missing an awful lot. Hopefully getting my teeth into this first story would help.

From a personal point of view – which was always an angle you needed to include to get the readers hooked – Wren Belkin had grown up in Ravens Hollow as Wren Dawling, though she left at the age of sixteen, when her dad got in trouble with the law and they'd moved over to the East coast. That was where she'd met her husband, Macoy Belkin.

There were dozens of photos of them at different events, and in every one, they looked totally besotted with each other. Dinners out holding hands across the table. Wedding snaps of that first kiss. Arms around one another as they walked together down the street.

Back when they had met, he had still been a young man, but it hadn't taken long until he'd become a prominent member of the mermaid mafia who had risen up the ranks at incredible speed. There wasn't any mention of his overly toxic mermaid venom that Diego had spoken about - or mermaid venom of any sort for that matter. Yet, some believed he was untouchable, and he'd certainly evaded arrest a fair few times, until he'd finally been charged with running a ring of soul-backed loans - yup, sea witches, mermaids and now this. I was starting to think that Hans Christian Anderson hadn't been as human as I'd always assumed.

Anyway, Wren had divorced Macoy soon after the allegations came out, at which point, she started increasing her number of exhibitions. While none of the articles said as much, it was easy to read between the lines - she had grown accustomed to a lifestyle, and without her husband's mafia money, she needed to be self-sufficient. Judging by the prices that her pieces went for, she was more than able to provide that lifestyle for herself.

'If it's not Ines and her crew, I think we could be looking at theft gone wrong,' I said to Bobby an hour later in his office.

'Even her small sculptures are worth tens of thousands. Someone could have snuck in before the exhibition was open, tried to steal one, and had to kill her when they got caught. Do we know if any of the sculptures are missing?'

Bobby pursed his lips.

'I could ask Raquel. I don't know if they've managed to catalogue the mess yet. They'd probably need someone from Wren's team for that.'

'Right. And are they planning on getting anyone in to do that soon?' I said. It seemed like the most basic of police work - seeing if anything was missing. But then, I had to remind myself that the murder hadn't occurred that long ago. It just felt like I had been in Ravens Hollow for weeks not hours.

'Any possible culprits you can think of?' I said to Bobby, my mind still on the idea of theft. 'Any Ravens Hollow characters that might try to pull something like this off?'

He scratched the patch of his forehead above his eyepatch. 'Got a few sticky-fingered fellas on the island, that's for sure,' he said. 'But to try to pull off something like that...? Wren and Macoy might be divorced, but I still can't see anyone daring to do anything that would risk getting the merman's attention. He's still got plenty of friends on the outside.'

'Friends who would want to hurt his ex-wife?'

'That's not something I can say.'

'Then maybe we need to do some digging there too,' I said

I may have only been in the office for a couple of hours, but I could feel myself getting itchy. I was desperate to go out there and start questioning people and following up leads. But without the daylight ward there was no chance I could do that. So instead, as I left Bobby's office and headed back to my desk, there was another itch I decided to scratch. One I had somehow resisted all morning.

'I know,' I said, looking down at Pongo, who had taken a

spot by my feet. 'I need to let it go. And I'm going to let it go. I just need to see it once, that's all. Then I'll be done.'

My hand hovered over the mouse. The Scoop. Isn't that what Chloe said it was called? If I knew what images Prue had posted of me, then I could see how bad it was and how many more introductory roars I was going to have to go through before it was forgotten. Or maybe, like Chloe said, there would be so many posts on the page that I wouldn't even be able to find me. Although, that wouldn't change the fact that Officer Whip had seen me in my onesie. If he was ever planning on seeing me in my bedclothes that would absolutely not be my first choice.

'Two minutes,' I said. 'Two minutes. I'm just going to check, that's all.'

Before I could talk myself out of it, I was typing Ravens Hollow Scoop into the search bar. One click later and the link had appeared.

'Last chance to back out,' I said to myself, knowing I had no intention of doing that at all. Holding my breath, I clicked again, this time opening up The Scoop's web page. A moment later, I was staring at a whole selection of portrait recorded videos. It looked more like a kid's TikTok channel than anything with journalistic integrity, but I couldn't help scanning down the page, until my eyes locked onto one of the titles: Ravens Hollow's new Roarporter.

My stomach sank. As I opened the video, the screen filled with the woman I had met the night before, with her bright red hair and sparkling smile.

'Hey, Scoopers! It's Prue Parsons here, and I have a scoop for you. We have a new arrival to Ravens Hollow. Elodie Evergreen, a journalist from the UK, is setting up residence on our little island, and it seems like she wants to make an impression, if the outfit she arrived in is anything to go on, at least.'

The image flicked from Prue to photos of me taken on the

plane. One had been snapped through the window before I'd even got back on board, while another three were taken when I was fast asleep. All from varied angles.

This was *not* journalism. Posting things about someone with no context or explanation – not that I could give them one – was not how this job worked. What the hell? And who took the photos?

Now I got why Chloe had wanted to steer clear of Prue at the festival. Although if I saw the sea witch again, she would discover that not all journalists at The Oracle were afraid of confrontation. Less than twenty-four hours in Ravens Hollow and not only had I got myself a murder to investigate and a serious crush on the local law enforcement, but now a nemesis too. That was good going, even by my standards.

I stopped the video and was about to close the webpage altogether when another post grabbed my attention.

Those Closest to Wren Belkin Mourn.

I didn't want to click this one. Chances were it was a load of drivel. Sensationalist nonsense made up for clicks. But then, Prue had been right about me being a new Ravens Hollow resident and my name, meaning she had to have done the smallest fragment of research. Knowing some people close to Wren would definitely help in knowing who to interview. Despite my better judgement, I once again pressed play.

Any doubt I had that Prue was a succubus of a newshound rather than an actual journalist was gone when I saw her holding her phone camera in front of a small group of clearly upset people.

'Can you just give me a word on what Wren meant to you?' she said, her voice loaded with false-sounding sympathy. 'Anything you'd like to say to those mourning the loss of a fantastic artist?'

'Get your phone out of our faces, now,' one of the men responded. His eyes flashed at the camera.

The hairs on the back of my neck rose. But it was when a tall woman with pure white hair strode towards Prue, shouting and waving her hands, that my stomach dropped away entirely.

'Let us mourn in peace, you vultures,' she said. 'Go on. Get lost.'

Whether she actually got to Prue or not, it was impossible to tell, as the video cut to Prue standing a fair distance away from the group.

'There you have it, folks,' the want-to-be journalist said, a fake forlorn expression on her face. 'The people of Ravens Hollow mourn Wren Belkin's tragic death and don't worry, we at The Scoop will be following this story very closely, so don't forget to hit that—'

The video continued to play, but I'd stopped listening. Every voice in that video I had heard before. Not just Prue's, but the man and woman she'd accosted too. I'd heard them speak, or rather argue, just before Wren had been found dead. Arguing about wanting to go to the police.

That couldn't be a coincidence. Could it?

TWENTY-ONE

'Bobby,' I said, already opening his door before I finished knocking. 'I need you to see this.'

I put my laptop down on his desk with The Scoop webpage open full screen. With a short inhale, he rolled his eye.

'Elodie, I'm sorry, we didn't—'

'No, it's not about me. That's fine. It's about these two people.'

I showed him the video, scrolling past Prue's introduction until the part where Wren's friends start talking to – or rather yelling at – Prue.

'These two. I heard them arguing at the festival,' I said. 'Actually, more than arguing. The woman was threatening him. He wanted to go to the police, and she said she would kill him if he tried.'

Bobby's eye widened. 'You're sure? Where were they? And was this before or after Wren was found?'

'Before,' I said. 'But I don't know where they were. I couldn't pick up on it with my hearing, you know, the same way I had trouble when those people dumped Pongo. I tried to pick them out, find them again, but I couldn't. Then, as soon as I heard them speak on the video, I knew who they were. I know it was these two. I'd bet my life on it. Not that that's really an option anymore.'

'Okay,' he said. 'Well, by the look of this video, they're staying at the Crow's Nest Hotel. When you've got your ward sorted, we can go chat to them.'

'Great. We should drop in on Ines and Sofia, too,' I added.

I still wasn't letting go of that thought. The idea of Ines and the protestors being responsible couldn't quite shift. It was the multiple injuries that were doing it for me. The way it seemed like the attack required a multi-faceted weapon or multiple people attacking at once. And she had the entire protest group on her side.

'Why do you think she didn't scream?' I said, the question suddenly rising in my mind. 'Wren, that is. I mean, with what happened to her, surely she would've screamed?'

Bobby cocked his eyebrow.

'Not sure. Maybe to do with the wards around the tent. Raquel told me they were pretty full on.'

'And we still need the name of the people that were bumped from that main tent. It would be good to get some quotes from them.'

I bit down on my lip. The busywork was done now. I needed to get out there, questioning people. Or at least, one of us did. Although it pained me to my journalist core, I was about to suggest to Bobby that he go ahead when Chloe appeared in the doorway.

'Hey, Elodie,' she said. 'Nyrah's here.'

'Nyrah?' I said. The person Whip had said was going to fix the wards around the tent the night before. The one Chloe didn't think would be free on such short notice. But here she was, ready to ward me.

'Amazing,' I said, moving to leave the office, only for a

woman to step into my path next to Chloe. With jet black hair, sharp features, and near black eyes. She looked more like a raven than anyone else I had seen in Ravens Hollow yet. Beautiful, yes, but canny, too.

'So,' she said with the slightest sniff. 'You're the one that Whip has made me rearrange all my appointments for. Let's get this started, shall we?'

'Guess you'll be needing my office for this, then,' Bobby said, already out of his seat.

'Oh, I don't want to—'

'Yes, you do,' Nyrah said before I could finish. 'I know this room. The energies. It'll be easier if I do it here than try to work out some different space.'

I looked at Bobby, who nodded in agreement.

'What about my dog?' I said. 'Can he stay?'

Pongo had been pretty much glued to my heel the entire morning. Nyrah looked down at him and sniffed.

'Does he have any magical residue?' she asked.

'What?' I felt my eyebrows rise.

'Has he been raised in an auric field? Exposed to enchantments? Anything like that?'

I stared at her blankly. 'I have no idea. He's a stray. I adopted him last night.'

Her lips pursed. 'Well, in that case, he should probably go. It may be alright to have him around during later wardings, but probably not a great idea for your first one.'

She turned to Bobby. 'I'll let you know when we're done. Until then, you know the drill. Do not disturb us.'

A moment later, the editor was stepping out of his office with Pongo in his arms, and Nyrah was pulling down the blinds.

The excitement I had felt at the thought of getting a proper ward done had rapidly been replaced by nervousness, and only part of that was because of the magic I was about to experience. The rest was Nyrah. From the way Bobby had responded to her, she was clearly a powerful woman, not to mention well respected. Yet she seemed less than pleased to be here.

'I'm really grateful for you coming here,' I started. 'And I'm sorry Whip made you rearrange your plans. I didn't know he'd do that.'

'No, it's fine,' she said, flashing me a quick smile. 'Sorry if I was snappy. It's just a hectic day after a long night, that's all. But when Chief Whip asks you to do something, you do it.'

'I can arrange a different appointment?' I suggested.

'There's no need for that, honestly,' she said, her smile holding firm this time. 'Besides, we owe you.'

'You do?' I asked.

'You staked a trafficker, right?' She stretched out her hand. 'I'm Nyrah by the way. And those traffickers are the worst scum of the world. You can definitely call in a couple of favours for that.' Now, she opened up her phone and promptly read something off it. 'So I'm here to give you a sixth-month sun light ward with an additional—' She stopped and pressed her lips together. 'Sorry, yes, complete sunlight warding. Six months' worth.'

'Wait, what?'

'Well, that's what's been booked for, anyway.'

'I'm sorry,' I said. There were two pieces of information I needed to process, but I was struggling to take in either of them. 'A six-month sunlight ward? You're saying that I'll be able to go out in daylight like normal for *six months*? Is it a necklace, or a potion, or...?'

'No, it's a series of spells. My own special calibration. I try to put a little bit extra on it, just in case people can't get to their next appointment in time, but normally clients try to book early, you know, just in case something happens.'

'And that's it?'

'That's it. Well, I mean, you've got twenty minutes of spells to sit through first, and some people find it gives them a bit of a headache the day after, but yeah, that's pretty much it.'

'Wow,' I said, only for the excitement to be replaced by a sudden weight in my stomach. Donna may have paid for my car as a ridiculously over generous gift, but I still had rent to pay, blood to buy and now a dog who depended on me. Costs were mounting up, and I know from my experience in London that even the cheapest wards, were far from cheap.

'Before you do this,' I said. 'How much is it going to cost, exactly?'

Her eyes avoided mine as she began pulling items out of her bag.

'This bill's already been settled.'

'Settled by who?' I already knew the answer. Whip. The moody chief. *He* paid for this? 'Is that something Whip generally does for new people who come to town?'

I tried to make my voice sound as casual as possible, but even I could hear the way my throat tightened slightly and the sensation wasn't helped by the way Nyrah's eyes were clearly avoiding mine.

'I wouldn't say it's exactly normal, but who knows with Whip? He likes to keep us on our toes,' she said.

That was one way of putting it.

TWENTY-TWO

'Well, you weren't joking about that headache, were you?' I said twenty minutes later as I rubbed my temples. It felt like several nails had been impaled behind my eyeballs.

The entire event had started out surprisingly relaxing. Nyrah had lit various herbs and candles, the scents of which had been most pleasant. But then she had started her chanting, and it was as if her voice was penetrating all the way into my body. My skull throbbed as my skin began to tingle, much like when the wards start to weaken, but while that sensation had been fleeting, the headache didn't feel like it was going to go anywhere for a while yet.

'You're feeling it already? That's interesting.' Nyrah said as she packed up her belongings. 'I don't mean this the wrong way, but what were you before they turned you?'

'What was I?' I said, confused. 'I was a human.'

'Right, but just a plain human?'

'Are there other sorts of human?' I asked.

At this, she let out a chuckle.

'Oh, there are lots of other sorts,' she said, stopping her

packing and perching on the edge of the desk as she spoke to me. 'That's the thing with keeping magic so hidden – people don't realise their ancestry. Or even the ancestries that are out there.' I must have looked as confused as I felt, because she shifted onto the chair opposite me, as if she was settling in to tell me something lengthy. And given that her voice seemed to be the one thing that help soothe this headache, I wasn't going to complain.

'Apparently,' Nyrah continued, 'the world was once fifty-fifty. Tips and paras. We lived for centuries, if not millennia, in peace. Then, something shifted. History books aren't exactly filled with details, but we can be pretty sure it was to do with power. Humans wanting more of it, I suspect. Anyway, early alliances formed between humans and various para types to bring other group's numbers down. Populations quickly diminished. Once that happened, the tips would form another alliance to bring down their previous allies. Eventually, there were so few that our ancestors went into hiding, forming small sanctuaries, like this one in Ravens Hollow. I think the plan was that once numbers got high enough, we would re-join the world, but the fear of the past holds strong. I don't know if we'll ever rejoin the tip world now. And to be honest, I'm not sure I'd want to.'

'Wow.' I said, the word leaving my lips in a near gasp It didn't seem quite the right word for the horrificness of it all.

'Yeah, well, the point I was trying to make was because of all the years that tips and paras lived in peace, there are a lot of tips out there with para genes they know nothing about. And they'll likely live their whole life that way. I mean, we had a vampire in here once who was one-sixteenth werewolf. Not enough to be affected by the moon, but oh my God, the blood-thirstiness at that time of the month? It was a nightmare. I probably spent the best part of a year working on a ward to sort that one.

'Sometimes you get people whose great-great-great-great-grandmothers were Fae folk or magic weavers. I mean, it normally manifests in some way, even if people can't tell. Like the vampire-werewolf guy, he was an amazing tracker. That's what he did as a human. And that carried over once he was a vampire. And of course, some full paras get turned too. And not just to vamps. You get some that are bitten by werewolves, others that get cursed for all sorts of random reasons. Then you get a whole other level of magicness going on.'

'Wow.' Again, I only had that same word to offer her.

'So,' she said, looking at me a little more pointedly. 'Did you have anything like that? Anything that made you remarkable as a human?'

I shook my head. 'No, not unless you count being a workaholic.'

Nyrah chuckled. 'I don't think that's limited to humans,' she said, flashing me another smile. Despite the slightly rocky start we had got off too, it was safe to say I liked Nyrah. And I sure as hell respected her. Fingers crossed the feeling was mutual.

'Well, the headache normally passes after forty-eight hours or so, but drink a lot of blood. That should help. Have you been up to Weirdoughs? They've got some post-ward blends I helped them develop. Recipes that are actually good. Try giving those a go.'

More and more people were recommending this bakery. I was going to have to go there at some point. And now that I could go out in the sun, I was thinking the sooner the better. Although first, I had work to get on with, and Pongo was going to get his first experience of being a journalist's dog.

TWENTY-THREE

'Oh my God, this is marvellous,' I said as I stepped out into the sun, slipping off my hoodie and wishing I had put on a pair of shorts instead of jeans. 'The sun here is so warm. Is it always like this?'

'Pretty much,' Bobby said. 'That's why you need air-conditioning.'

I had lived my entire life in the U.K. where the sight of the sun was an event worthy of celebration, and even then, it didn't mean the day was warm. No, clear blue biting winters were a definite thing and the number of times I had been tricked into thinking it would be warm outside by a clear sky was ridiculous. I couldn't imagine ever wanting to be cold on purpose. This was a part of life in Ravens Hollow I was not going to take for granted.

'So, where are we going first?' I asked.

'Well, if you really want to speak to Ines, that seems like our best bet. I'm still waitin' on Raquel to see if she knows whether anything was stolen, so we might want to hold off on talkin' to Wren's people until we know that for sure.

'Speaking of which, I did some diggin' while you were getting warded by Nyrah. I've got some names for you. The two people you pointed out were Esmeralda Unker – Wren's agent – and Thor Nolan, her head of security.'

'Agent and head of security. So, two people who were definitely close to Wren and on the inside.'

The back of my neck prickled. People that close to a murder victim, threatening silence and police involvement *before* the body was found, didn't feel like a coincidence.

As Bobby headed for his truck, I moved to follow him. 'You wouldn't mind if I drove, would you?' I said. 'I'd just need to pop back to mine to get Maureen, but it shouldn't take me a minute.'

'Maureen?' That singular eyebrow quirked.

'Maureen the mini,' I said, though I wasn't sure why that needed an explanation. 'I haven't had a chance to take her out yet, and I need to get used to driving on the other side of the road.'

'As long as you're sure,' he said. 'We need to go to the southwest of the island. That's where Ines lives, with the rest of her pack.'

'Ines isn't the same pack as Diego, right?' I asked, as we changed direction. Apparently, we were walking to my place together. And I was fine with that. More time in the sun, and more time learning about the people of the island, was a win-win for me.

'You figured Diego out then,' Bobby said with a grin. 'Not that he's a tough one to figure out. Theodora'll be a harder nut to crack.'

Theodora was the copy editor who'd offered me a very swift good morning before sitting down at her desk and putting her headphones on. *A harder nut to crack* in more ways than one, I suspected.

'So how many packs are there on the island in total?' I asked.

'Five,' he replied. 'And two of them live out in Wounded Woods . You won't ever see them. The two in Wraith Wood are a bit more sociable, but I use the term loosely. Diego's a rarity amongst them. Ines's beta for the Amber pack in the Welcoming Woods.' He let out a belly chuckle. 'Don't take that name as a given, though. That lot tend to come out for the events, but whether you want them there is another matter. Like last night.'

Five wolf packs, and at least three woods. I was learning the island little by little, though I suspected I had a long way to go.

It was only when we reached the house that I realised how badly I had misjudged asking Bobby to let me drive. It wasn't that I didn't think I could handle being on the other side of the road. No, the issue was whether he could deal with sitting cramped into the tiny passenger side, his knees under his chin.

'This was a mistake. We'll take your truck,' I said, as he wound the window down so he could rest his elbow outside.

'Don't fuss, I'll be fine,' he replied. 'But maybe that dog of yours will be best on the back seat, rather than on my lap,' he said as Pongo licked his face.

'Yes, sure.' I lifted the pup and planted him directly behind me. 'So, you just tell me where to go,' I said. 'And if I'm in the wrong lane.'

'I'm sure I can manage that.'

Ten minutes later, and we had left the suburbs of Ravens Hollow behind.

'I can't believe how much jungle there is here,' I said. 'I don't know why—I just didn't think it would be so... jungley.'

'Got the weather for it,' he said. 'There's a place at the end of the island where there used to be a zoo once. Non-magical creatures, believe it or not. Had things like guinea pigs and badgers.'

I laughed. 'I couldn't possibly imagine going to a zoo to see a guinea pig. What happened to it?' I asked.

'Hurricane,' he said. 'We don't get them the same way they do over on the east coast, but every now and then we get the tail end of one. This one was particularly nasty. Destroyed most of the enclosures. Didn't seem any point in rebuilding it.'

'Oh.' A zoo would have been a nice place to take Pongo for a walk. Not that there weren't plenty of other places to explore also. 'What happened to the animals?'

'A lotta the ones that survived got rehomed. And, well, there are a fair few crocs still about, some wild sun bears, though I'm not convinced they ain't shifters. Oh, and there's an impressive flamboyance of flamingos. Those ones are definitely regular birds. Had to have a protection order to stop some of the bigger shifter residents hunting them.'

A protection order to stop the residents from eating flamingos? This place was absolutely bizarre.

'Take the right here. It's five minutes away.'

The jungle had given way to a small cluster of about twenty or so houses. Most were single storey, though there didn't seem to be front yards or fences separating the properties. It all felt like a communal space.

'Is he gonna be alright?' I asked, motioning to Pongo. 'Wolves don't eat dogs, do they?'

Bobby raised his eyebrows. 'No. Let's just say it's a good job you said that in front of me and not one of them. They might do something just to spite you.'

Right. Remembered. Do not anger werewolves.

'Probably best if you let me do the talking as well,' Bobby continued. 'You know, given that everyone knows me and everything.'

I wasn't going to argue with that. Not because I didn't

want to speak, but because I liked observing. I was good at observing. Meaning if Ines was involved in the murder, I'd spot the clues. Of course, that was before I had all the issues with my vampire sense. But I wasn't going to worry about that for now.

TWENTY-FOUR

We parked the car behind a rusty old truck, and despite what Bobby had said, I brought Pongo with me. I didn't want to leave him in the car on his first work outing, particularly when there could be people around. Not to mention the heat. No, Pongo stayed by my side, and the sooner the people of Ravens Hollow saw us like that, the better. Though as for hoping my senses would play ball, we were still ten feet from the house when I learned that wasn't going to happen. Although this time it wasn't my hearing that was going haywire. It was my sense of smell.

It was like having my head dunked into a vat of perfume, although I was still able to make out every aroma as they clogged my nostrils. Pine trees and cactus flowers were the first scents that struck. How the hell I knew they were cactus flowers I had no idea, but it was so powerful, I could practically taste it. Beneath those aromas came the next layer: moss and damp earth, wood-burning stoves and ... formaldehyde? That one didn't seem in keeping with the rest of the smells, but it was there. More and more subtle aromas began to creep in. Leather boots, lavender incense sticks, freshly baked bread....

'Elodie, you okay there?' I shook myself out of the aromas to find Bobby staring at me, his eyebrow quirked in concern.

'Yes, yes,' I said, blinking away the echo of the scents that still lingered in my mind. 'Sorry, just taking it all in.'

'As long as you ain't getting peckish? Wouldn't be a great place to do it.'

'No worries there.' I flashed him a quick smile to show my completely fangless mouth, then hurried to catch up to him.

As we reached the door, Bobby lifted his hand to knock, but it swung open almost immediately. Standing there, in jeans, a vest top and... what would you know... leather boots, was Ines Ortega.

She offered us a slow roll of her eyes.

'I had a feeling it would be you,' she said. 'And I'll tell you now, I've already spoken to Whip. I've got nothing to add other than what I told him. No, I did not kill Wren. No, I do not know who was responsible for killing her. Yes, I do have witnesses for where I was the entire time before and after he dispersed us. No, I am *not* sad that she's dead.'

'Well, that was to the point,' Bobby said, a smile flitting onto his lips.

Clearly, his advice about not getting on a vampire or were-wolf's wrong side applied to me rather than him.

'Is there any chance we could just ask you a couple of questions?' I said, ignoring the warning about keeping quiet. If Bobby could ignore his own advice about being polite, I could ignore him about not speaking. Just for a bit, anyway.

'About?'

'About a few things,' I said. 'I still hope to do a follow-up on your protest. Would it be alright if we come in though? I'm not quite used to the heat yet.'

It was true, obviously, but also, I wanted to see if there was anything in her house. Anything that could be a clue. Word-lessly, she stepped aside and let us in.

It was clear that Ines Ortega was an outside type of person. There were very little in terms of homey touches in her house, like the cushions and candles Chloe had sorted for me. But there were several taxidermied animals, including a raccoon posed to be swigging from a beer bottle and a ferret wearing sunglasses with a revolver in a holster, which explained the formaldehyde scent.

'My aunt does them,' Ines said as she saw where I was looking. 'We have to keep a couple on display for when she pops over. Now, what was it you wanted to ask?'

I didn't wait for an invitation before taking a seat on the sofa. Bobby promptly sat next to me, while Ines took a seat opposite.

'Is your sister in?' I asked. 'I assume you two live together.'

'We do, and no, she's not,' Ines answered curtly. 'Were you intending on harassing her too?'

'We're not planning on harassing anyone,' I said. The protective big sister vibes were practically rolling off Ines. But was that because Sophia needed protecting because she was guilty, or just because that was what she always did? Either way, I decided to leave it for now. 'I'll get straight to the point,' I said. 'Other than your group of protestors, is there anyone you can think of who would have wanted to harm Wren?'

'*Other than my group?*' Her lips twisted. 'When exactly did I say I wanted to harm her? I said she was vile, that we didn't want her on our island. Having her there was a disservice to all the people who had put in months of work to prepare for the festival. Particularly since she stole their places.'

'Who did she do that to?' I asked.

'Obviously, the people who were supposed to be in the main tent and got pushed out.'

'And do you have some names?'

Her eyes narrowed slightly. It was true, I could look this up myself, but I wanted to see how easily she would throw another name out there if the heat was on her.

'These people aren't killers. They're artists,' she said.

'I know. But I would have asked you this anyway, even if she hadn't died. We were going to write a piece, remember? That's what we said yesterday. And if we're going to cover this properly, we need to know who the displaced artists were. Otherwise, we won't be able to give an accurate account. You understand that, right?'

She pressed her lips together.

'Suzanne Livermore,' she said. 'She's a bird shifter. Lives by the jetty over near Pepper's Bay and she does these amazing pieces of art out of sea glass and driftwood. She was meant to be in that tent, along with someone she works with. Instead, they got shoved under a tiny canopy in the middle of nowhere. She was pissed, yes, but she's *not* a murderer. You'd be better off looking into Esmeralda.'

'Esmeralda Unker? Wren's agent? Why's that?' I asked.

Ines bit down on her bottom lip. 'We're not the police,' I reminded her. 'If you tell us something, we can tip them off, but your name never comes into it. I promise you that. I value my journalistic integrity.'

Unlike some people on this island, Prue Parsons.

Ines let out a long sigh, but I knew she was going to tell me. 'It's not common knowledge,' she said eventually, 'but Esmeralda's husband was killed working for Macoy.'

'What?' I said. 'When was this? Before or after Wren and Macoy's divorce?'

'Before. Just.' Ines hesitated. 'Some people reckon that's the real reason Wren divorced him. That it had nothing to do with the conviction at all.'

'How do you know this?'

She chewed on her lip, glancing away for a moment.

'I was born and raised in Ravens Hollow. So were my parents. So was Esmeralda. After her husband died, she came back here for a couple of months. Kept it quiet. She was staying with her mother down on Pepper's Bay. I only knew because... because—' She stopped, her eyes widening slightly as she looked at Bobby. Clearly, she had said too much.

'You were out hunting at Folorning Forest?' Bobby suggested.

I didn't know where or what Folorning Forest was, but from the reaction, it wasn't somewhere Ines was meant to be.

'We *weren't* hunting. We were doing pack drills,' Ines corrected. 'You know, endurance training. Stuff that helps with survival. Keeping the packs out of Folorning forest is damaging. Harming biodiversity. This woodland here has halved in size over the last twenty years while Wraith Woods has been so overly hunted it's criminal. And it's not just normal creatures whose numbers are plummeting. Sprites in that woodland are suffering because of all the hunting. Not to mention other shifters using their homes as scratching posts, amongst other things. If the council actually knew anything about the ecosystem on this island...' She shook her head. Clearly Wren Belkin wasn't the only thing Ines had had issue with. Not when it came to the environment, anyway. 'Now, do you want to hear what I heard, or not?'

'Yes, yes, we do,' I stressed firmly.

Ines let out another sigh before she continued. 'I was out on the far side, sticking to the area close to the coast, when I heard Esmeralda talking to her mum. She said Wren could have stopped it. Those were her exact words. It sounded like she hated the woman. She'd lost her husband, her money, everything. Who could blame her? But then, six months later, she's back touring with a new exhibition, standing at Wren's side, all happy smiles. It just doesn't sit right with me.'

'Thank you,' I said. 'I appreciate you taking the time to

answer that.' Given the way she had threatened Thor and now this, Esmeralda had gone up to the top of my list of suspects. Meaning I wanted to talk to her. Now.

I got up, ready to leave, when my eyes fell on something in the corner of the room. I had no idea what it was, but it didn't look friendly. Three heavy-looking balls were connected by a piece of string. If that was swung at a person, I reckoned it could do a serious amount of damage. Crush someone's chest even.

'Sorry, what's that?' I asked.

'That? It's a bolas,' Ines said, like I should know what that meant.

'Sorry, what does it do?' I asked.

Rather than replying, Ines moved and picked it up. 'You might want to step back,' she said, swinging it lazily over her head. The thing looked deadly.

'It's a hunting tool,' she said as she continued to move it. 'Our pack believes in more than using our teeth. This is one of the traditional techniques I've been trying to master.'

'The idea is that when this is spinning fast enough, you let go, and it entangles the animal's leg. When it falls to the ground... well, you get the rest.' She slowed her spinning, then lowered the item to her side. 'A couple of the kids have been interested in learning other methods of hunting. Pretty sure it's a pride thing, you know? Shifters always make them feel crappy about not being able to change whenever they want. So I've been teaching a couple of them. Like Rami Hawkins, Fabian Thomas. Basically, I'm just trying to keep the teens out of trouble. Though I get the irony, given that I'm the one with the police and papers on my doorstep right now.'

She let out a light chuckle, though I responded only with a small smile.

'Where are the boys now?' I said, trying to sound as casual as possible. 'It would be great if I could speak to them.'

'Speak to them?' She asked, her eyes flickering ever so slightly.

'We want to speak to as many people as possible who were there last night,' I said, you know.

'Oh, they weren't there,' she said. 'They went off the island with their dads. Not the artistic type,' she said, letting out a chuckle that sounded a fraction too tight. 'Now, if there's nothing else I can help you with, I need to get on. I'm sure you can see yourself out.'

TWENTY-FIVE

I got into the car and turned on the engine, eager to discuss everything that we had just learned. But as I opened my mouth to speak, Bobby cut straight over me.

'Who's a good boy?' he said, ruffling Pongo's fur. 'Yes, you are. A very good boy.'

He was speaking unusually loudly. Even though he was fussing over Pongo, he was looking directly at me the whole time. Then, he tapped his ear and turned on the radio.

Right.

No doubt Ines was listening in on our conversation. I would have thought being a vampire would make investigations like this easier. And I suppose in some ways, it had. After all, Esmerelda wouldn't be top of my current interview list had I not overheard her speak. But matters like this - being overheard even when you couldn't see anyone was going to take some getting used to.

We drove away from the houses, and only when we were a good couple of hundred metres away did Bobby turn down the volume and start talking.

'I know what you're going to say.' He shook his head as he spoke. 'But I just can't see it.'

'Bobby, Ines had a weapon in her home. She even told us that it was for hunting.' I knew exactly how exasperated I sounded, but this seriously looked like a home run to me.

'I know,' Bobby replied. 'But that in itself has to be a sign. If she was the murderer, she'd know the cause of death and assume that we did too. It would be a risk to show us that. Besides, she didn't say the weights that did the damage, it was the rope that was used.'

'What about the kids she said she was teaching? There were two names, weren't there? Not to mention she could be covering for her sister. Sofia was riled up last night, and obviously they have a strong stance on how the council handles environmental issues on the island. I bet three teen were-wolves swinging those things could cause an awful lot of damage.'

It wasn't a bet I was actually willing to take, given that I'd never seen a teen werewolf, but if these were the type of kids that wanted to prove themselves against others, then at that age, with hormones running riot, strength was bound to be a big thing, right?

'At the very least, we need to let Whip and the rest of the department know,' I said, refusing to drop the point. 'They need to come and take that thing as evidence.'

Bobby wrinkled his nose.

'Ines said Whip had already been round there himself. He wouldn't have missed somethin' like that. Not a chance. Not to mention, you'd have been able to smell if there was blood on it, and as far as I'm aware, you didn't, did you?'

'I hadn't even thought about doing that,' I admitted.

'Don't think you needed to think about it,' Bobby replied. 'Pretty sure if there was human blood on that thing, you'd've picked it up.'

I thought briefly about when I had stepped into the tent the night before, and the thick, cloying aroma that had my fangs tingling. But there had been a lot of blood in that situation and there was a good chance that my olfactory senses were just as out of whack as my hearing was.

'I know you think she couldn't have done it,' I said. 'But she was really angry at Wren being there. And in the time between Whip dispersing the crowd, there definitely would have been time for her to sneak in and kill her.'

'Okay, so say I agree,' Bobby contemplated. 'What about that stuff she said about Esmeralda? About her husband? You seemed pretty adamant that she was involved, too.'

'Maybe they both are,' I said. 'Maybe they were in cahoots. Ines saw us closing in, and thought throwing Esmeralda under the bus would help take the heat off her.'

Bobby let out a low hum.

'Right now, it's all speculation, and until we know who had access to the tent, we'll just keep going around in circles. Let me give Raquel a quick ring and see if she's got any more details.'

He tapped on his phone. I'd been hoping to use my vampire hearing and see if I could tune into his conversation, but he flicked it onto speaker.

'Hey, Dad,' a cheery voice answered. 'Let me guess, you just wanted to call and see how my day's going and tell me you love me dearly and that I'm your favourite daughter, right?'

'You're the only daughter that stayed on the island,' Bobby replied. 'Does that count?'

'Not at all,' she chuckled. 'But it's fine, because I know I am. So, let me guess, you want to know more about this case?'

'Just a quick question. So we write things accurately, you understand.'

'Of course,' she said, her tone flat. I could almost hear her rolling her eyes. 'It's not because you're busy sticking your nose into official police business.' Bobby, for his part, chose to stay entirely silent, at which point Raquel let out a long sigh. 'Go on then. What's this quick question?'

'The wards around the exhibition tent. How easy would it have been for someone to get past them? I assume you've had a witch there to assess what magic was in place before the murder?'

'Yeah,' she grunted. 'Nyrah was here most of the morning unpicking everything, after she'd put her own in place.'

A pang of guilt struck me. No wonder Nyrah had been so tired and grouchy. I'd be exactly the same. If there's a sleep-related term for hangry, I got it. Badly. It was only adrenaline and jetlag getting me through today.

'Everything in there was very tight,' Raquel continued. 'Wren didn't like anybody seeing her exhibition until it was open. Not even most of her staff. The only person who could raise and lower the barriers to let people in were her agent and her head of security.'

'Esmeralda and Thor,' I said.

'That's them,' Raquel replied. 'Hi, Elodie. How's your first day going?'

'Definitely busier than I expected,' I admitted.

So, Esmeralda had the ability to open and lower the wards to let people into Wren's exhibition, and she had been arguing with Thor and threatening to kill him. Yeah. These coincidences around her were too big to ignore. But that didn't change how I felt about Ines' weapon.

I was definitely leaning towards the idea that the two of them had worked together, but there were still a lot of people I needed to speak to before I dared put anything in print.

Bobby said goodbye to Raquel before he hung up the phone and turned to look at me.

'So, where's our next stop? Are we going for Suzanne or Esmeralda?'

'I think you know the answer to that,' I said, feeling that journalist flutter building within me.

'Esmeralda it is.'

TWENTY-SIX

The Crow's Nest Hotel was a modern building, a mixture of yellow stone and glass, far more minimalist than anything else I had seen in Ravens Hollow so far. Not that I had seen much, yet. Though I drove my little Mini in through the Bentleys and Porsches, it was clear this was a very different part of town to where Ines and Sofia lived.

'I'm not sure they're going to like dogs in here, so you need to stay quiet, okay, boy?' I said to Pongo as we walked past the manicured lawns and into the foyer where a glistening chandelier hung from the ceiling.

While Bobby walked over to the reception desk, I stayed by the door. Partially because I was holding Pongo, but also to work on my hearing skills.

'Afternoon,' he grunted. 'We're here to speak to Esmeralda Unker.'

The concierge sniffed. Either it was a seriously loud sniff - which was possible - or I was tuning in well. I hoped it was the second. 'And who should I say is calling?'

Bobby opened his mouth, but before he spoke, a thought

struck. With a clear line ahead of me, I vamp sped over to him, determined to get there before he could say anything else.

'Somebody with a message for her from Pepper's Bay,' I panted, before Bobby could get a word out. 'Sorry, boy,' I added, glancing down at Pongo, who was blinking in confusion. Bobby looked at me, raising his eyebrow.

'Trust me,' I whispered.

There was no way, after the incident with The Scoop, that Esmeralda was going to come down if they said it was the press. Making her think it was something to do with family might get her down.

'Is lying a common technique for journalists in the U.K.?' Bobby asked while he waited.

'I prefer to think of it as manipulating the truth,' I replied.

'Yup, that's lying.'

The moment Esmeralda appeared in the foyer, I recognised her from the photo and the video online. She was tall, with slender shoulders and that bright white hair, which was currently piled high in a sixties style back comb. From a distance, it looked like she might hit Bobby's height, although as we moved over to meet her, even with the hair, she was still a few inches short.

'Esmeralda Unker?' I said.

'I'm sorry, I don't know who you are, but I'm here to meet someone.'

'Yes, someone from Pepper's Bay, right?'

Her lips pinched inwards as her nostrils flared.

'Let me guess. Press. Here to hound us again. I've already had enough of that, thank you very much.'

She turned to leave, but a definite advantage of vamp speed was that I was already standing in her way before she'd taken a step. And this time, I'd remembered to put Pongo down on the ground first.

'I wanted to ask you some questions about your husband's death,' I said.

'Sorry?' She started slightly. The question had clearly caught her by surprise. Obviously, she'd assumed I was going to ask about Wren. 'What do you know about my husband's death?'

'That it was an unnecessary tragedy.' I was clutching at straws and terrified she could see it. But it hadn't been the first time I'd used someone's body language to tailor my questions, and more than once, I'd been rewarded with a damn good lead. 'And I know that some people think the Belkins were to blame.'

Esmeralda's nostrils flared again as she visibly sized me up. 'You have no idea what you're talking about,' she snapped.

'You're right, I don't, not really. And I'm not somebody who writes speculation. I'd much prefer to hear your point of view.'

She ran her tongue over her lips, but she still offered no response. 'If you are somehow insinuating that what happened to my husband was a motive for Wren's death, then I can assure you, you are barking up the wrong tree, Miss...'

'Evergreen,' I said. 'Elodie Evergreen.'

'Well, Miss Evergreen, let me tell you this. Wren was not just my employer. She was my very best friend, and I can assure you, she remained that way until her death. I would never, ever do anything to hurt her. Did I always agree with her decisions? No, I did not. Did those include marrying Macoy Belkin? Possibly. But like you said, what happened to my husband was a tragic accident. I no more blame Wren than I do myself. Now, if you don't mind, I have people to see. As you can imagine, the interest in Wren's pieces has soared, and I am left to handle that.'

For a second time, she turned to walk away, and Bobby

looked at me, satisfied that we had got something out of her. But I wanted more. No, I needed more.

'Miss Unker,' I said. She snapped back around to face me

'It's Mrs Unker,' she said. 'Just because my husband is dead doesn't mean I have reverted to my maiden name.'

'I understand, I do, and I apologise. I just wanted to ask one more question.' Her face remained impassive, and I knew any second she was going to march away. So I got it in fast. 'Who were you threatening last night?'

Her face blanched. You didn't need vampire sight to see the way the blood had drained from her cheeks.

'I'm sure you're mistaken.'

'Actually, I'm sure I'm not,' I said. 'You were threatening somebody because they wanted to go to the police, and you said that you would murder them if they tried.'

A muscle twitched along her jawline. 'I do not believe that was my word of choice at all.'

'I think it was as good as,' I said. 'So, are you going to tell me who it was?'

'What, so you can pester another innocent person about Wren's death?'

'It was Thor Nolan, wasn't it?' I said. There was no point playing this back-and-forth game. Not when I actually knew the answer. 'What was he going to do?' I asked. 'What had you so worried?'

She snorted. 'You don't know anything.'

'That's why I'm asking. All I know right now is that you threatened a man, to murder him, very close to the time that someone you knew was also murdered. I'm also aware of the fact that the only people who could go through the wards into her exhibition before it was opened was Wren herself, you, and Thor. Doesn't look very good, does it?'

A long blow of air billowed from her lips.

'It's all irrelevant now, anyway.'

'Why? Because Wren is dead?'

'In a manner of speaking.'

She glanced around, only now seeming to realise that we were standing in the foyer of the hotel, with little to no privacy.

With a despondent sigh, she nodded her head towards the bar.

'We'll talk in there.'

TWENTY-SEVEN

As Esmeralda strode away in front of us, Bobby whispered into my ear.

'Donna weren't joking when she said you take no prisoners, was she?'

'Just doing my job,' I said, but I felt a flicker of satisfaction rise in me. I wanted my new boss to see that I was good at what I did. Fingers crossed, that meant I'd get to stay on the investigative side of things. There was no way I could cope with fluff pieces. Not when there were stories like this out there that needed covering.

Esmeralda moved to a seat at the furthest corner of the bar and sat down.

We followed suit, and I tucked Pongo under my feet. Somehow, I didn't think the bar staff would take too kindly to him. It had a very, no kids, no pets, no fun vibe about it.

'So,' I said, hoping that would be enough to prompt Esmeralda into talking. It was.

'You have to understand that when Wren and Macoy divorced, she struggled. It's always a struggle for an artist to keep themselves afloat. For the vast part of her career, Wren had had Macoy to support her, but then he went to prison, and the funds... dried up.'

As her gaze went to me, I offered a small nod, but stayed silent. Hadn't I thought exactly the same thing to myself earlier in the day? Good to see my journalistic skills were still intact, even when my pulse wasn't.

'So what happened? What did Thor have on her?'

Tension rippled through Esmeralda. Which was good. It meant whatever she was going to tell us had meat to it.

'The first couple of exhibitions she had after the divorce did well. I think a lot of it was hype. You know, the convict's ex-wife. But then sales began to drop. Substantially. In fact, at one exhibition, she had zero sales at all.'

'So what did she do?' I asked.

Esmeralda pressed her lips tightly together before she spoke. 'She put her pieces up for auction and got people close to her to bid on them, then buy them at the inflated rate. Just a few times, but with a lot of money behind them. The type that immediately catches art collectors' interest.' She let out a scoff. 'It's ridiculous, really. The sculptures were worth just as much as they'd always been worth, but until you get yourself that name...' She sighed again, as she shook her head. 'Anyway, she could've done it no more than half a dozen times before she didn't need to anymore. She was earning big bucks again.'

'Right.' I said, linking what she'd told me to my original question. 'So I'm guessing Thor thought it was immoral? That was why he wanted to go to the police?'

'I mean, he didn't think his pay check, which was completely inflated, was immoral, but hey, there you go.'

'And this was what you were threatening to kill him over?' I said.

'It was an exaggeration,' she said. 'I wouldn't have *actually* killed him. Caused pain, dismembered him perhaps, but not killed.' Even though a smile lifted her lips, I wasn't sure if she was joking or not.

'And Thor? He'll back up this story of yours?' Bobby said at my side.

'I believe so,' she replied, although there was something about the way her eyes flickered ever so slightly as she said the words.

People had tells. Chloe had held my gaze absolutely when she lied about not knowing why people were roaring at me. Bobby fiddled with the strap of his eye patch. I wanted to test a few more lies to make sure.

'So, generally speaking, you and Thor work well together? You got on?'

'Generally speaking, yes.'

There it was. That erratic flicker again. She was definitely lying.

'Can I just ask you another question?'

'I have the feeling that you're going to. But you should know, my patience is wearing thin.'

'It's a quick one,' I promised. 'We were hoping to get the answer from the police, but as you're here, you might be able to answer it for us. Do you know if any of the pieces were stolen from the exhibition?'

She shook her head. 'Numerous pieces were broken, but as for stolen, I don't believe anything was, no.' There was no eye twitch. Interesting. I wasn't planning on pushing my luck with any more questions, preparing to thank her and say my farewells, when a sharp ringing broke the silence at the table. Esmeralda looked down and pulled her phone out of her pocket.

'What do you know? Actual family. From Ridgecreek, this time,' she said. 'Now, if you don't mind, I need to get going.'

'Of course not,' I said, stretching out my hand. She didn't take it. 'It was nice to meet you,' I added anyway.

'I won't say the same. But at least I can hope my face won't appear on some tacky video.'

'No cameras here.'

'Very well.'

A moment later, she was striding away.

Having learned my lesson from last time, I stayed quiet until I looked at Bobby.

'So what do you think?'

'I think she's lyin' about a few things,' he said. 'Raising prices to flood interest is unethical, but it would hardly be something to threaten to kill a person over. Assuming you heard that right.'

'I did.' I wasn't taking his doubt personally. Overhearing a comment in a busy situation would never hold up in court. Nor in a decent paper.

'There's still the situation with her husband,' I said. 'Something about it just didn't fit right with me.'

Bobby nodded, obviously in agreement. 'So, time to speak to Thor?'

'Absolutely.'

It was time to start unravelling Esmeralda's lies.

TWENTY-EIGHT

Unfortunately, before we had a chance to ask the concierge to ring down Thor and try a similar trick as we had on Esmeralda, Esmeralda had informed them that we were not relatives of anyone, but the press, and that we were not to speak to anybody in the building. In fact, she had requested that we were escorted off-site.

'She's going to speak to him, make sure he confirms what she said,' I told Bobby as we got into the car.

'I agree. So what are you thinkin' we oughta do now?' he said to me.

I contemplated the question momentarily.

'Honestly, I still want to go talk to Suzanne Livermore and the artists who were booted from their marquee, but I also want to check what Esmeralda just told us about the money. If Wren was inflating her prices, then there'll be some evidence in the bank, right? The money going out, then coming back in again. Do you have access to that kind of thing?'

'I've got a contact, but they ain't the most reliable. We'd likely be waiting a good few days to hear back.'

'Maybe I can ask Donna,' I said.

'Donna?'

'It's a big story, and I'm guessing we're not the only people she knows in paranormal journalism, right? Or the only contacts she has. Maybe she'll have someone who can help us get some of those bank statements. After all, there's a good chance Wren's payments were international. You know, to make it look more realistic.'

'Good thinkin',' he said. 'Wanna give her a call on the way to Suzanne's?'

'That sounds good.'

Unfortunately, despite trying several times, we weren't able to get through to Donna at the office, or on her mobile. It was annoying, but not unexpected. I sometimes found it a miracle that Donna made time for any sort of life outside of work at all.

As I gave up trying to contact her, I switched my focus to the scenery around me. We were well outside of Ravens Hollow town, and driving parallel to the coast, down a thin drive which finished at a wooden shack with a veranda that seemed almost as big as the house itself. The entire thing was decorated with artwork–hanging sea glass, light catchers, and upright garden sculptures. Chickens strolled leisurely around as they pecked at the ground or else took up roosts on various bits of furniture. It was incredible.

'Yeah, something tells me you'll be okay without a lead here,' I said to Pongo. 'Just stay next to me, okay?' He looked up and raised his paw, before following the action with his standard two barks. I had to give it to him, this dog was nothing if not consistent. 'I'm going to take that as a yes,' I told him, before heading up the steps and knocking on the door. A few seconds later, I tried again. After the third attempt, I called out.

'Hello, Suzanne? Are you in? Hello?'

'Hello! Is someone there? I'm round the back!'

With a quick glance of acknowledgement at one another Bobby and I walked around the back of the building, where a large workshop stood with the doors open wide. A woman was standing with driftwood and glass sculptures filling the space behind her. I wasn't sure what I'd expected Suzanne to be like. Probably somebody between twenty and forty. That seemed to be the average age of the people I'd met so far. Yet the woman we approached could have been anywhere up to eighty. She had a mass of silver and auburn hair woven into a great plait that draped around her shoulder at the front, and a face creased with laughter lines. Definitely not what I thought of when I envisioned a murderer, but I knew better than to let looks deceive me.

'Hi, Suzanne? I'm Elodie.'

'Elodie Evergreen,' she smiled, sweeping those creases even higher up her face. 'I see you've gone for more formal wear today.' She grinned. Great, so even Ravens Hollow pensioners read The Scoop. At some point, I was going to kill Prue Parsons for those damn photos of me on the plane. And whoever it was that took them.

'Yes, well, it's always good to travel in comfort,' I told her. 'I was wondering if I could ask you a few questions?'

She pushed her hands on her denim overalls and stepped all the way out of her studio. 'Well, I was going to stop for a little bit and make a cup of tea, if you fancied one?'

'Yes, that would be lovely, thank you.'

'How are you, Bobby?' Suzanne asked as we moved towards the house. 'Been a while since I've seen you. June doing okay?'

'She's good, thanks, Su.'

'And Raquel? Getting on well at the station? I'm sure Whip and Alex have already got her in their pockets.'

'Oh, you'd be surprised how well she holds her own against the Chief,' Bobby said.

While the fact that Bobby and Suzanne clearly knew each other shouldn't have come as a surprise – after all, this was a small island – I was surprised that Bobby hadn't said as much. Still, as we headed towards the house, I couldn't help but cast my gaze back into the workshop. Was there something in there that could have been used as a murder weapon? Something that could have caused those multiple heavy strikes to the chest? Most of what I saw was driftwood and pieces of glass, but I was sure that someone with enough skill could use that to fashion a weapon, couldn't they?

'So, I'm guessing that even though I've told the police my alibi, you're going to ask for it, too?' Suzanne said as we entered her kitchen. 'Because it's pretty tight.'

Bobby looked to me. Apparently I was taking the lead on this.

'Actually,' I said, 'there were a few things I wanted to ask you about. But I did want to ask about Wren. I was told you didn't get any warning that she was going to push you out of the main exhibition tent, is that right?'

'Well, about an hour. Had to pack up all my things. Hadn't even finished putting them in boxes before they were bringing hers in. That was when I was kicked out. I don't know how fast they expected me to move. I can only carry one of my sculptures at a time. They're not light.'

'What happened to all your stuff?' I asked.

She raised her eyebrows.

'Oh, they brought it to me afterwards. God forbid I see her masterful work before it was time. I'll be honest, from what I heard of her last exhibition, it all just looks like papier-mâché. No real style or signature to it. But hey, what do I know? Only been doing this most of my life.'

She filled a teapot from the kettle, then fetched a milk jug out of the fridge. I couldn't help but feel a snug sense of warmth. I hadn't realised that people over here used teapots and wondered if they were common. I'd already heard that some people made tea by putting the bag in water in the microwave and I wasn't sure how I felt about that. But today, this was a proper brew and I planned on enjoying it.

'Did you see Wren?' I asked.

'Yes, yes, she thanked me for giving up the space – like I'd had a choice – and that was it. Then that witch of hers got to making the wards. And that was when I was kicked out.'

'Right, that's it. You weren't the only one though, right? Are there any other exhibitors who maybe weren't as matter-of-fact about it as you?'

'You mean ones who would kill her?' She smirked. 'Not that I can think of. I mean, really, you'd be looking at outsiders. I'm not saying Ravens Hollow doesn't have its problems. It absolutely does. If Bobby hasn't filled you in on pack politics and all that kind of nonsense, then I'm sure he will. But festival days—whether it's the art festival, the music festival, the food festival—those are the days we come together. We put those quarrels aside. Act like a small town is supposed to. I can't think that anybody would want to disrupt something so special in that kind of way.'

'But your friend Ines was there protesting,' I said.

She shrugged. 'Yes, I know. She was being a friend. That's what that one does. But I don't know. I'd look at the people close to Wren if I were you. You know, her security manager worked for Macoy before he came on board with Esmeralda? And we all know what a rotten egg Macoy is.'

I exchanged a glance with Bobby. So Thor was okay working for the mermaid mafia, yet wasn't okay with Wren inflating the price of her artwork. That wasn't adding up too well, in my opinion, anyway.

'Can I ask how you know that?' I said. 'I'm pretty sure members of the mermaid mafia don't announce themselves, do they?'

She chuckled. 'No, they don't. But I'm one of them. Not the mafia part, that is. The other bit.'

'You're a mermaid?' I tried to look like this wasn't the most exciting thing I'd heard, but my eyes involuntarily shifted down to her legs, disappointed to see they were exactly that. Legs. Still, I didn't have any reason not to believe her. God, what would my ex think of me talking to a real mermaid? Well, he'd think I'd lost my mind.

When my eyes returned to meet Suzanne's, I blushed at the smirk on her lips.

'No tail at the min, but I promise I am what I say. And gossip in the sea is just as bad as it is here.'

'And gossip's how you know that Thor was working with Macoy?' I said, trying to ignore my social faux pax and return to a state of professionalism.

'For years and years. And I'm not sure why Wren kept him on, because the rumour is they hated each other. But maybe Macoy had something to do with that. After all, it's rumoured she got a very big payout from the divorce.'

'It is?'

'It is. Big enough that she didn't have to keep making those sculptures of hers, that's for sure.'

I scratched Pongo absent-mindedly. It felt like the more we learned about the situation, the fewer matters were adding up.

'Well, Suzanne, we won't take up any more of your time,' Bobby said, saying what I was thinking. 'I'm sorry about you not getting your spot. If you'd like, I could send Diego down, get some shots, and give you a bit of a double-page spread in the paper. You know, make up for the lost publicity.'

Suzanne's smile broadened.

'Oh, would you? That would be lovely, thank you,' she said. 'If I could get the other artists who had to miss out involved too?'

'Sounds good to me,' he said. 'Just ring the office and arrange a time.' Suzanne gave Pongo a rub before letting us back out the way we came. 'Nice to meet you, Elodie Evergreen. I'm sure I'll see plenty of you in the future. And if you need something nice for your garden.' – she pointed to one of her sculptures – 'you know where to come.'

'Thank you,' I said. 'I'll bear that in mind.'

We weaved our way back through the chickens and into the car.

'So,' Bobby said, as he squeezed himself into the passenger seat. 'What are you thinkin' now?'

I assumed mermaids weren't one of the para types we had to worry about overhearing us. Either that, or he wasn't convinced we need to hide things from Suzanne. I was tempted to agree.

'I'm thinking we've got a lot of different rumour mills saying a lot of different things,' I told him. 'If Macoy gave Wren a massive payout from the divorce, then why would she need to inflate the prices of her sculptures? We need a look at her money. At least then we can work out who's lying.'

TWENTY-NINE

I was feeling the effects of a full day's work for the first time in weeks. My body ached, and I would quite happily have curled up and slept for the rest of the week. But it had been a good first day, and even better because it was a day out and about. Three interviews later, and I had seen a fair chunk of Ravens Hollow. Certainly more than I would've done had I been shut in an office the entire time.

'I'll try Donna again later,' I said to Bobby as we drove back into town. I'd had no luck getting through on her mobile or at the paper, and asking someone to break the law wasn't something you did via text message.

'Right, well, probably best to drop me at the office and head home.'

'Are you sure?' I said.

'For sure. My truck's there, and I gotta check a few things before I head home.'

'Anything I can help with?' I asked.

Bobby shook his head. 'Nah, you've done plenty. You go home. Have a rest. You deserve it. Busy first day and all.'

I dropped him off at the office before driving back to my

place. From what I could tell, there weren't that many roads in Ravens Hollow, but I was still impressed that I knew where I was heading.

'So, what do you think, Pongo?' I said as we drove away from the office. 'Did you like your first day of being a reporter's dog?'

The moment Bobby had got out, Pongo had jumped onto the front seat, and it was clear that was where he was most comfy. Though I couldn't help but notice the size of his paws as he pushed them up against the window. They really were big. But that didn't mean he was going to grow to be a big dog size, did it? No, of course it didn't. All puppies had big paws, right?

It was only as we turned onto Magnolia Drive I realised I'd totally forgotten to go to the police station to see what they had in the way of harnesses and leads. It hadn't been an issue, but as a responsible dog owner, it was careless of me not to have got those things sorted. I didn't even know what the laws around here were. There was a possibility I'd been breaking them all day by not having him on a leash, although most of the time he'd been in my arms, or close enough to grab. And it wasn't like he could actually run away from me. No matter how fast he could go, I could guarantee I was faster.

I drove towards the house, ready to do a U-turn and head back to the police station, when I discovered there was no need. There, standing in my driveway, in a black T-shirt and casual jeans, was none other than Chief Inspector Whip himself.

'Good God, he looks good,' I muttered to Pongo, before remembering my mistake. It had only been a murmur, but still. How good was his hearing? I didn't even know *what* he was. Something brooding and dangerous – that was all I'd got so far. Of course, there was the other fact about him that I couldn't ignore. The fact that I, and everyone from what I could tell, seemed to do everything he asked without a moment's deliberation. Was it just his pretty privilege? It was possible, but I didn't think it was likely.

'Just play it cool, okay, buddy,' I whispered to Pongo as I drove the car into the driveway to see that Whip hadn't come empty-handed.

There, by his feet, was a large dog bed and a duffle bag. If I was to hazard a guess to what was in the duffel bag, I'd say it was dog harnesses. Goddamn it, he was bringing me gifts. And he was hot. If I hadn't sworn off men after the Andy debacle, I would, I would... What would I do? There'd been no world in which I'd ever been brave enough to make the first move on a man like Whip.

But then again, the last time I'd been in the dating pond I had been human. Maybe vampire Elodie Evergreen finally found the guts she'd always wished she had.

'I wondered when you were going to be back,' he said, his deep drawl enough to make me tingle in places that definitely weren't my fangs. 'I was just going to leave this here for you.'

'Thank you. You didn't have to do that. I would've gone to the station and picked them up. It's just been a bit of a busy day.'

'I heard. Got an angry telephone call from Esmeralda Unker.'

'I can't say I'm surprised,' I said.

Whip raised an eyebrow. Somehow it made his cheekbones even sharper.

'You think Esmeralda is behind it?' he said.

'I don't know. There's something there. But hey, you're the detective.'

'Chief Inspector, technically,' he corrected. 'But enough work, how did the sun ward go with Nyrah?'

Oh crap. 'I'm so sorry. I should have rung and said thank you.' A wave of guilt flooded through me. How the hell had I not done that? I prided myself on my manners. It should've been the first thing I'd done. But after Nyrah had left, it just hadn't entered my mind.

'No worries, really. As long as it works.'

'It's been amazing. So much better than the bracelet Donna got me in London.'

'Oh yes, speaking of which.'

He dug into his pockets and pulled out the bracelet he'd taken from me that morning.

'I had Nyrah take a look at it,' he said. 'That ward should've lasted for months. And I wanted to talk to you about the moonlight issues you mentioned. You struggle to go out when it's too bright. Is that right?'

'Well, yeah, but I've just had issues with the full moons so far. All that reflected light really takes it out of my type, I guess.'

I smiled in what I hoped was a carefree – not to mention attractive – manner but Whip's expression remained a picture of seriousness.

'Not normally, it doesn't. I've never known anyone to have a problem with that before. And I've been quite close to a couple of vampires.'

Quite close. Did that mean... no, I wasn't going to think about that.

'My stepsister,' Whip clarified before I could get another word out.

'Your stepsister?' I said.

'Of a sort. Let's just say that my family situation is a little more complicated than the average person's. Or even paras. But I knew her from pretty much the day she was turned. We went through a lot together. So, while I'm not an expert, I've seen what it's like to go through the adjustment firsthand.'

So Whip's stepsister was a vampire, but I had no idea what he was, other than not like me. Still, the fact he was sharing personal details felt like we were making a shift into a new territory. Friendship perhaps.

'Is your stepsister in town?' I said. 'I'd love to meet her. You know, to actually meet another of my type.'

His smile was fleeting, and I couldn't help but notice the sadness that flickered in his eyes. 'No, I don't have any family in town. And it's been a long time since I've seen my sister. But she'd have liked you. I'm pretty sure of that.'

Liked. There was definite use of the past tense there, which meant what? His sister had passed away. If that's true, given that she was already a vamp, the situation couldn't have been good.

Silence swelled between us. Silence I desperately needed to fill.

'But the moonlight thing makes sense, doesn't it?' I said, blurting out the first thing I could think of. 'Moonlight's reflected sunlight. It's still the sun, right?'

A slight grin lifted the corner of his lip, making his dimple reappear. He didn't look like he was finding me cringeworthy. Just amusing. Was that better? Marginally, I supposed.

'Do you want the easy answer, or the long, scientific answer?' he said.

I'd never been one to shy away from knowing the full truth. Yet before I could respond, Pongo barked at my feet.

'Sorry, I need to give him some food,' I said. 'And I'm sure you've got places to be.'

He bit down on his lip, his pearly white teeth causing a fluttering in my abdomen. Good God, he was gorgeous.

'Actually,' he said, 'I was just gonna start by carrying these into the house for you. Like a gentleman,' he said, glancing at the dog bed and duffle bag. 'Then I was going to head back to the crime scene. There are a couple of things I want to check out.'

As he looked at me, he seemed to realise he had made a mistake.

The tiredness I had been feeling as I drove home now pushed to the back of my mind.

'Let me guess,' Whip smirked. 'You want to come with me?'

This was nothing to do with Chief Inspector Whip. No, this was old Elodie Evergreen, who had no intention of missing out on anything that would help me write the best possible story.

'You can tell me about the moonlight on the way,' I said, grabbing my keys from my pocket.

'Sounds like a deal,' he flashed that damn smile again, and unless I was reading it wrong, there was a twinkle in his eye. Maybe I had a chance with the chiselled-jaw mystery para after all. Not that I would date him. No, I was off men. One hundred percent.

Unfortunately, the more time I spent in Ravens Hollow, the harder it was to believe that was true.

Unsurprisingly, Pongo wolfed down his food, and I'd barely had time to open the duffle bag to see if there was a decent-sized harness for him before he was at the door, ready to go again. Apparently, the pup was as keen for me to get back to the crime scene as I was. Still, I found a collar and lead, which I clipped around him. The collar was far too loose, and I was sure he could have slipped out of it without much trying, but thankfully, he was perfectly happy to walk to heel.

'So this moonlight thing,' I said to Whip as we turned off Magnolia drive. 'Why doesn't it affect vampires the same way if it's just sunlight?'

'It's due to polarisation,' he said.

'Polarisation?' I asked.

'It happens to light when it's reflected. Polarised light doesn't affect us in the same way. Like polarising sunglasses. Theoretically, you could cover your entire body with that type of glass and walk out in the sun quite happily. Not that I'd advise it. Unless of course, that's something you'd be into, then just let me know.'

He flashed me a grin. Whip was flirting with me. There was no doubt.

'So moonlight didn't affect your sister?' I checked again.

'No, it didn't. But different vampires can have different tendencies, depending on if there's anything else in their lineage.'

That was exactly what Nyrah had said to me earlier. I pondered the question. Bobby had told me that people held their cards close when it came to their magical powers, and it was a wise choice, safety wise, but Whip was the chief of police. Surely he would be a safe type of person to talk to. Besides, I'd already told him about killing the second vamp.

'And you think that's what caused the other vampire to die when he bit me?' I asked.

He turned to look at me. I hadn't thought it would be possible for somebody to look cute and confused, but he absolutely did.

'I really don't know. I've never heard of that happening, just like I've never heard of the moonlight thing, but I'm starting to think I should watch myself around you, Evergreen.'

There was something about the way his lips twisted that set my stomach on fire. Yes, he should watch himself. And I would happily watch him too.

No, Elodie! I immediately caught myself before my ogling became even more obvious. Bad thoughts. Mustn't have bad thoughts.

'What about sleep?' he asked me. 'How do you sleep at night?'

'On my own. Well, with Pongo next to me now,' I grinned. 'And you?'

Was I flirting? Yes, one hundred percent. And from the way Whip grinned back at me, he wasn't exactly hating it.

'Also on my own,' he smirked. 'But I meant more about

hours. Do you find you need to sleep, or are you drinking enough blood to stop you from doing that?'

There was a lot to unpack there. The first thing being that Whip had volunteered information about him being single. And the second, was that I'd learned something new and useful about being a vampire.

'Drinking blood can stop us from needing sleep?' I said, feeling it was more appropriate to question him on this than go down a line of finding out exactly how he slept on his own. Boxers or in the buff? Fully under the sheets or just partially? God, it was like I was in heat, though after years with Andy, I could hardly blame myself for that.

'Yes. It's not advised all the time, and not for a new vampire either – you'll get a bit too much of a taste for it. It's actually a good way of knowing whether you're having the right amount or not. If you're wired day and night, you're probably drinking too much. If you've regressed to the teenage stage of not wanting to leave your bed, then you probably need more.'

My mind skipped back to the last few weeks in London. Whip had got the description spot on; a teenager who didn't want to get out of bed. If it hadn't been for Donna making me do things, like get wards or pack for the move, I probably wouldn't have got up at all some days. Yesterday and today had been the busiest days I'd had since I'd turned, and I was feeling the effects. The thought caused an involuntary yawn to escape. Whip chuckled.

'Given that it's only six, I'll take that as a sign that you probably need to drink more,' he said.

'I had a horrible feeling you were going to say that.'

'Don't worry. You're not the only one who's not a fan of the taste. That's why Weirdoughs has such a loyal cliental. Apparently, one bite of their shakshuka, you'll be hooked.'

'I'll have to take your word on that.'

'Or maybe I'll just have to take you there. As a part of a group, that is,' he added hurriedly. 'It's a hangout for lots of the vamps. It would give you a chance to meet some of the others in town. I'm not a very good person to show you the ropes. There are other people in much better positions. Actual vampires, I'll give you their number. So you don't have to contact me every time you need something.'

There was a shift in his tone that prickled my skin, and not in a good way.

'Right...' I said. 'Well, I wasn't aware I'd contacted you for anything at all so far, given that you were the one who's turned up at both my house and my job today. But I'll just put that generosity down as an anomaly.'

'Elodie,' he started, but I quickened my pace and pretended I didn't hear him, which was stupid, given the vamp hearing and everything. But hell, it was a good job my heart wasn't beating – going from hope to zero that fast would have hurt. So much for thinking that the flirting was recipro-cated. I swallowed my disappointment and tried to focus on the positives. This was a good thing. There was something about Whip that was disorientating. The power he had over people was unnerving, not to mention the way my thoughts flip-flopped around him. I had a job to focus on, and the last thing I needed was a distraction like Whip.

We were nearly at the park where the exhibition had taken place, but it was looking one hell of a lot different now. The tents were gone – all except the central marquee, and with all that open space I could see all the way down to the beach. There were several other details about the park I'd missed like the cycle track, various pagodas and children's play areas. With so few people, I tried to narrow in on some of the sounds and see what I could pick up on. The waves were pretty loud, and I was fairly sure there was a sports match going on somewhere in the distance. But I wanted to hear details. Pick up on the little things closer to me. Drawing in a deep breath, I tried to tune out the distant noises.

Focus Elodie, I muttered to myself.

Rather than quieting, as I had hoped, a crescendo of crashing waves and cheering crowds roared through me, but then, almost as quickly, it was as if I had been plunged into a vacuum. There was nothing. No sound. An absolute absence of noise. And a deep thud, thud of heart beat, joined by another two slightly farther away. Three heart beats. Whip and two other people in the tent? Yes, I was sure that was what I was hearing.

'You have to know that I'm not going to let you roam around the crime scene.' Whip's voice startled me out of the moment and I turned around to find him standing far closer than I expected.

'Sorry?' The shift from complete control back to normality was more than a little disorientating. 'I missed that. What did you say?'

His cheeks pinched inwards, sharpening the sculptured look of his face even more.

'I said I can't let you roam around the crime scene,' he repeated. 'We've got a necromancer coming in from the mainland to see if they can pick anything up, and we need to keep the area as clear of spiritual contention as possible before then.'

Well, that had my attention. Even more than wanting to know if I was right about the single other heartbeat in the tent. 'Necromancers? They're real?'

'Yes, but we don't have any on the island.'

'Why not?'

'They're not always the most sociable of souls. In a small town like this... no.'

He didn't need to say more.

'So what is it exactly you're looking for?' I said.

'Honestly, I don't know. But I find it's always worth a second look at things. And it might help having you here in the dark, you know, when your senses are at their strongest.'

Assuming I could get them to work, that was. Still, knowing that my senses were strongest at night was another tick in the box for things I'd learned about vampires. Not wanting to try the hearing again, I decided to put that theory to the test with another sense.

'Is that blood I can smell?' I said, noting the same aroma that had hit me when I'd gone into the tent the night before. 'Wren's blood?'

'I suspect so,' Whip said. 'That's probably the most easily recognisable scent for all of you.'

'Right.' So maybe looking for something more subtle *would* be a good idea, although now all I could smell was blood and sea air, so maybe using a different sense would be a better tactic.

'The ground there looks very wet,' I said, pointing to an area at the back of the tent. 'Nothing else is like that.'

'No,' Whip agreed. 'I think that's probably to do with the exhibits they brought in. Some of the sculptures were suspended in different coloured liquids. I don't know what they were. Something abstract and blobby.'

'Something abstract and blobby?' I couldn't help but raise my eyebrows. 'Wow, what an excellent description. Can I quote that in the paper? You really sound like you're an art fan.'

He flashed me a grin that caused my stomach to melt, but I quashed the sensation as quickly as I could. I was not being pulled into it again. He was a player. Someone who flashed hot and cold to keep a woman interested. Well, I was too old to be playing games.

'That one was very much off the record. I'm afraid.'

'And what do I have to do to get you on the record?'

A moment passed between us as our eyes locked. A lump formed in my throat as I willed my feet to stay where they were, and not move involuntarily towards him. Was this just because I hadn't had an attractive man look at me in nearly a decade? It felt like it was more than that, but I could hardly say that, could I?

Unless I could phrase it as wanting to know more about vampires. Did he know whether increased horniness was a vampire thing? There was no way to ask that question without looking like I was hitting on him. But the way his gaze lingered on me made it hard not to.

'I just feel like I'm missing something,' Whip said, suddenly shaking his head and breaking the moment. 'Like the answer is there, here, and I can't quite put my finger on it.'

A heavy exhale flew from my lungs. Of course, his intense look had been because he had been thinking about the case, not me. I cleared my throat and flashed him a smile.

'Well, if you ask me, the answer is Esmeralda and Thor. Possibly working together.'

'Maybe,' he replied. 'They're on my list to question again tomorrow. Hopefully, I'll be able to get some more information from them.'

For a second, I considered telling him about my money trail idea, but I hesitated. After all, he was the police. I was a journalist. There was a fine line between us. And it wasn't just me doing this research. I needed Donna's help. The last thing I wanted to do was let Whip know I was pushing my friends onto the other side of the law. No, the best thing to do would be to tell Whip when I had the evidence. Besides, I still hadn't spoken to Donna.

I looked at the time. It was early evening, which meant it

wasn't even midday there. Donna would be in the office now, but I should still be able to get hold of her.

'Hey chief, I was hoping you were going to pop by.' A voice from by the tent caused us to turn around. Alex was standing there in his uniform, staring at the pair of us; we were far closer than I had realised. I tried to shuffle back subtly, while breathing a lungful of Alex's honeysuckle scent. 'Had the mainland calling for you. Wanting to know when the bridge is going to be open again. And according to Raquel, Josephina is pissed that you've not been in all day. The radio's playing up, and she needs you to re-tune it in.'

'Any of you can re-tune the radio, you know that, right?' Whip groaned.

'Sure we do,' Alex grinned. 'But then she'll start nagging us to do it too.'

At this, Whip rolled his eyes. 'And I don't get how she can't tune the radio, but has no problem putting YouTube on at any time of day.'

'One of Josephina's many mysteries,' Alex said, as he flashed me a quick smile. 'Hey Evergreen,' he said. 'Good day?'

'Busy,' I said. 'Alex, is there another person in there with you? In the tent? Or are you alone?'

His lips twitched. 'You're asking if I'm on my own? That sounds like a proposition,' he grinned. 'I'm not saying no, just that maybe we should slow it down a little first.'

'Or maybe she's just a new vampire trying to test her skills,' Whip growled behind me.

I flashed Alex a quick smile, not sure why I felt quite so bad. Maybe because I was almost sure he had been flirting with me. Again. And what the hell had I been thinking the last time we'd met, when I'd got hung up on the idea of Alex being all brawn and no brain? He was actively pursuing vampire traffickers. And he clearly had a wicked sense of humour.

Maybe I had been spending time daydreaming about the wrong police detective.

'I do still want to talk to you on your own about the traffickers,' I said. 'But yeah, I was trying to see if I was hearing things properly. There's someone else in there, right?'

With what was as close to a serious expression as I believed Alex could do, he cast a glance back at the tent before looking at me and nodding. 'Yeah, got a security guard from Mayor Hillard's team in there.'

'Just the one?'

'Just the one.'

'Is that what you thought you heard?' Whip asked, his focus purely on me.

'Yes,' I answered. 'It was.'

'Then that's good.'

Another moment was buzzing between us. A moment where I was going to work out why he was being so hot and cold? I doubted it, but I could hope. But then, before either of us could say any more, Alex cleared his throat.

'So now that we've cleared that up,' he said, as his face slipped into a grin. 'Why don't we set a date for you and I to get together to talk about traffickers? Maybe over dinner? I'm a good cook. Just in case you like a man who cooks.'

Hell yes, that was flirting and the fact that he was continuing to do so was surely a sign that I'd improved since my humiliation with Whip when I'd first arrived on the island.

I opened my mouth to respond, but before I could, Whip spoke.

'You should head home,' he said, turning to face me. 'I have enough to do here without risking civilians contaminating the crime scene.'

'Sorry,' my jaw dropped again. He had practically invited me here. Whatever was going on with him, it was seriously starting to piss me off. 'Alex,' I said, ignoring Whip entirely, 'thank you, I would love to take you up on your offer of dinner at some point. Just give me a call at the paper.'

His grin widened.

'Don't worry, I will.'

With that done, I turned to Whip. 'I should let you get to it. I'd hate to contaminate anything. Thank you again for the dog things. And the wards. And don't worry, I won't be asking for your help with anything from now on.'

'Right. Of course. I mean...'

He opened his mouth, as if he was going to say something more. His eyes locked on mine and I felt it again. A static humming buzzing between us. For a split second, I was sure it was going to be one of those lines from the movies. You know the ones. Where the guy apologises for being a dick.

Whip leaned forward and pecked me on the cheek. The brush of his skin against my cheek created a thousand tingles that spread out from the place his lips touched me.

'I'll see you soon, Elodie,' he said, before swivelling around and disappearing into the tent. What the hell was this guy playing at? He was like a sauna-plunge pool combo. Constantly hot and cold. Was that how he got everyone in the town to do his bidding? Because they were hoping that one day, they'd finally get their way with him? Well, that wasn't the type of game I wanted to play. And yet I could already tell how much fun it would be to win.

It was only when I heard a throat clear to my left that I realised Alex was still there, looking at me. His smile widened as he glanced down at his watch.

'You know, I get off in half an hour, if you fancy going for that drink tonight?' he said. 'Could show you a bit of Ravens Hollow night life?'

'Alex!' Whip called from inside the tent. 'Get in here now!'

A slight smirk twisted on Alex's lips as he rolled his eyes.

'Next time Evergreen,' he grinned. 'Next time.'

As he disappeared, I let out a long sigh and dropped down next to Pongo.

'I'm starting to think that Ravens Hollow might be the death of me, boy,' I said. 'And for someone in my state, that is not good at all.'

THIRTY-ONE

'What happened to settling in slowly?' Donna said when I rang her from home an hour later. 'Interviewing potential murderers doesn't feel like taking it slowly to me.'

'I'm ever so sorry. Next time I move house, I'll make sure no one gets killed until I've had time to unpack my bag, shall I?'

Her laughter down the line caused a warmth to spread through me. It was good to talk to her like this. To her face, even if it was just on the screen.

'But from what you've seen of it so far, do you think you'll be happy there?' Donna carried on. 'Happy in the para world?'

'Well, the island is beautiful and the people I've met so far seem cool enough. I've not seen much of anyone at the office yet other than Bobby, and he's great. But Chloe and Diego seem lovely too. Chloe has done such a thoughtful job with making the house homey. And in case I haven't told you enough times already, the car is amazing.'

I had texted her the night before with a photo of the car

gushing over how much I loved it, but in my opinion, for a gift like that, my appreciation couldn't be overstated.

'I need a photo of you in it,' Donna replied. 'I can just imagine you driving by the beach, windows down.'

'Right,' I grinned. 'With my new companion in the passenger seat.'

'Companion?' her voice hitched. 'You met a guy? Already? How?!'

I had filled Donna in on a few aspects of life via text, but I hadn't wanted to tell her about Pongo until I could give him an official introduction. From the excitement fluttering through me, and the way his big blue eyes were staring up at me, I knew I'd made the right decision. He deserved all the fuss in the world, even if this was coming virtually over a video call.

'Not exactly...' I said, stretching out the tension. 'I've got a dog.'

Donna's jaw dropped as her hand flew to her mouth. 'Oh my God, that's even more commitment than a guy. Let me meet him. Come here!'

For the next five minutes, Donna ooh-ed and aah-ed over Pongo. I had only had him a day, but I could already feel the change in his weight as I helped him up to the screen. It was only when she finally had a thirty-second break from telling him what a cute, fluffy monster he was that I finally mentioned work.

'So, I rang you earlier,' I said, trying to sound as casual as possible. 'Tried the office, too.'

'Sorry, I know,' she let out a long sigh. 'Meetings with unions and freelancers,' she said. 'I take it you wanted to intro-duce me to this fellow?'

'Yes, but also, I wanted to ask a favour.'

She rolled her eyes. 'Already? And let me guess, this is linked to the latest story you're investigating?'

I couldn't help but smile. I loved working with someone

who knew me so well. And while Bobby seemed great, I doubted we would ever have a relationship even close to what Donna and I'd had. After all, she hadn't just been my boss. She was my best friend.

'Is there any chance you know someone who would be able to look into people's bank accounts? Magical bank accounts?'

'Magical bank accounts?'

'Bank accounts of magic people. Paras,' I said, though I wasn't sure why the comment needed that much of an explanation.

'If they're paras who mix or need the tip world, then they tend to keep their money in tip bank accounts. That's the easiest thing to do. It means you can change it into whatever currency they require and you can pay for tip things - flights, hotels, groceries, you know. Only paras with no communication to the tip world would keep their money in a community bank. But to be honest, those have become fewer and fewer. You'd have to find out if Ravens Hollow still has one.'

She was right. That probably was something I would have to do at some point, but at this precise moment, I didn't think it was necessary.

'Okay, so if I wanted to look at, say, Wren Belkin's finances since her divorce, the best way to go about that would be...?'

Rather than replying straight away, Donna let out a long sigh. 'Wren Belkin. Really? Do you want to do this?'

'I do. I know that following the money will give me the answer. And I really want to do a great job on this. You know – so the guys at the paper know what I'm capable of.' It wasn't just Bobby I was thinking of, though. There was no doubt that a small part of me was looking forward to the look on Chief Whip's face when I'd managed to unravel all of this. Yes. That feeling of satisfaction was definitely gonna be a good one.

'I actually know somebody who worked with Wren when

she was doing her London exhibition a couple of months ago,' Donna said. 'I can probably find out a little bit of information. When do you need it by?'

'As soon as possible,' I said.

'How did I know you were gonna say that?'

'Well, whoever did the murder is still on the island. They closed the bridge. So if this isn't just a vendetta against Wren, and there are other people on the murderer's radar, then there's a risk.'

'Okay. I hear you,' Donna said, waving her hand slightly. 'Are you going anywhere tonight?'

'Nope. Just me and Pongo.'

'Alright then. I'll see what I can do.'

I moved to hang up the phone when Donna spoke again. 'I forgot to say, I got some satellite photos of the basilisk's egg, though. Looks like you found a great spot for it.'

'Satellite photos?'

'Yeah, they monitor the area, you know, just to make sure there are no issues. They can get images of the whole island.'

'And you didn't think about looking at those images before I went?' I said. 'You know, so we could have picked the place I should leave it before I landed? And, oh, I don't know, avoid one or two of the swamps?'

I watched as the realisation dawned on Donna's face. Her mouth opened, though for a moment, no sound came out.

'You know, I should really get on to my contact at the bank, see if I can't find those details about Wren Belkin for you.' Then she flashed me a grimace before hanging up for real this time. God damn it. If I hadn't blamed Donna for the lion onsie introduction to the town before, I did now. Maybe I'd just have to go back through my photo albums and see if I could find some of her as payback. Then again, not until she'd found those details for me.

IT WAS THREE HOURS LATER, when I was dozing on the sofa with Pongo on my lap, when Donna messaged.

> Okay, I do not know how many laws have been broken to do this, but hey. That's the job, right?

I wasn't sure that lawbreaking was technically in our job, but I wasn't gonna say that right now. Instead, I wrote a more appropriate reply.

> You got them that fast?! You're amazing!

> I'm emailing them through. They're encrypted, so you'll need the passcode. I'm going to text it to you, just in case your computer is stolen.

> I don't think that happens in Ravens Hollow.

> Murder did, though.

She had a good point. A moment later, my computer buzzed.

> Okay, pinging through the password now.

A minute later, I was typing the eight digits into my computer.

As I clicked enter, the screen flashed open with pages and pages of documents.

> DONNA! There are nearly 4000 pages here!!

> Well, you did say you wanted it all.

She was right. I did. Now I was going to test exactly how

long a vampire could go without needing sleep and whether vamp speed applied to reading too.

THIRTY-TWO

Ten minutes later, and I had found that vamp speed definitely applied to reading. I actually wished that I knew just how long it would have taken me to get through a bank document before, just so that I could compare. But I reckoned I was at least five times faster than I had been. Unfortunately, with nearly 4000 pages of numbers to look through, it was still going to take a long time to make a dent. And it didn't help that I wasn't exactly sure what I was looking for. Just that there had to be something.

I looked down at Pongo, who had shifted his head from my lap to my feet as he sat on the sofa next to me. The dog bed Whip had brought around was still completely untouched. But then maybe Pongo would just want to use it at bedtime. I considered. I could at least hope, after all.

'What am I missing, boy?' I said. 'What were the lies that I needed to match up? The inflated prices, that was what Esmeralda had said, but we also need to find that divorce settlement. See if it was as big as the rumours had Suzanne believe.'

Deciding to switch tactics to look at specific dates, rather than going for the unknown needle in a colossal haystack approach, I opened a search bar on my laptop and it didn't take long for me to find the details of Wren's divorce. Although there were a lot of details to scour through. Facts about Macoy's role as head of the mermaid mafia, and various para tabloid pieces about how the pair had got together and throwback photos of their wedding and honeymoon. Then there were rumours of the separation and impending divorce, but it wasn't until a fair bit of searching that I finally found one about the divorce having been settled.

Having found an approximate date, I flicked through the documents to the corresponding pages of bank statements. My jaw dropped. Seven-and-a-half million dollars had gone into Wren's account on the day her divorce was settled. From the account of M. Belkin. That had to be the divorce settlement, didn't it? Which meant that I knew for certain that Esmeralda was lying. Wren hadn't been short of cash after her divorce at all.

Unless...

Using that point as my starting place, I carried on scanning upwards, wondering if maybe she'd made some big purchase. Like a massive house. Or several massive houses. That would explain where the money had gone. But instead, I found a cash withdrawal of $200,000, only a few days later. Then another. Then another, and another.

The entirety of the seven-and-a-half million dollars had been withdrawn within three months. If that wasn't suspicious, I didn't know what was. My fingers were flexing, as I went back to the Internet. There wasn't just money going out, there was money going in too. And I knew Wren Belkin sculptures were worth a lot, but still...

As I sat, staring at the computer screen, my stomach was a mix of knots and butterflies the way it always was when I knew I'd hit on gold. There was even more of a story here. Yes,

Ravens Hollow was going to get one hell of a first piece from Elodie Evergreen. That was for sure.

For a second, I contemplated ringing Bobby, telling him what I'd found. But it was late at night, and he'd had a long day, just like me. But there was someone I suspected would still be awake. And so much for me going to him for help. This was me helping him with his job and God, I wanted to shove it down his throat. With that in mind, I stood up and walked over to the kitchen, where I pulled out a pint of O negative. I had no plan on sleeping anytime soon.

I WAS DOING THE LOGICAL, responsible thing, I told myself as I lifted Pongo into my arms. He had been asleep the entire time that I'd been waiting for Donna to email me, and while I had been going through all the files, so I didn't feel too bad taking him out. It was definitely a better option than leaving him in the house, on the chance he'd wake up and feel alone. There was no way I wanted him to ever feel like he'd been abandoned again. So, I popped him on the seat of the Mini and drove to the police station.

Just as expected, there were a couple of lights on in the station, although it hardly looked like a hive of activity. With Pongo once again in my arms, I opened the door, ready to call out Whip's name, when an apparition swept in front of me. At least, I assumed it was an apparition by the fact that the body was almost translucent.

'A bit late to be out, don't you think?'

The woman was wearing a yellow floral dress and a bonnet with her dark hair sprawled out from beneath it. If I had to guess her age, in terms of appearance, she looked around fifty, although I already knew from Bobby that she was substantially older than that. In ghost years anyway.

'You must be Josephina,' I said.

'I am,' she said, pushing her shoulders back, clearly pleased her reputation preceded her.

'Elodie. Elodie Evergreen,' I said, stretching out my hand, only to realise my mistake. Could ghosts shake hands? Did I want to shake a ghost's hand? Thankfully, she didn't give me a choice in the matter as she lifted her arms up in delight.

'Oh, my goodness, the one in the lion outfit! Do you know people have been showing that to me all day? You are that Elodie, yes? It's difficult to tell without the mane.'

I gritted my teeth. 'Yes. I'm that Elodie Evergreen,' I hissed. 'The one in the lion outfit.' It appeared that my reputation had preceded me too. And it was one hundred percent not the impression I had wanted to make.

'Is Chief Whip in, Josephina?' I said, keen to get away from her before she asked me to roar or do something else, equally humiliating. 'I have something I need to speak to him about.'

'Well, he's upstairs in his apartment, but I can get him for you if you want.'

Whip had an apartment above the station? And I thought I was a workaholic.

'It's fine,' I said. 'He's probably asleep. I'll come back in the morning.'

I turned to go, only to hear the sound of footsteps on the floorboards above me.

'Josephina, if you've managed to get YouTube on again, I am going to unplug your speakers.' A door at the back of reception swung open and Whip came marching outside, only to stop in his tracks when he saw me. 'Elodie? Sorry, I just thought that Josephina had YouTube on again.'

'Yes, I heard,' I smiled. A ghost who loved YouTube but couldn't tune the radio. I was keen to know how that worked. 'No, sorry, it's me talking to her.'

'Is everything okay?' His perfect brow was furrowed. 'It's late.'

'Yes, I know. It's just – I found something, and I thought it was important to show you. I think that Wren was killed because of money.'

He let out a scoff. 'It wouldn't be the first time. Why do you think that?'

'Please, can we...' I motioned inside to the office.

'Don't mind me. Just been here for years, and everybody just talks through me like I'm not even there,' Josephina said.

I turned back to look at the scowling ghost. 'Sorry Josephina, you're right. And I meant to say thank you for fishing out all those things for Pongo,' I said. 'I assume it was you who knew where they were?'

Her scowl softened.

'You're welcome. Although he's probably not going to fit them in a couple of months' time. The biggest dog we ever had here was an Alsatian.'

'I'm sure he won't grow bigger than that.' I said, my voice quivering with a hint of a question. And yet Josephina shock her head as she rolled her eyes. I had never been given a condescending look by a ghost before, and yet there it was.

'Well, maybe you'll be right. But I wouldn't hold my breath if I was you.'

I looked down at my furry companion. Sure, he was big for a puppy, but then I didn't know how old he was. Maybe he wasn't even a puppy at all, he was a fully grown dog, and this was a big as he would grow. Big enough for me to carry around and take up a reasonable portion of the sofa. I wanted to believe it, but the tightness in my belly was making it hard.

'I should show you these documents,' I said drawing my eyes away from Pongo to look at Whip. If he was going to get big, then I would just have to deal with that when it happened. Right now, I had a story to write. And a murder to help solve.

CHAPTER
THIRTY-THREE

We walked through a set of double doors from the reception area of the police station into the space where I assumed the rest of the officers worked. There were desks and computers, not dissimilar to what we had at The Oracle, although straight in front of us was an incredibly thick door with a reinforced window and sizeable lock that I assumed lead through to cells of some sort. Whip and a cell. Had I not been so consumed with what I'd just found on the bank statement, then I would have likely lingered on that thought a little longer.

But Whip lead me through to an office at the end of the room, where he pulled out a chair for me to sit on. Though rather than moving around to take his place on the big comfy chair on the opposite side, as I expected him to, he sat directly next to me.

'So, what is it?' he said.

I was acutely aware of how close his knees were to me, but I had something more important to think about than the inspector who constantly flashed hot and cold.

'You're not allowed to ask any questions about where I got

what I'm about to show you,' I said, gripping my laptop tightly. 'I need you to agree to that.'

I'd taken a massive risk in coming to him like this and if I'd judged him wrong, well, then I might have found myself seriously entangled with the law on my first week in Ravens Hollow. And not the way I wanted to be entangled.

His smile twitched, revealing that dimple, but I kept my eyes away from him. This was more important than that. Donna had got me this info, and I wasn't going to do anything to risk her integrity.

'And what if I say no?' he said.

'Then I'll leave now. And you will be three steps behind in this case and The Oracle will have a scoop that'll mean everyone knows.'

He drew in a long breath, his chest rising slowly.

'You're not giving me much choice, are you?'

'I think I am, but it's up to you. I won't risk my sources for anything. But I think you need this.'

'Fine,' he said with a dip of his chin. 'What have you got? I'm guessing it's important, as you're here now. Either that, or you took that need for more blood a little too far.'

Ignoring the blood comment, I considered what to do next. Was that an agreement that he wouldn't ask me any questions? I was going to take it as a yes. It was my turn to take a deep breath as I lifted my laptop onto his desk and opened it up.

'I was looking through Wren's bank statements,' I said.

'Wren's bank statements? How did you— ' I shot him a glare, and he fell silent, shaking his head. 'Right. No questions. My apologies.'

With another breath in, I scrolled down and continued. 'She was given a big payment after her divorce. A very big payment. But then she took all the money out, little by little.'

'Right,' he said. 'I mean, could just be living expenses.'

'Six hundred thousand dollars every week? Living expenses? I mean, that is a whole different lifestyle,' I said as I shook my head.

'And that's just the start of it. About six months after the first withdrawal, that's when she gets her first big payment back in – two hundred and fifty grand. And then a week later, another three hundred grand went in.'

Whip's eyebrows were getting closer and closer to his hairline. 'So where does it say the money's coming from?'

'Through the galleries and her exhibitions. Particularly international ones,' I said. 'But the way she withdraws all that money to start with... I feel like she was using it to invest. Seed money, for whatever it was she was up to.'

'Okay, so this is good, Elodie. I think you're right – it does look like there's something behind it. Thank you.'

He reached out his hand to shift the laptop around, only for his fingers to brush against mine. A series of sparks ran up my arm. The type of which I had never felt before. My breath caught short as his eyes locked on mine. Those green-flecked eyes. My body melted. God, I wanted to kiss him. That was the only thought running through my mind. I wanted to kiss him so much, and the way his fingers remained against mine, and his eyes stared into me as his lips parted ever so slightly, made me think he wanted the same thing. My mind raced. Should I do it? This was brave Elodie Evergreen after all. The vampire Elodie who'd moved to the other side of the world. She could take a risk, couldn't she?

I felt my body leaning forward towards him, my eyes involuntarily starting to close, when without warning, Whip straightened up his shoulders and jumped across the room. And by jumped, it was like he had vamp speed. Papers flew up around him as he stood with his back against the wall. He'd gone as far as he could get away from me without leaving the room altogether.

Embarrassment flooded through me. I stumbled to my feet, ready to apologise, although it was Whip who spoke. But rather than looking at me, his eyes were trained on the ceiling.

'I need to ask you something,' he said. 'And it's going to be awkward, but I need to know. So, I'm going to apologise right now. But I promise, I wouldn't ask if it wasn't important. And I really need you to answer with the truth. No matter how much you might want to lie to me, please don't.' My nerves churned. He looked... pained? Still, he finally lowered his gaze to look directly at me. 'A moment ago, before I moved, did you suddenly feel like you wanted to kiss me?'

My eyes widened.

Of all the questions I'd expected him to ask, that absolutely wasn't one. How the hell was I meant to answer that without feeling even more humiliated than I already did? And while he'd asked me to be honest, part of me suspected he would know if I was lying.

'Yes. Yes, I did.'

My ribs felt like they were going to crack from the tension wrapping itself around my body, as Whip pressed his lips together and nodded.

'Well...' he said, before letting out a lungful of air. 'That's shit.'

THIRTY-FOUR

I had been out of the dating scene for a long time, but when a guy said it was shit that you wanted to kiss him, it was not a good sign.

Goddam it, it was me and my crazy rebound mind. The first attractive guy to smile at me and I had just jumped in there with a crush, like I was some sixteen-year-old schoolgirl. And not only had I thought about kissing him, but I'd admitted to it, too.

'I should get going,' I said, going to pick up my laptop, only to suddenly find Whip standing there again between me and the door.

'Look, I'm sorry,' he said, shaking his head. 'I didn't word myself very well, just then. I didn't think it was shit that you wanted to kiss me. Not at all. I wanted to kiss you, too. But that's the problem.'

He took a couple of paces back and forth. This was a long way from the cool, collected Whip I had met previously and there was no sign of even half a dimple in sight.

'Okay,' he said, letting the word out with a sigh. 'This was something I was going to tell you at some point, but...I guess you have a right to know. Especially if what I think is happening is happening. It's not fair on either of us.'

I wasn't entirely sure he was making sense, although whether I wanted to understand him was another thing entirely. He had said he'd wanted to kiss me too, right? That hadn't been my imagination? Couldn't we just leave the conversation there and take off where we'd been before he bolted across the room?

'Us wanting to kiss, I'm afraid it's all been rather one-sided."

Wow, if that wasn't the harshest brushoff I had ever heard, I didn't know what was. As my jaw dropped, I saw the horror on his face. 'No. Crap. I didn't mean you... I mean... crap...' He let out a long breath.

'I should go,' I said, trying to move around him.

'No, please wait. I need to explain to you. I don't want you to think... because. It's not that at all. Not at all.'

How was this the same man I had met before? Sure, he looked the same. And he was equally as hot, but this nervousness? That wasn't the Whip I knew at all. Not that I really knew him yet. And by the way this conversation was going, I wouldn't be getting to know him any better, either.

'Elodie, I—'

'No, really, I should get Pongo home. I showed you those statements. That's what I meant to do. Now I should go.'

I slipped my hand past him, ready to race out of the room and bury my head under a pillow for the rest of my unlimited years or however long it took for the embarrassment to go, yet as I took a step through the door, I found my path blocked.

'For goodness' sake, woman, just listen to him, will you?'

'Josephina!' Whip barked. 'This was meant to be a private conversation.'

'Well then, you should have had it somewhere private. Not somewhere I can stick my ear through the wall,' she said, before turning her attention back to me. 'Trust me, you're gonna want to hear this sweety. Now be a good girl and take a seat.'

I was stunned to silence. Being called a *good girl* by a ghost was incredibly patronising, and after the humiliation I had just been handed, part of me wanted nothing more than to march through Josephina's translucent body and out of the police station. But there was something about the way Whip was looking at me. The pleading in his eyes.

'Fine,' I said, 'You have one minute. And you,' I looked at Josephina. 'Need to get out of here.'

'You know I can just—'

'Out!'

'Out!' Whip and I said simultaneously.

With an exaggeratedly ghostly noise, Josephina flew at the wall, disappearing through it and rattling the filing cabinets as she went.

Silence filled the room.

'Well, she's going to be mad at me for a while after that,' Whip said quietly. He tried to grin, but when his eyes met mine, the expression faded almost instantly.

Once again, the quiet took hold, and he ran his fingers through his dark hair. It was amazing how my vampire sight could pick up every single emotion shifting across his face, but there were so many, it was hard to know which ones were the strongest. There was anxiety, sure, but also hurt, and doubt and, for some reason, anger.

As the silence swelled, I was about to tell him his one minute was very close to running out. But that didn't seem fair, given how nervous he obviously was.

'There is a reason I am very good at my job,' he said. 'A reason people tend not to object when I ask them things.'

I knew it! I was tempted to fist bump the air and say the

words aloud, but thankfully, I kept them in as Whip exhaled sharply before meeting my gaze.

'I'm different,' he said. 'Like you, I was turned, but not into a vampire, And I was well aware of the paranormal world before that happened. Because I was born into it. I lived my entire first life as a para.'

'You were a para, but you were turned into... a different para?' I said, feeling a lump in my throat that I couldn't swallow down.

'Yes.'

There was a question he wanted me to ask, and I knew it, but I was still trying to get my head around it first. To be a para before he was turned. There were a lot of options, right? Fae? Merman? Something godly. I wouldn't have ruled that out for him. And what had he been turned into if he wasn't a vampire? A werewolf? That was the only thing I could think of, but in the end, I knew any suggestion I made would just be clutching at straws, and, with the lump still thick in my throat, I bit the bullet and asked.

'What were you?' I said quietly. 'What were you before you were turned? And what are you now?'

He pressed his lips tightly together, before releasing the words. 'I was a siren,' he said. 'And in some ways, I still am. But I was changed to be more. I was changed to be a weapon.'

THIRTY-FIVE

I wasn't sure what the average number of times a person blinked in a minute was, but I was one hundred percent sure I had exceeded it by a lot. The thing was that was currently the only movement my body seemed capable of. Blinking.

'Sorry, you're going to need to say that again,' I said. 'I think I must've misheard you.'

Whip smiled, but it wasn't enough to form the dimples I had previously seen.

'I was a siren,' he said again.

'A siren,' I said, scratching my head. 'I'm not too sure about all my paranormals yet. They're water creatures, right?'

'Yes, but they're most famous for luring men. Voices, their song.'

The memories stirred in the back of the mind. Weren't they something in Greek mythology?

'But I thought... I thought the ones in stories were always women,' I said, voicing my thoughts aloud.

'They were, mostly. A male siren is born about once every two hundred years.'

'Wow,' I said.

Whip was running his hands through his hair again. It was clear he wasn't a fan of this conversation.

'Yeah, I was a rarity. And a pretty powerful one, too. Male sirens have an ability – just by considering something they want, it makes those thoughts shift to the people they're talking to. It makes them automatically want to please us.'

Oh my God. A series of knots built up in my stomach.

'It explains why you're such a well-liked police chief then,' I said, trying to make light of the situation. Though it was hard. My head was spinning. Did that mean I didn't want to kiss Whip? That seemed silly. Who the hell wouldn't want to play a little tonsil hockey with a man who looked like him? Not to mention the fact he was charming and well mannered. And he had brought me dog gifts for crying out loud.

Yes, he was an ideal specimen. But it also explained Nyrah's whole thing about ancestors and the chance of me not being entirely a tip. Was she surreptitiously trying to tell me about Whip? It definitely didn't feel like a coincidence.

'Does everybody know?' I said. I was grateful I hadn't brought up how attractive I'd found him to Chloe at the station earlier. Or even Donna, for that matter. No, I was relieved this was something I could keep to myself.

'No,' he said. 'Not many people at all. Raquel and Alex. June, Raquel's mum, is a siren too. The one who got me the place here. So, she and Bobby know. Mayor Hillard has her suspicions, but has never said anything outright to me, as is the case with a few people, I suspect. And it wouldn't be hard for me to manipulate their thoughts so that they forget. Not that I do that,' he added, locking his eyes on mine, as if to prove he wasn't lying. 'Beyond that, it's just Nyrah, who does the wards. I trust her explicitly – she's been helping me with this for a long time. But no... the general public can't know. They don't need to. I don't use my powers in any way to benefit me. I'm all about the town. And for them to find out would undermine me a lot.'

'You were turned because of your power?' I said. 'Turned into what?'

'An immortal. And technically, the correct word I should use is cursed. Not turned. I was cursed, so that death could never reach me. And believe me, it works. It wasn't just that, though. The curse strengthened my powers. For years, I had almost no control over them. It didn't matter who I was around, my thoughts affected everyone. And I know it doesn't sound like it, but it was hell. To be trapped in your own thoughts, constantly. To know that every word leaving someone's mouth wasn't their own but yours.... it's a torment I can't explain. It took decades to control the power and my stepsister was the one who helped me. Jeez, she saw some rough things. Then again, we both did.' His eyes drifted momentarily away as if he was thinking back to those times, before returning to me, with the saddest glint of a smile. 'The thing is, I thought I'd got control of them. Until you.'

My heart throbbed in my chest for him, as a heat of tears pricked behind my eyes and there's so much I wanted to say to him, but in the end, it's only one word that finds its way out of my throat.

'Why?' I said. 'Why would someone do that?'

'Why else? Power. Someone very wealthy and very unscrupulous thought that by changing me, they would have an all-powerful, immortal weapon on their hands. I could start and end the wars they wanted without so much as raising my fist. Didn't ever have to worry about me dying and losing their weapon.'

'Shit,' I said, not sure what other words I could offer.

'Yeah,' he said. 'Well, that was a long time ago now. And I've left that life behind.'

'So why are you telling me this?' I asked. 'Others don't know – why have you told me?'

'Because I can't ever trust someone's feelings. And I get if it sounds like I'm throwing myself a pity party here, but that's not what I'm doing. I promise. But I can't ever know if the people I think I like – people I want to get to know more – actually want to know me because of me or because of what I am subconsciously making them think.' He let out a dry chuckle. 'I mean, when I'd heard from the mayor's office there was a new vampire who had already staked a trafficker, I knew you were going to be something,' he said. 'But when I saw that photo of you on the plane, I guess I became more than a little intrigued. And then I met you...' He let out a sigh, as if he was recalling the moment we met by the protest, just the way I was doing, only he was the one finding me attractive. Which didn't make sense, given he looked like a god. 'I knew from how you spoke to me that there was something there, but I was sure it was all coming from me.'

'So, the thing about whips, you put that thought into my head?' I said, feeling the need to inject just a little humour into the situation. Whip offered a brief chuckle in response, but it faded almost immediately and with it, another thought sprung to my mind. 'The first time I met Alex, my thoughts kept yo-yoing,' I said. I knew that wasn't the first time it had happened, but it was the clearest one to think about. 'One minute I was thinking... well, that he was attractive, you know. And the next...'

'More brawn than brains?' Whip said, solemnly. 'Yes, I'm sorry. That was me. Not deliberately. It's just, lots of women tend to find Alex's charms irresistible, and I got rather inse-cure there. Stupid with my thoughts, too. The guy is one of the smartest people I know. Like I said, normally I can decide when my thoughts will have a direct impact on someone else, but when they're as strong as they are around you...let's just say it's not so easy to stay in control. I'm sorry.'

I leant against the wall as I tried to take it all in. He wasn't joking about being a powerful weapon. He hadn't even tried to influence my thoughts and yet I'd been deciding Alex was a definite no go.

'No wonder they wanted to use you,' I said, eventually.

He nodded in agreement but didn't reply immediately. 'That ward I put on you – I got Nyrah to place on you – wasn't just a sunlight ward. It was meant to work against me, too. But I'm not sure it is. She told me you were struggling with headaches the minute it finished, and then there's the whole thing about the vampire dying when it bit you. A standard ward might not have covered it.'

He paused, and I used the moment to put the pieces together.

'Meaning this...?' I waved my fingers between us both.

'On my part, it's real,' he said. 'One hundred percent. But on yours...we can't be sure. I'm sorry. If there was something I could do, if I could ward myself against it, then I would, but we've tried. Trust me.' He stepped forward as if he was going to take my hands, only to hesitate. 'Should I have told you?'

No. Why the hell did he tell me? And how the hell could he not think I would find him attractive on my own? He was a work of art with his clothes on, and out of them...

No. I stopped the thoughts before I could let them fully form. There were other things to think about.

'Okay, so you paid for that ward because you wanted to know?'

He exhaled. 'But if it's no good, then it's probably best if you avoid me for a little while. Is that okay?'

Avoid him. That was the last thing I wanted to do. If I hadn't wanted to be near him before, I sure as hell did now.

But he wouldn't believe that it was me who really felt like that. And how could he, when I wasn't even sure myself?

'If that's what you think is best,' I said, unable to hide the sting of disappointment in my chest. 'Absolutely understand.'

'Well, you should probably head home. Do you know how to get back?'

There was no question in his voice. I had very much been dismissed, but before I turned to leave, I looked him in the eye. 'You don't have to worry about me telling anybody.' I said finally. 'Well, maybe my best mate. But she won't tell anybody. I'd swear on my life.'

'I trust your judgement, Elodie,' he said, before sighing slightly. 'As long as you're not around me.'

Two minutes later, I was standing outside the police station with Pongo in my arms.

'Well,' I said with a long sigh. 'It's safe to say that that was definitely not how I expected the night to go.'

CHAPTER

THIRTY-SIX

The good thing about the time difference was that even though it was two-thirty in the morning in Ravens Hollow, I knew Donna was still up.

'Did those statements help you?' she asked when she picked up the call.

'Statements?' I said, before realising she'd assumed I'd rung about the investigation. 'Well, actually I took what I found to the police chief, and that's where the night got really complicated...'

For the next twenty minutes, I proceed to fill her in on every interaction that had happened between Whip and me.

'Sorry? He was a male siren before he was cursed to live forever, and because of that siren part of him, everybody loves him and agrees with everything he says, and normally he's okay with that, but he didn't want you to be. So twenty-four hours after meeting you, he put a ward on you so that you wouldn't be affected by his siren charm, and yet he's worried that you *are*, so he's keeping his distance because he *likes* you so much that he even tried to stop you liking his equally good looking colleague?'

'That's pretty much it,' I said, impressed at how succinctly she had summed up what I had spent thirty minutes getting across.

'Wow, that is...'

'Overwhelming,' I said.

'Romantic,' she suggested.

'Really?' I couldn't lie. I had thought the same, but if he was determined to draw a line under anything happening between us, it didn't seem worth contemplating ideas like that.

'Hell yes, why did you wait this long to tell me about him? I mean, this *guy is seriously* hot, right?'

'Is he?' I said with a groan. 'Or is it just his siren energy getting into my head?'

'Mate, I've just searched him up. I'm looking at a photo of him now. I mean, I'm not even attracted to men, and I wouldn't say no to him.'

Great. So he was actually hot. That was even worse.

'I'm not sure if that helps, Don,' I said. 'What do I do? Do I just avoid him? It's not like I can stop thinking about him. Not when I know he likes me. Do you know how long it's been since a decent guy liked me?'

Maybe I was being mean to Andy, thinking like that, but he had banned me from ordering garlic bread in restaurants, as the smell affected him too much. He also put a limit on the number of house plants I could have in my home.

'And what if Alex is the one I actually like, but this stuff with Whip just made it impossible for me to see that?' I said.

'Alex?' Her eyes widened. 'Who the hell's Alex?'

An overly dramatic sigh rolled from my lungs. 'He's the one looking into the traffickers, I've told you this. Traffickers that I want to be looking into too. The good-looking colleague Whip tried to make me think was an empty muscle head, but actually seems really sweet. And funny.'

'Right, sorry,' Donna said. 'I'm just not used to dealing with you and the idea of love triangles. And I thought you were keeping what happened with you and the traffickers quiet?'

'Yeah...' I let the word roll out. 'Turns out that's easier said than done somewhere like this.'

Rather than replying, Donna's lips pinched together.

'I know what you're thinking,' I said, getting in there before the lecture could start. 'But it's okay. Honestly. Bobby thinks it's a good idea. You know, they can't just knock me off without drawing attention to themselves. And let's be honest, if they're an elite global vampire trafficking ring they were going to find out where I was eventually, right?'

Her lips remained twisted a moment longer before she spoke again.

'Just don't go putting yourself in danger, okay? I've been doing some digging and these guys are serious.'

Why did people think I actively went looking for danger? I went looking for stories. The two were not the same.

'I promise. Now can you please help me work out what to do with Whip?'

It was clear from the creases that remained in Donna's forehead that she wasn't happy to let the issue of the Guardians go for long, but thankfully, she seemed to realise it wasn't best to push it right now.

'Okay,' she said, with a slight exhale. 'Just to backtrack a bit, is there any reason to think these wards aren't working properly?'

'Well, I had a bad headache afterwards.'

'A bad headache? That's the evidence you're going with here. And neither of you contemplated that the wards could be working, and you just wanted to kiss each other at the same time? That is how it's supposed to happen, you know. A two-way wanting thing.'

It was true, I hadn't contemplated it. The way I wanted to kiss him in the office hadn't felt any different to the way I'd been attracted to him before. Apart from that time, I'd actually been willing to act on it.

'Maybe,' I said, before drawing in a deep breath. 'But maybe this is better. I've got enough to get on with without worrying about bringing men into my life. I'd already decided that I wasn't gonna date anybody until I felt ready, and I definitely don't feel ready. No, I'm just gonna avoid Whip, enjoy my little fur baby, and get used to my way of life. That's what I'm gonna do.'

'Well, I can't wait to hear how that goes,' Donna said, her voice thick with sarcasm.

'It's fine. Bobby deals with the police when it comes to The Oracle. His daughter works there. I'll send everything we need through them.'

'That sounds like a good idea. But then maybe you could just say screw the not working ward and screw the—'

'Do not finish that sentence,' I stopped her. I was not letting my mind go there. She let out a light chuckle.

'It'll be fine, El,' Donna said. 'Have a good night's sleep, and everything'll be better. You'll see.'

And I honestly believed that, even as I curled up in bed with Pongo.

No way was I going to let whatever was between Whip and me interfere with me starting over here.

After all, he was called Whip, for crying out loud.

That wasn't even a real name.

I would be completely fine.

By the time I got off the phone with Donna, it was gone three o'clock, but the knowledge that I could just load myself up with a couple more pints of the red stuff in morning and keep going was a relief. Still, I turned my phone to silent, curled up next to Pongo, and fell asleep.

The next morning, I was woken by a substantial licking on my face.

'I guess we're going to try that dog bed tomorrow,' I said.

IT WAS AMAZING the difference a walk in the sun could make. Did it really matter that Whip's ward hadn't worked on me? Sure, it meant I couldn't date him, but there were loads of positives to take from the situation. Clearly, I was dateable – and after the way my last relationship had ended, I hadn't been entirely sure. But now I was. And for someone like Whip – smart, intelligent, obviously hot as hell – to like me? That was a definite confidence boost.

Then there was the other factor. If only one of the wards was going to work, then obviously, I wanted it to be the sunlight one, right? How crappy would it have been if, yes, Whip and I could get it on – in the type of dirty way I had already envisioned far too many times – but I could never see daylight again? No. I definitely got the best out of the situation.

Feeling a sense of positivity and control, I walked into Weirdoughs and ordered myself a cappuccino with a double shot of AB from the gentlemen behind the counter. From his stocky angular features, and fists the size of boulders, I had a sneaking suspicion this was the para Bobby had assumed was a troll.

'Sit Pongo,' I said to the puppy at my heels, expecting him to offer his paw in response. But for the first time ever, his bum plonked onto the ground, although he still followed it with the standard two bark response. 'Look at you!' I said, grabbing him a doggy treat from the tub they kept on the café counter. 'Who's a smart boy? Who's the only man I need in my life?'

He let out a little bark that made my smile grow wider.

'That's a smart dog you've got there.'

I twisted around to find myself staring at a vaguely familiar yet incredibly distinctive face, with ears that left her head at a forty-five degree angle and a face framed with emerald green hair. It was the elf woman from the art festival. Had she told me her name? I was sure she had, but I struggled to remember what it was. Damn, I was sure vampires were meant to have perfect memory, but I guessed I'd just put that down as another lie, or else something I was incapable of.

'Amira,' she smiled broadly, apparently sensing my issue. 'Amira Holbridge.

'Of course. Amira. Lovely to see you again.'

'And you, Elodie. Is this your first time here?'

'It is,' I said.

'Well, in that case I must treat you.' She moved her attention to the non-troll behind the counter. 'You can put this on my account.'

'That's very kind of you,' I said. 'But I've actually already paid.'

'Oh, of course.' Her lips tightened in embarrassment, and I was tempted to tell her that if she was that keen she could buy Pongo a puppuccino, but that just felt silly. 'Well, next time? I would really like it.'

'Yes, yes, I'm sure I'll be back here soon enough.'

'Why don't I give you my number? I remember what it's like, being new in town, and not having anyone to go for a drink with. Not that I think you're having problems like that. I'm sure you're already settling in perfectly well with Bobby and the other folk at the paper.'

Was that annoyance in her voice? It certainly sounded like it. My vampire senses tingled. I had read enough true crimes to know how easy it was for someone to think they'd found a firm friend only days after moving somewhere new only to discover their chum was a possessive crazy person.

'One double shot cappuccino,' the non-troll said, breaking the awkward silence between Amira and I.

'That's me,' I said, flashing her a smile as I picked up the drink and took my first sip, only to let out a slight gasp. It tasted like... coffee. Really good coffee.

'Sorry,' I said, turning to the barista and wondering how a man that size could turn into something as small as a hummingbird. 'Did you add the double shot of, you know... blood?'

'All in there,' he said. 'Is it not strong enough? I can make it a triple if you want.'

'No, no. It's perfect. Absolutely perfect.'

'Definitely the best in town,' Amira said. 'At least that's what the vampires say. Anyway, I should let you get about your day, Elodie. It was nice to bump into you.'

'Right, you too, Amira,' I said, while making a mental note to ask Chloe about the fae in the near future or at least have a proper look at the book she'd leant me. So far I'd not even flipped through it. Fingers crossed Amira was just being friendly, and like she said, knew what it was like to be the new person in town. If not... Well, if not, then I guess I would have to train those vampire skills of mine so that I was warned when she was coming.

Despite the strange encounter, my dead heart skipped in my chest as I made my way to the office. Pongo had successfully sat, and I had no doubt that every penny of my salary was going to end up at Weirdoughs, but hey, I didn't care. I would've done it even if I hadn't needed blood in my drinks.

'Come on, boy. Aren't you a clever pup? Now, let's see if we can show that new trick to the others in the office.'

I knew Chloe would be equally excited by this progression, but as I walked into the building, I discovered that once again, I was one of the early birds. The only other person who was in was Bobby, but rather than being at his desk, he was standing beside it – almost as if he were waiting for me.

'Bobby, everything alright?'

'For you and me? Yes. But for Esmeralda and Thor? Not quite so much.'

Had Whip had enough to arrest them?

'Are they at the station?' I said, unable to hide the excitement in my voice. I loved this part of an investigation – when all the puzzle pieces finally fell together, and I actually got to write the article. My first piece for The Oracle, and it was going to be a corker.

'No,' he said. 'They ain't at the station.'

'Where, then?'

'They're at the pier.'

'The pier?'

'Yup. They're dead. And it looks like the murderer was the same folk who killed Wren.'

Now that was a spanner in the works I hadn't expected.

THIRTY-SEVEN

'Raquel said the two bodies were found just outside the yacht club,' Bobby told me as we walked. 'By a stretch of public beach.'

Beach. I had been dying to visit it properly since I arrived here. But maybe dying to visit was the wrong expression to use, considering.

'Any idea of the cause of death yet?'

'No,' he said. 'Don't know any more than you. But I'm guessing it's similar if they're thinking it's the same murderer. Young lad who works at the yacht club found 'em. Ran straight to the police, then rang me. Wanted to give me a quote. Make sure it was put in there that they were the first one to find them.'

'Well, everyone's entitled to their five minutes of fame one way or another, right?' I said.

Bobby rolled his eyes.

'Who was it that found them, anyway?' I asked.

'Some kid. Rami something?'

'Hawkins?' I suggested.

He looked at me, that single visible eye narrowing. 'Yeah, that was it. Why's that name familiar?'

'That was one of the kids Ines had been teaching bolas to. You know, the one we didn't bother speaking to because we just believed Ines when she said he was off island with his dad during the festival?'

'That's right,' Bobby replied.

'But if they were off island for the festival, how would they have got back in?'

'They wouldn't o' been able to get past the barrier.'

My stomach coiled. What an idiot. I had taken a woman at her word, even though I'd had a gut instinct about her and that weapon from the start. Well, we'd be going to speak to Rami and Ines after this – and it looked like the former might get his wish of seeing his name in the paper for far more than just one line. First, though, we needed to see whatever was going on here.

As I looked around at the lapping water, trying to work out where we should head, I noticed a woman walking directly towards us. It was the first time I had seen her properly, given the rush that everyone was in at the festival, and it was heart-warming how similar she looked to her father. She was shorter than he was - not that that was hard - but had the same kind of brown-amber eyes, the same round, warm cheeks. And at this precise moment, the same kind of tight frown I had seen him wear repeatedly. A flash of disappointment rippled through me. I had half been hoping to see Whip again, but it was probably better if I didn't. It wasn't like I knew what I'd say to him anyway.

'Raquel,' I said. 'Thanks for keeping the paper in the loop. So does it look like the same M.O. as the last murder?'

I was straight to the point, well aware that she would be very busy. The last thing I wanted to do was take up any more of her time than necessary. She smiled.

'Yes and no,' she said.

'Helpful,' Bobby grunted, at which point, his daughter shot him a glare.

Although the expression immediately flicked to a smile which faded again the moment she started talking. 'Both victims have their chests caved in. Like with Wren. But we'll have to get the coroner out to know for sure. This time, it looks like it was just one large impact rather than several small ones.'

I grimaced at the thought.

'Yes, it's pretty gruesome. And that's putting it bluntly.'

I glanced behind her. It was time to see if I could get this vamp sight thing to work. I focussed on the area where I believed the body to be, narrowing out the rest of my vision. Suddenly it was like I was looking through a telescope.

'Now this is cool,' I muttered under my breath. I could have done with this for some of my previous stories, that was for sure.

Even though the bodies had been covered, there was still a spill of red spreading across the wooden slats of the jetty, along with several other items that had small flags beside them, no doubt for photos and forensics that needed to take place before they could be moved. By the looks of things, there were a couple of bags.

'What did they have on them?' I said, turning to look at Raquel. 'Anything that might point to a murderer?'

Raquel pressed her lips tightly together. Clearly, I was pushing her limits of what she was comfortable sharing with the press.

'We found a broken dart gun on the ground,' she said. 'And an ocarina.'

'An ocarina?' I question.

'It's an instrument,' Bobby answered for me. 'You blow into it. Makes a pretty sound.'

'Do people use dart guns here a lot?'

'Nope. And considering Esmeralda's a bear shifter, I can't imagine there are many people she couldn't take down.'

'Is there anything out in the water they would want to dart?' I said. 'Could that have been what they were doing here?'

It was Raquel's turn to purse her lips, though she looked to her father to answer the question.

'The only thing we've got in these waters are the island paras, selkies, shifters, merpeople.'

'Merpeople like Macoy and Thor?'

'Where is your head going with this Elodie?' Bobby said, his single visible eye trained on me.

'I'm not sure,' I said truthfully. 'But I feel like there are some dots here I'm not joining together. Does the barrier stop people coming in through the water, or just via the bridge?'

'Whole island. There ain't no way in or out. Not when it's at full strength.'

Joining dots was a normal part of investigative journalism, but I was definitely on the back foot with my lack of knowledge of the different paras. The next time I got a free evening I was going to read through that book Chloe had given me. For now, though, I needed to think down more traditional routes.

'Any witnesses?' I asked. 'CCTV cameras?'

'No. It's a dead area. Nothing at all. I've asked...'

Whatever or whoever Raquel was asking, I was no longer listening. My ears had turned into a different voice. One closer to the bodies.

'And how long have you known this?' he growled with a voice that caused a rumble down my spine. It was Whip. And he was angry. 'Well, I now have three dead bodies on my doorstep,' he continued down his phone. 'And I can promise you, if your ineptitude is the reason, there will be blowback.' With that, he promptly hung up.

I glanced back to Raquel and Bobby who were still in conversation, but it was hard to join back in with them given what I'd just heard the tail end of. And even harder now that Whip was walking across to us.

'We don't need the press holding us up right now,' he said, looking at Bobby. 'You can wait for the official release.' A second later he was looking at Raquel. 'Alex needs your help. Now.'

If I hadn't known that Raquel was also a siren and immune to his powers, I would have sworn Whip had used them on her, the pace at which she scurried away. Bobby tapped me gently on the arm, implying we needed to do the same. But I couldn't leave just yet.

'Who was on the phone?' I said. 'It didn't sound like good news. Is it to do with the case?'

His eyes snapped hard on me. The same eyes that had looked at me the night before and told me how he couldn't control his thoughts around me. Yet at that moment, they were tired. Tired and fearful.

'That was police business,' he said. 'And using para skills to interfere with police business is a criminal offence. I'll assume you didn't know that, and let you off with a warning, but if you try it again...'

'If it's something that the public has a right to know, then you need to tell us. And before Prue Parsons and her damn Scoop gets wind of it. Is this something she could find out?'

His nostrils flared as he rubbed the back of his neck. His jaw locked.

'This is not to be printed,' he said finally, his gaze fixed on Bobby. 'I'm asking, but I can *tell* you if that's what it takes.'

Wow, powerful scary Whip, was also incredibly hot. Even if it was an inappropriate time for me to think such a thing.

'Won't be necessary. I know how this works,' Bobby replied.

'And you?' Whip turned to me. 'Can I trust you to keep quiet?' From what he'd said the night before, I wasn't sure it was entirely necessary. He controlled my thoughts even when he didn't want to. Wasn't that the problem? Still, I dipped my chin in a nod.

'That was a buddy of mine on the mainland,' he said. 'I've just got news that Macoy Belkin's missing.'

'What? When did he escape?' Bobby asked.

Whip scratched his temple again.

'They're not sure.'

'What?!'

'He was first flagged as missing twenty-four hours ago. But he could have been gone for up to seventy-two.'

'Three days,' I replied. 'You're saying that the leader of the mermaid mafia might well be on Ravens Hollow and responsible for all these killings?'

'That's exactly what I'm saying,' he said. 'And if history teaches us anything when it comes to Macoy, it's that there are likely to be a few more deaths before we get hold of him.'

THIRTY-EIGHT

On the one hand, I was pleased. My instincts about Thor and Esmeralda trying to shoot something or someone in the water had been spot on. I just hadn't realised it had been Macoy. On the other hand, I wasn't happy to agree to Whip's demand about keeping this quiet.

'The people of Ravens Hollow have a right to know.'

'No. The public has a right to be *safe*. And they are safer if they don't know.'

We had been going round the same argument for the last twenty minutes, neither Whip nor I willing to budge on our point of view.

Despite Whip telling us to leave, I hadn't gone anywhere. When the coroner had come to move the bodies, I had followed Whip into his police vehicle, taken a seat, and was refusing to leave until he saw some sense.

'The bridge to the island is closed,' he said. 'We're keeping it safe that way.'

'We're on an island,' I said. 'And this man is the head of the freaking mermaid mafia.' It didn't matter how many times I said that – both in my head and out loud – it would never stop sounding ridiculous to me. 'Surely if someone knows a way around the water barriers, it would be him?'

'You think I don't *know* that Elodie?' Whip snapped, then paused before letting out a long sigh. 'I'm sorry. You're right. It's just... people like Macoy Belkin, they don't think like you and me. Trying to predict what they'll do is impossible – they're always three steps ahead. The only way you can have any hope of winning against them is by controlling every possible variable. And the people of Ravens Hollow are variables I have no hope of controlling if this gets out. And he'll use that to his advantage. People like that always do.'

He wasn't just talking about Macoy Belkin. I could see that. This situation – someone powerful and deadly using others for their own ends – struck way too close to home for him.

I was hit by the sudden urge to ask more. To ask if maybe he needed to step back for a little and let Alex or Raquel take the reins. But I knew how well I'd take a comment like that, and I suspected he was the same.

'What about Suzanne?' I said instead. 'She seems to have her ear to the ground when it comes to mermaid gossip. Maybe she's heard something about Macoy's whereabouts.'

Whip nodded. 'Yes. I was going to talk to her myself now.'

That was good. He could go that route. I would go and see this Rami Hawkins and get to the bottom of that, too. I moved to open the car door when Whip lightly grabbed me by the elbow. A shudder of static rolled through my chest.

'Elodie, do me a favour, will you? Don't take any risks for this story. It's not worth it. Macoy's a powerful para. Please, don't take any risks.' As his eyes locked onto mine, I was hit by the sudden urge to say sure – only a different feeling replaced that one. Anger. When someone says that to someone like me – someone whose entire job involves taking risks – what they're actually saying is don't be you. Don't follow your gut.

Would he have said it if I were a six-foot-three muscle-bound *guy* who'd staked a trafficker while still human? I doubted it.

'I have a job to do, just like you do,' I replied instead.

His lips curled slightly as his nostrils flared, and for a second I thought he might try to tie me up, lock me in the truck, just to keep me safe, but he didn't. Although maybe that was just my mind going places it shouldn't be again.

'How about this, then?' he said, more softly than before. 'If you think what you're walking into might be even the slightest bit dangerous, you call someone so you're not alone. Okay? Someone who knows the para world. I know you're a vampire, but you don't know this world yet. So, call me. Call Bobby. Call Alex even. I don't care. You just don't go into one of those situations alone. Okay?'

I cleared my throat, ready to respond – to tell him I didn't tell him how to do his job and I'd appreciate the same in return – but he was right. I had gone into a para situation before and left it without a pulse. Next time, I might not be so lucky.

'Fine,' I agreed, opening the car door and stepping outside. 'I promise I'll ring someone.'

I just needed to get those leads first...

THIRTY-NINE

'You and the chief seemed to be having a pretty heated conversation in there,' Bobby said as I joined him in my car. Once again, we had taken the Mini and he'd pushed the seat back as far as it could go, but he still didn't seem to have much room. Pongo, meanwhile, was spread out full on the backseat and seemed to be taking up more room than ever. But that couldn't be possible, could it? I'd only had him for a couple of days. 'Is everything alright?'

'Fine,' I said. 'Whip told me about what he is. And that you know, too. And a couple of others.'

'He did?'

Bobby looked genuinely surprised by this news, but he didn't say any more.

'How do you feel about him in his position?' I said. 'You know, given his powers and everything.'

Bobby scratched at his eye patch. In the place where his right eye should have been. He was clearly contemplating his answer carefully.

'I weren't sure, when I first met him. I'd heard rumours, see. Things he'd done... but he's been nothing but good for this town. This island. Think maybe he feels like he's got some good to make up, and that's what he's doing in Ravens Hollow. Then again, he spends a lot of time off island too. Sometimes for weeks at a time, and none of us are sure where he goes during that time...'

It was my turn to consider how to reply. Whip had said he'd been cursed to be an immortal weapon, but I'd never considered the fact that he might have actually been used as one. In the end, I went for a change of topic entirely.

'Raquel seems lovely,' I said.

'Aye, she's a good one,' he said, flashing a grin. 'Takes after her mum.'

'In that she's a siren?' I said. 'Because if she'd taken after you, she'd be...'

I let the sentence trail off, only for Bobby's grin to widen. 'Oh, you think you've got my mark, do you?'

I pressed my lips together. He had said I should try to work out what type of paras I was dealing with, and given that he was the one I'd spent the most time with, it seemed logical that he was the one I should figure out first. And every day, I kept coming to the same conclusion, though it sounded ridiculous to say aloud.

'Will you get offended if I get it wrong?' I asked.

'Depends how wrong you are,' he said.

I hesitated. 'The thing is, I don't know all the correct terms to call people yet. All the sects and things.'

'Just spit it out,' he said, shaking his head, but as much as I wanted to, I couldn't. So I opted for another route instead. An indirect route.

'What's under your eye patch?' I said.

His smile lifted.

'Why's that?' he asked.

'Well, I just have my suspicion that maybe there's nothing under there at all.'

Bobby raised his single eyebrow, but it was a look of pride that filled his face.

'Is that right? Well, now that that's sorted, how do you want to handle these werewolf kids?'

THE ADDRESS we had got for Rami was only three houses down from Ines'. Bobby came with us, probably to stretch his legs after the Mini. Pongo and I led the way, and after a couple of knocks, a young lad – maybe fifteen or sixteen – opened the door.

'Rami Hawkins?' I said.

He grinned. 'Yeah. You're from the paper, right? The one in the lion suit. Are you here to get my quote? I've got one ready.' He straightened his back only to hesitate and frown. 'Don't you need to write this down or something?'

'No, I'm good,' I told him.

'Well, the bodies were gross. And I reckon something had eaten their hearts for a ritual to raise some ancient god-thing. So when it happens, you need to remember you heard it here first. From Rami Hawkins.'

Even if I had been coming for a quote, there wasn't a chance I would ever let something like that go to print. Thankfully, that wasn't why we were there, and it was time to let Rami know as much.

'Right,' I said. 'Thank you, but actually, we're not just here to talk to you about the bodies.'

'You're not?' His grin turned into a frown.

'No. I wanted to ask you about the night Wren Belkin died. The night of the art festival. Do you remember where you were?'

A muscle ticked along his jaw and his eye twitched slightly. Yeah, no need for vampire sight here. It was *very* obvious that this boy had just got nervous. Although... deciding to test my hearing skills, I tuned in on his heartbeat. Yup. I didn't even need to compare it to Bobby's to know that it was far faster than it should have been.

'So?' I pressed. 'Where were you?'

Rami swallow. 'I...I was out hunting with my dad. On the mainland. I went with my friend Fabian Thomas, too.'

'Is that right?' I said, nodding my head slowly.

'Yeah, yeah it is.'

I pressed my finger against my lips as if I was genuinely considering what he'd just told me. 'Now, here's the thing. The bridge has been closed,' I said. 'No one's been in or out since Wren's death. So, if you were away, how did you get back?'

His cheeks flushed in colour.

'We...we got back just in time,' he said. 'Like *literally* as Floyd was closing the gate.'

'Like *literally*,' I said, mimicking the teen's speech. 'Right. Well, then, Floyd should remember, right? If you were *literally* there as he was closing the gate?'

'I—I don't know about that. I mean, it was dark, and there were lots of people. *Lots* of people at that time.'

'Right. Well, I'm sure we'll be able to clear it up with Floyd,' I said. 'Unless you're lying. Because if you're lying, well, then you haven't just become the person who found the bodies. No, you're a whole different thing now. Someone who lied about their whereabouts on the night of the murder, and then *found* the next two bodies. That doesn't look good. Does it, Rami?'

He'd gone from red to white, and now his skin had taken on a greenish hue.

'I just said what she told me to say,' he said, his voice breaking. 'That's it.'

'Who? Ines?' Bobby was standing beside me now.

Rami was biting down on his bottom lip. 'It's not like I had a choice. She's my beta.'

'Right,' I said. 'Thank you. So can you tell me where you were, please?'

His jaw locked tightly together, his arms trembling. The poor kid looked terrified. Like he was going to pass out. But he still didn't say anything.

'Rami, I need you to answer this. Unless you want me to go to the police?'

'He *can't tell us*, Elodie,' Bobby said. 'If Ines specifically told him that he had to lie about this, he can't go against her orders. Not without breaking himself from the pack and that's not something we are going to be responsible for. You need to let this go.'

I looked at the young lad and suddenly noticed the pain he was in. Bobby wasn't joking. This wasn't just a case of keeping someone's secret.

This was a whole lot more.

'Okay. It's fine,' I said to Rami, terrified he was going to pass out if I didn't say something soon. 'You don't have to tell me anything. I'll talk to Ines now.'

I left the poor boy bent double, clutching his knees, gasping for air, like he'd been underwater. A flicker of guilt rippled through me. Not that I had anything to feel guilty about. No, the only one in this situation who needed to feel guilt was Ines for putting a kid in that situation in the first place.

Yet as I reached Ines's door, a car appeared on the track behind us, the tires screeching as it braked to a stop. When she jumped out, her eyes flashed with anger.

'How *dare* you question a pack member of mine?' she said.

I didn't know whether she'd been close enough to hear the conversation or if someone else had called her, but it didn't matter. She was here, and I wanted to talk to her.

'How dare I?' I replied, spitting her words back at her. '*You* lied to us. When we are investigating a murder.'

'You're not investigating it. You're journalists.'

'*Investigative* journalists,' I said. 'And we are very much investigating Wren's murder. What you told us derailed a whole load of things.'

'I didn't derail anything!' She said, her hands on her hips. I didn't know if it was my imagination or not, but I could have sworn her eyes were starting to glow a little. Who would win in a fight? A werewolf or a vampire? I felt like that was something I probably should have looked into before now. 'The boys weren't at the festival,' she continued. 'They were still hunting with their dad. They weren't responsible for anyone's death.'

'So why not just tell us the truth?'

'Because... Because...' she stuttered as her eyes flickered to Bobby beside me.

'Because they were in the nature reserve, weren't they?' Bobby said, with a groan. 'That's why you told us they were off the island, isn't it? Because they were hunting at Folorning Forest?'

'Folorning Forest is the only place on the island that hasn't been over-hunted,' Ines said. 'Wounded Woods has never been big enough for two packs, and Wraith Woods is practically devoid of wildlife with everyone hunting there. Not to mention you can't even hunt near the Scorched Circle. It's safest for the environment that we keep an equal spread of our hunting grounds. I'm doing what is best for the environment by having my pack hunt in the place that is best for this island. Not just the people. Everything that inhabits it.'

I had to admit it was an impassioned speech. Ines was clearly a born leader, and while I knew nothing about werewolf politics and whether the shift from beta to alpha was possible, something told me she'd be running the show at some point soon. With a fire like that, I wasn't surprised she'd been able to rile a group to protest Wren's presence at the Art Festival so quickly, but while I was unexpectedly moved, Bobby was less than impressed. Instead, he let out a low growl.

'That ain't your call,' Bobby growled. 'The island only

works if folk stick together. You got a bone to pick with the hunting grounds, take it up with the council.'

'We have tried. They don't listen.'

'Try again,' I said. Her eyes flashed to me with a glow that was very much not human. But I wasn't human anymore, and I'd refused to be intimidated even when I was. 'Look. If what you're saying is true, and we are putting the ecosystems at risk here, then everybody should know about it. I will back your corner. If you've got the evidence to support it, I will stand up with you and go to the council and write articles that articulate your point.'

'You would?' she said, sounding genuinely surprised by this. 'But the paper doesn't take sides with pacts or sects. It never has.'

'From what you said, this is nothing to do with pacts or sects. It's to do with the island's ecosystems.'

'Yes, it is. Absolutely.'

'Then, like I said, you get me the evidence. Real hard evidence, not just personal observations, and I'll share it. But not if you go around lying. You pull stunts like that again, and you can guarantee any goodwill I have will very quickly disappear.'

I didn't look at Bobby as I said any of this. I didn't need confirmation that he would allow me to go ahead and write something like that. As far as I was aware, if what Ines was saying was true, then it was the paper's duty to report it. For a moment, we stood in silence, Ines's lips pressed tightly together. She nodded.

'Fine.'

'And you steer clear of Ridge Creek. That's the edge of the boundary and you shouldn't be going anywhere near it or the forest, until it's approved by the council,' Bobby added. 'Can't have the paper supporting trespassers.'

Her teeth ground together as she admitted a low hiss.

'That's the condition,' I said. 'Take it or leave it.'

With a final grunt, the rest of her resolve evaporated.

'Fine, but you should know that giving a werewolf your word is no small thing,' she said, looking directly at me. 'You better not mess me around on this.'

'Just keep your part of the deal, and we'll be fine,' I said, sounding as confident as I could. Although it didn't stop the twist of nerves in my abdomen. Less than a week on the island, and I was already making deals with werewolf betas. This really was an entirely new world.

CHAPTER
FORTY-ONE

Back at the office and it was the busiest I had ever seen. Chloe and Diego were both in the kitchenette, Dylan was arguing on the phone with some potential advertiser and Theodora was busy on the copy edit so we could go to print at the weekend. It was a far cry from London, where the paper had had a daily, rather than weekly edition and before arriving I'd assumed I'd find the pace far slower because of it. As it happened, I didn't feel like I'd slowed down at all since I'd arrived.

Attracted by the smell of homemade banana bread, Bobby and I joined Chloe and Diego in the kitchenette.

'There's mango ice cream in the freezer too,' Chloe said. 'I made it from mangoes in my garden. If you don't know what to do with yours when you get too many, I can do the same for you.'

'Or you could get Mick and Larry to make you some mango hooch,' Diego suggested.

'Mango hooch?' I questioned.

Chloe rolled her eyes. 'Larry, Mick's brother, makes it.

They run the auto shop on the south of the island. You would have passed it when you first drove in here.'

'Well, Mick, runs it,' Diego replied as he took another slice of the cake. 'Larry mostly makes liquor, which he sells out of the auto shop to avoid paying taxes. Everyone drinks it. It's crazy good.'

From the scowl on Chloe's face, it was clear she wasn't a fan of her future brother-in-law's business enterprise. Or the way Diego was demolishing another slice of banana bread.

'Well, I would love a slice,' I said, needing to break the tension that was filtering in the room. As I took a slice from out of the tray, Pongo sniffed loudly. 'I'm not sure this is for dogs, boy,' I said, only for Chloe to grab another piece.

'Sure it is. There's no chocolate in it,' she said. 'Perfectly dog safe. And it'll stop Diego eating it all.' She dropped it down by Pongo's feet. 'Enjoy.'

'I think Whip's going to be disappointed if he thinks he can keep Macoy Belkin's release quiet,' Diego said as Pongo tucked into his portion of the cake. 'I had a buddy from main-line call me about it twenty odd minutes ago. And I'm sure I'm not the only one who's heard.'

A pang of sympathy tugged in me for Whip. One hell of a lot of responsibility fell on his shoulders. I didn't think I could cope with that.

'Do you think it could be him?' I said to the group. 'Macoy? I mean, the injuries are pretty horrific. What are mermaids like when they turn? Can they cause that type of damage?'

'Their tails could,' Chloe responded. 'They're kind of fan-shaped. And sharp as hell.'

'Yeah, I've seen some that actually have spikes at the end,' Diego commented. 'I think mermaids' fins are like zebra's stripes though, you know, completely unique. But freaking strong. It's just muscle, really.'

Spikes at the end. Could that explain the different points

of impact? The coroner's reports hadn't mentioned that type of impaling, but then I supposed it depended on what part of the tail Wren was hit with. And what Macoy's tail was like.

'It's scary,' Chloe said. 'I heard in Florida, when his group took control, you didn't know who you could trust. There were killings all the time, apparently. I don't want that to happen to Ravens Hollow.'

'It won't,' Bobby said gruffly. 'If it is Macoy, we'll catch him and be done with it.'

'You really think he'd do that? Kill his wife?' Chloe said.

'His ex-wife,' Diego interrupted. 'They were divorced.' He reached for another slice of cake, but Chloe slapped his hand.

'You know I made that for the whole office, not just you? Theodora still hasn't had any, and it's Dylan's favourite.' She looked back at me. 'I always thought the divorce was more to do with him going to prison than anything thing else. Like he was giving her permission to move on with her life. The photos I saw of them online, they looked really loved up.'

I had thought the same, but didn't say as much. 'Yeah, but that's online,' I said instead. 'You can make anything look however you want in a photograph.'

'I guess you're right,' Chloe admitted. 'I mean, we could make Diego look as if he was taller than five foot nine.'

'Hey! I'm five foot eleven, and you know it!'

'Yeah. With a wonky ruler,' she said.

As the banter continued, a thought struck me. There had been water outside the tent where Wren Belkin had been killed. I had pointed out as much to Whip. Could that have been because Macoy had slipped in from the water? It wasn't impossible.

'Well,' I said, my head too full of questions I didn't have answers to. 'I'm gonna look more into this thing Ines said about the ecosystem. Not my normal type of investigation, but it feels a bit safer. And it'll keep me busy until something else comes up.'

'Why don't you just go home?' Bobby said. 'Today's been full-on. I know you've got your daylight ward and everything, but there's no need to test it to the limit. Or if you want to test it, at least see more of the island than you've seen following up stories. Have you even been to the promenade yet, had a look at the sea? The shops.'

'I saw the sea this morning,' I reminded him, only for him to shake his head.

'A crime scene does not count.'

'Maybe, maybe not. But I'm not much of a shopping person either.'

'Oh, but these are great shops,' Chloe interrupted. Runes and Tunes is amazing. And Nyrah has her salon there. Nails and Naughtiness. She does amazing beauty therapies, as well as wards and things.

'Nyrah has a salon?' I said, my interest finally piqued.

'Yeah, it's normally rammed, so if you want something, like your ward redoing, you need to book a month in advance.'

Did what I want require a booking? It wasn't a ward, but it would likely take up some of her time all the same. And, for the first time since moving to Ravens Hollow, I would be doing something that wasn't to do with work. I couldn't tell if I was excited or not.

'You know what,' I said, popping another small piece of banana bread into my mouth. 'I think I might take off early after all.'

FORTY-TWO

I glanced through the window at *Nails and Naughtiness*. There was no sign of Nyrah, but I stepped into the shop. There were a total of six people. Three working, three having treatments done. The two women who worked there were almost identical, from the purple at the end of their braids to the iridescent sheen on their skin, while the man had deeper-coloured eyes that looked almost luminous next to his complexion. As for the clientele, well, Chloe hadn't been joking about saying everyone went there. A large man, who looked more bear-like than an actual bear, was getting a pedicure, while the two women getting facials both had wings poking out beneath their backs.

'Sorry,' I said to the woman working nearest to me.

'Can I help?' she asked.

'Sorry, I was hoping to find Nyrah.'

'She's on her break,' she replied.

'Right,' I said. Breaks were precious for anyone who worked, and given that it was already early evening, I assumed that meant she would be working late. But as much as I didn't want to impose on Nyrah, I really wanted to talk to her. 'I've just got a question about a ward she did for me. It's the first time I've had one like that and I just want to make sure it's all working correctly.'

The colleagues exchanged a look.

'Nyrah's wards always work properly,' the second woman said.

'Oh no, I'm not saying it's anything she's done,' I said hurriedly. 'It's me that's the issue. It'll just take two minutes of her time.' Hopefully, I thought, but I didn't add that part.

'She's in the back garden,' the first one said, gesturing to a door at the back of the room. 'But if she curses you for disturbing her, that's on you, not us.'

A lump stuck in my throat, but I gulped it back down and nodded my thanks before walking through the door. The second it opened, a gasp escaped my lips.

I had grown up in a world full of flowers. That was one thing I missed most about my house in London. Andy had been allergic to almost all kinds of pollen – the most he could deal with me having was a few potted succulents, provided they didn't bloom too often. Although for some reason, every plant I got had an irritating habit of blooming far more often than the internet said it should. Much to Andy's annoyance. Along with a dog, a healthy, colourful garden was at the top of my list now I had moved, but there was colourful... and then there was *this*.

It was incredible.

Above my head, a canopy was covered in purple passion-fruit flowers, while different types of ivy climbed the trellises. Was that wisteria? It didn't seem like the right climate for it. And yet, it was there. There was a blur of reds, oranges, pinks, and blues in between – some flowers I recognised, others I had no idea about. For a minute, all I could do was stare.

'Elodie?' I turned around to find Nyrah looking at me. 'Is everything okay?'

Her hands were deep in the soil of a tub. Unlike the rest of the plants in the garden, this one looked surprisingly wilted.

'That doesn't look too healthy,' I said, completely ignoring her question.

Nyrah sighed. 'My brother's in charge of the garden, but he's been away for a month. He comes back next week, and if I've let anything die, he'll never let me live it down. Not that I *want* to let anything die – I need this for my wards. I just can't work out what's wrong with it.'

I walked over and looked at the plant a little more closely. 'You've been giving it lots of water?'

'Yes.'

'I think that might be the problem.'

'Sorry?'

'Its leaves – the waxiness of them – it's a type of plant that doesn't need much water. And is the sunlight it's getting direct?'

'Pretty much.'

'Try moving it to a more shaded corner. Maybe under the canopy, let the light filter through instead. I think you've been killing it through kindness.'

Nyrah looked at me, a small, curious smile playing on her lips.

'Okay. I'll give it a try.' She pulled her hands out of the soil and dusted them off.

'Oh, and you might want to break up the roots a bit too. Gently,' I added, looking at the state of the soil. 'If they're too clogged, it could be hard for the water to reach them properly.'

She tilted her head. 'Well, you really like your plants.'

'I would have,' I said, sighing. 'Actually, looking at all this, I wonder if at some point I could take some cuttings? For my own place.'

'That'll be a question you'll have to ask Vincent – my brother. But I'm sure it'll be fine. Especially if you end up saving this one.' She tilted her head to the side as she looked at me. 'Is there anything else I can help you with? Or did you just come to talk about flowers?'

The lump that had filled my throat before I'd stepped into the garden returned, although I was now decidedly less worried that Nyrah would curse me for invading her time.

'No, the flowers were just an added bonus,' I admitted. 'There are a couple of things I wanted to ask you about. About the wards you put on me.'

Her expression tightened. 'I figured as much,' she said, before she glanced at her watch. 'Well, I don't have another appointment for forty-five minutes. What do you say we grab a coconut, go down to the water and chat?'

'A coconut?' I raised an eyebrow. 'An actual coconut?'

Nyrah laughed. It was the first time I'd heard her laugh like that before, and it was a beautiful sound. Melodic. Ethereal even. 'Oh wow, you've never drunk coconut water before?'

I shrugged. 'Well, I've had those little cartons of coconut water from the supermarket, if that's what you mean.'

She shook her head, still laughing as she led the way out of the garden.

'It's not. It's definitely not. Come on. You're in for a treat.'

FORTY-THREE

How was this my life? I was a vampire, sitting on a beach, about to drink coconut water out of an actual coconut while sitting next to a... a what? A witch, I assumed, but I wasn't sure. Either way, it didn't feel real. And not just because of the para aspect, but because of the view. The sun was low in cloudless sky, while waves gently lapped against the shore. Seagulls - or at least I assumed they were seagulls and not shifters - were dipping in and out of the water as music drifted from somewhere in the distance. This was the type of place I had dreamed about visiting. Not somewhere I thought I'd go, let alone live. Ravens Hollow was one heck of a place, that was for sure.

Nyrah had led me away from the shop to a little shack on the beach, where a woman with a massive cleaver had cut a hole in a green coconut, stuck a straw in the top, and handed it to her. And just as she'd said, it was delicious.

'You can have it with a shot of mango hooch if you like,' Nyrah said. 'It's the way most of the locals have it.'

I was definitely tempted, given how the others had spoken

about it before, but it felt wrong to add something to my very first coconut.

'Maybe next time,' I said, to which Nyrah nodded.

'I'll have mine straight, too,' she said, before paying, picking the two coconuts up and handing me mine. 'So, the fact that you're out in the day is a good sign. That sunlight ward I put on you is obviously working.'

'Yes,' I said. 'It's incredible. I'm so grateful. But it's not that one I wanted to talk to you about. It's the *other* ward.'

Nyrah's lips pinched together, and she nodded slowly. 'I thought as much. Whip told you?'

'He did,' I said.

Her expression remained pinched. 'I'm sorry I did it without your knowledge. That's not something I normally do, put wards on people without them knowing. I get if you're mad.'

It hadn't even crossed my mind to be mad at Nyrah, or Whip, for that matter. They had both thought they were doing a good thing. And they were. But now I realised that was why she'd assumed I'd come; to have a go at her for meddling with my mind.

'I'm not,' I told her. 'I mean, I fully understand why you would do it, but I need to know if there is any way to test if it's working?'

'What makes you think it isn't?' she asked.

How much detail did I want to go into here? I thought. Not much, that was for sure. 'There's just been a couple of... incidents,' I said.

A slight smirk lifted on Nyrah's lips, and she tilted her head, eyeing me with amusement. 'Let me guess – you saw the police chief again, and you *still* wanted him to get his handcuffs out?'

'Pretty much,' I admitted with a sigh.

Nyrah took a long sip from her coconut before drawing in a

breath and looking at me. 'Thing with that particular ward –
it's easy to know if it *is* working, harder to know if it's *not*. But
there are a couple of things... well, one mainly, that you can
use to test.'

'Okay, what's that? What do I need to do?' The sooner I
could find out, the better.

'You don't need to do anything. Not really, I just need to
know if he has annoyed you at any point since I put the ward
on you?'

'Sorry?' I said, confused by the question.

'Has he irritated you? Have you found yourself with a
desire to yell at him? Seen him as anything less than perfect.'

'Well, obviously,' I said. 'I mean, before he told me about
the power, there was a moment... and then there was the argument we had in his car about Macoy Belkin, him telling me
when I can and can't take risks in my job, despite the fact he
barely knows me, so yes, I would have happily tried to slap
some sense into him.'

'Then it's working,' Nyrah said.

'Sorry?'

'The ward is working.'

I frowned. 'Are you sure?' I said, remembering the feeling
in his office, when I had been so desperate to lean forward and
kiss him. Surely there had to be some kind of magical power at
play.

'Absolutely. That's a *seriously* powerful sign. Even people
who disagree with him still can't get properly annoyed with
him – they just kind of... take it. And from what he said about
you, and the effect that his emotions had had on you the first
times you'd met, the only way you'd actually be angry at him
is if his powers were having no effect on you.'

'So, the fact that I wanted to kiss him...' I said, not sure if I
even wanted to hear the answer.

Nyrah's lips twisted into a smirk. 'Was all you, I'm afraid.'

'Shit,' I muttered, letting out a long sigh. I was into Whip. And Whip was into me. It should have felt good, but what it actually felt was... well, terrifying. Like I needed life in Ravens Hollow to get any more complicated.

FORTY-FOUR

After our discussion about Whip, Nyrah needed to head back to the salon. Apparently, they were open twenty-four hours a day, to cope with all their clientele's sleeping habits, but by the sounds of things she had plenty of staff, meaning they didn't have to pull long shifts too often. I didn't envy her. It was only late afternoon, but I was feeling ready for bed myself. Pongo, bless his little furry paws, had walked all the way to the shop, and I could hardly blame him when, still ten minutes away from home, he refused to walk any further.

'Why do you feel even heavier?' I said as I carried him the final part. 'You know, I'm not getting another car, so if it ends up with you and Bobby fighting for space, we're going to have problems.'

As a soft snore rolled from his lips, Pongo didn't so much as flick his ear in response. So now, I knew where the saying *it's a dog's life* came from.

'Evergreen?' I turned around to see Alex, and his lion's mane of hair striding towards me. A smile involuntarily rose on my lips which was immediately reciprocated by a grin from

him. Alex was a man who oozed boyish charm. While Whip
had a dark mysterious air that drew you into him, Alex had
this ineffable ease that seemed to do the same. While Whip's
presence made me excited in a way that I wasn't sure I'd ever
felt, Alex's somehow relaxed me to the same degree.

'You taking a bit of time to see the town?' he asked when
he'd caught up to me. 'From what I hear you sure as heck hit
the ground running.'

'That's definitely one way of putting it.'

'But you're settling in okay?' he said, an unusual level of
seriousness forming in his expression. 'You don't need
anything?'

'I'm good, I think. Although from what people have said, I
really need to try this mango hooch.'

'Done. I'll grab you a bottle when I next go past the auto
shop.'

I let out a laugh. 'You don't have to do that,' I said.

'I know I don't. I want to.'

As he grinned, his eyes locked on mine and caused a deep
fluttering in my chest. What the hell was this. I couldn't have a
crush on Alex, could I? No, not when Nyrah had only just told
me that the ward was working meaning the feelings I had for
Whip were genuine. But what were those feelings exactly,
other than physical attraction?

'I... I should get back,' I said, clearing my throat as I
attempted to swallow the lump that was filling my throat. 'He
needs his sleep.'

'Sure thing,' he said. 'Catch you later, Evergreen.'

Back at home, I placed Pongo in his dog bed - which I'd
positioned at the foot of mine - and let out a wide yawn. The
effects of Weirdough's cappuccino had well and truly worn off
and I vaguely contemplated the idea of having some more
blood, but after the deliciousness of the coffee, I wasn't sure I
could stomach a blood bag. Besides, would it be that terrible if

I went to sleep at 6pm? After all, I probably wasn't past all the jetlag yet, and I definitely wanted to sleep.

I drew the curtains, blacking out the room, curled up in bed, and I was asleep as soon as my head hit the pillow. And there was a good chance I would have stayed that way all night, had it not been for the ringing of my phone.

The noise may have been what woke me, but the moment my eyes flickered open, I was distracted by the pressure on my legs. As if something heavy was pushing down on them. Apparently, putting Pongo to sleep in the dog bed didn't mean he would stay there. Good to know. Shuffling him off me so that I could move, I reached to my bedside table and picked up my phone. My eyes went first to the name. Then to the time. It was five to eleven in Ravens Hollow meaning that it was what, three-ish in London? And yet Donna was ringing.

'Donna? Is everything alright?' I asked.

'Yes, yes, everything's good. Is now an okay time? It's evening there, right? I thought you'd be up and about. Oh god, I've woken you up, haven't I?'

I stretched out the cricks in my neck as I switched on the side lamp.

'It's absolutely fine. It really is. Is everything okay?'

Donna paused, as if she wasn't sure whether she could carry on, but given she'd already woken me up, I was glad she did.

'Well, just thought you'd like to know I got some more satellite pictures through,' she said. 'Of the basilisk egg. And it's hatched.'

'It has?' I was surprised by how relieved I was to hear the news. I guess I'd been worried about the incubation abilities of a lion onesie, not to mention the egg's journey across land and my chosen hatch-ground.

'Anyway, I thought you'd like to see them,' Donna continued. 'I mean, it's not very exciting, I'm afraid. They didn't get the basilisk in the snaps. But the hatched egg is there. I'll send them over now.'

My messages pinged a second later, and I opened up the photo. Sure enough, there it was. The picture was grainy, given that it had been zoomed in by quite a distance, but still, I could make out the long grasses and the fresh water of the stream, not to mention the hatched egg. A shudder at the memories of that journey poured through me. If I never went to that entire island again, I would be happy. I was about to say as much when I looked more deeply at the image.

The edges of the egg were blurred slightly. The clarity was lost due to the magnification, but its texture looked vaguely familiar. Almost like papier-mâché.

All the hair on my arms rose as my stomach lurched and a sense of deep uneasiness flooded through me.

'Sorry, Donna,' I said. 'I've got to go.'

FORTY-FIVE

I felt guilty that this was the first time I had actually looked properly through the book Chloe had lent me, but I was also infinitely grateful that I had it. While the tome was massive, like Chloe had said, it was logically organised, and something told me I knew which section I needed to go to.

'If I'm right about this, you have to stay here, you understand?' I said to Pongo. 'You are way too little to face whatever this is.' He looked at me, his head tilting to the side.

I continued turning through the book, searching for something capable of inflicting those multiple blows that had killed Wren Belkin. As my eyes skimmed across one of the pages, the air rushed from my lungs in a gust.

'God, I hope I'm wrong,' I said aloud, grabbing my telephone and scrolling straight down my contacts list.

It was all very well for Whip to saying I needed to contact somebody as soon as I discovered something, but I didn't have his number. So I tried Bobby first. Nothing. Then Chloe. The same. Twice I tried the police station, and both times it went to answerphone. I only left a message once. Fingers crossed if

Josephina could find a way to turn on YouTube, then she could find a way to forward it to Whip, but I didn't hold out much hope.

'They're still guarding the tent, right?' I said, to Pongo, pretty sure he didn't have a clue what I was saying. 'Three days. That's how long the Mayor said they needed before they could move the exhibition. If Alex is there... or Whip...' I leaned down and pecked Pongo on the head, who seemed to finally grasp that he was about to be left. He let out a low whine. 'I promise, when you're bigger, boy. But not now,' I said.

Slipping my phone into my pocket, I grabbed the book and ripped out the page I'd been reading

'Crap,' I said as it came off in my hand. 'I could've just taken a photo.' Still, it was too late to worry about that now.

As I raced toward the marquee, I tried the police station again.

'Josephina, this is Elodie Evergreen. You need to tell Whip to get to the marquee, okay? Wren Belkin's exhibition tent, and fast. I know what—'

The message was cut off as I reached the end of the answerphone call, only a few metres away from the tent. Though before I moved any closer, I stopped. Blood. I could smell blood. And not just blood, but blood, and salty sea air, and honeysuckle.

'Alex!' I sprinted those last few meters to the tent opening. Alex was there, face down on the ground, a large gash on the back of his head.

'Please be alive. Please be alive,' I whispered as I dropped down next to him. His body was prone on the ground and for a split second, I considered rolling him over to his back to check if he was breathing, but I stopped myself. The last thing I needed was to worsen his injuries. And it wasn't like I actually needed to feel for a pulse. I needed to listen.

'Come on Elodie, focus!' I hissed at myself before gritting

my jaw. A moment later, it happened. That surge of noises that evaporated into nothing but silence, and then... the sound I wanted; a weak thud-thud of a heartbeat, accompanied by a shallow wheeze of air moving in and out of his lungs. Alex was alive, but he needed help.

I reached for the phone again, realising I had no idea what the number for the emergency services was. Was it 911 for para emergencies too? That didn't seem likely. I raked my mind, trying to work out what to do, when I heard a noise coming from inside. I jolted upwards. How many people guarded the tent?

This time, the effect was instant. No surge of noise. Just the silence and then sounds coming from inside the tent. Buzzes. Light, fast buzzes, and then... another heartbeat. A raised heartbeat, far faster than Alex's. Was whoever was in there in danger? Did they need my help? If pulse rates were anything to go by, then the answer was a resounding yes.

'I'll be back,' I whispered as I pushed myself up to standing. 'You're going to be fine. Whip'll be here any minute.'

I wasn't sure if I'd said the last bit about Whip turning up for Alex, who probably couldn't hear, or myself, but either way, it was a thought I was going to hold on to. Whip would show any second. I just needed to make sure everyone stayed alive until he got there.

Steeling myself with a breath, I whipped open the entrance curtain to the tent, searching for the sign of the security guard with the pulse. Only two steps in, I discovered I wasn't going to be so lucky.

There, on the floor, was a security guard. Like Alex, he was face down on the ground. I didn't bother kneeling beside him as I narrowed my hearing onto the body, desperate to hear that repetitive thud-thud, of the airy wheeze of inhales and exhales, but as the seconds passed, I had to face the truth. He was dead.

And yet, that heartbeat I had heard before I entered the room continued to beat. My eyes lingered on the body for a moment longer, before I shifted my gaze around the tent. There, standing behind one of the largest sculptures, was a man.

I'd never seen him before in person, and even in the images I'd seen, he hadn't looked like this. Mainly because in those he'd been fully dressed.

Now, his torso was bare, while his bottom half wore only a pair of boxer shorts. Calvin Kleins. His sandy hair was swept into a side part, glistening with salt water, yet somehow he managed to maintain an air of superiority. Something told me this was a man who liked his expensive suits and watches. His piercing blue eyes held the colour of the ocean within them while in his hand, he was holding one of the exhibition's smaller sculptures. The item was only around five inches tall, and covered in black resin.

'Macoy Belkin,' I said. 'I need you to put that egg down and step away.'

FORTY-SIX

Despite the dead body at my feet and the fact that the man in front of me was the notoriously ruthless head of the mermaid mafia, I was strangely calm. Was it because I was a vampire and possessed phenomenal strength? Was it because Macoy was just in his tighty-whities? Or was it because no matter how scared I should have been, the thought of a mermaid mafia was still enough to evoke a giggle?

Then again, maybe my confidence came from a different place. Maybe it was because I had worked it out. I had figured out who, or what, had killed Wren and her colleagues. I knew what she and Macoy had been up to all these years. And that gave me a whole different sense of power.

Coldness emanated from Macoy's body as he took a step towards me.

'I don't believe we've met,' he said, as if we'd just been introduced at a party.

'No, we haven't,' I replied coolly. 'My name is Elodie Evergreen. I'm the one who's gonna be writing an article on how you and your wife have been smuggling mythical creature eggs around the world – using your connections and her art to transport them. I'll also be the one to bring you into police custody.'

I would have thought my words would have given him just a little cause for concern, but he looked completely at ease.

'Elodie Evergreen.' He stretched out the syllables in my name, a smirk twisting at the corners of his lips. 'That name is familiar. Where have I—' His head tilted to the side, his eyes narrowing before his lips parted into a round, *oh,* shape. 'Oh. You're *that* Elodie, aren't you? The one who got the better of the Guardians in London. And you chose to come to Ravens Hollow? Interesting.'

My stomach flipped. The Guardians weren't the ones who turned me directly, it was one of their sires, but still, tomato-tomato. Every decent person I'd met referred to them as vampire traffickers.

Macoy's smirk deepened. 'Well, that's interesting, isn't it? I know some people who will be *very, very* pleased to know where you've ended up. From what I've heard, there's been quite a search for you.'

The hairs on the back of my neck prickled, but I refused to let the feeling settle.

'The police are on the way,' I said. 'You're not going to get away from this. Your egg trafficking enterprise ends now. If you turn yourself in, maybe the judges will see that as a show of good faith.'

If Macoy was perturbed, he was once again doing a damn good job of not showing it. Instead, he lifted his hand and twisted the sculpture containing the egg within his grasp, as if he had all the time in the world.

'Whatever happens tonight, I can assure you that both myself and my enterprise will survive,' he said eventually. 'Certainly, it will change. There's no doubt about that. But that's what us survivors do. We evolve. We adapt. That's what keeps us at the top of the food chain.' His eyes had a silvery coldness to them, and I desperately wanted to look away. But how fast did mermaids move? Faster than vampires? I didn't think so, but did I want to take that bet? No. What I needed to do was stall him until Whip arrived. Whip would be able to sort the situation out. Wouldn't he?

God, I hoped so.

'You know, I'm pretty sure I've sabotaged one of your plans before now,' I said. 'A basilisk egg? One that was trafficked in London? It's now hatched and living in the wild in a place you'll never find it.'

'Is that right?' His eyebrow arched.

'Yes, it is. I've seen the photos. Safe to say it's thriving out there.' Yes, I was embellishing a little, but he didn't need to know that. 'So what's that one?' I said, looking at the item in his hand. 'It's far smaller than the basilisk's egg was, so I assume it's something different?'

He held up the sculpture. It was impossible to believe that it was the same shape of the egg it held within, but Macoy gazed at it as though it was the most wondrous item he had ever observed. 'This little beauty is worth a fortune. And It's going to pay for my passage to wherever I want,' he said.

'More expensive than the basilisk egg?' I said, keen to keep him talking as long as possible, but also out of genuine interest.

He sniffed. 'Substantially. It's a Lidérc egg. Wren herself was going to look after the hatchling. But now...' He shook his head, brushing his cheek as if a tear had fallen – though I could see no sign of such a thing. 'Anyway, like I said. It's rare and expensive, and that's all you need to know.'

That wasn't true. From a journalistic point of view, there was a lot more I needed, or at least wanted, to know. Like, where was he getting these from in the first place, and who the hell was he selling them to? But I thought it unlikely that he'd disclose those pieces of information. I didn't even know what a Lidérc was, but I wasn't going to let him know that either.

'What about the hydra? Was it more expensive than that?' I said. 'You know about the hydra egg, don't you? The one that killed Wren when it hatched before her exhibition. I assume Thor and Esmeralda died trying to catch it for you?'

He scoffed as his face hardened. 'No. They got themselves killed. Thought they could catch a bloody hydra of all things. I mean, the old ocarina trick works to attract them, but then you have to know what you're doing once they come to you. And they did not.' His expression softened as he shook his head and let out a long sigh. 'But my poor Wren. I told her she needed to think of the temperature changes. Creatures hatch quicker in warm weather. I thought after all this time, she had come to grips with that, but obviously not. That's what caught her by surprise. My poor, poor darling.'

I recalled the photos I had seen of them together online. The way they had looked so very in love.

'So the divorce was all for show, right?' I said. 'To make sure people never suspected Wren and you could still be in cahoots.'

Rather than responding, his eyes narrowed. 'Ms Evergreen, as much as I am enjoying the conversation - and learning what a great asset you'll be to The Guardians when they find you – and they will – I have grown tired of your delay tactics. And I think we can both agree that if reinforcements were going to turn up, they would be here by now, don't you think?' He smirked before clicking his neck from side to side, rolling his shoulders as if he was warming up for a fight. 'Tell me, Ms Evergreen, have you learned much about mermaids? About the magic they possess?'

I bit my lip.

'Oh, my goodness.' His smirk widened. 'In that case, this is going to be even more fun than I thought.' And with a flick of his wrists, he put down the egg, only for a full fist of claws to flick out from his knuckles.

This was not good. Not good at all.

FORTY-SEVEN

Mermaids had claws? Since when? That hadn't made it into any of the fairy tales I'd read or watched as a kid. You could mark my words that if – sorry when – I got through this, I was going to write Disney a very strongly worded email.

Still, I was a vampire. I had super strength, super speed, super hearing – I was *not* going to be killed by a mermaid, of all things. There was no way I'd live that down. It would be far too humiliating.

Unfortunately, the mermaid in front of me definitely looked like he had murder in mind. I should have seen if Alex or the guard had a gun on them. Not that I had any idea how to use one.

'There's poison at the end of these, you know,' he said, flexing his fingers so that the dim light reflected off his claws. 'It fills the tips of our spines, much like a lion fish.' He glanced down at his hand, twisting his wrist, admiring the weapons he had protruding from his knuckles. 'It has an effect on most creatures,' he continued. 'Not all, but most. And unfortunately for you, vampires are not impervious. I've seen it firsthand.

More than once.' The smile he flashed me was full of menace and enough to override any amusement I'd found at seeing him in his underwear. He wasn't bluffing. He had used those claws before. Many times, if his reputation was to be believed. Yup, perhaps the reason Macoy felt so comfortable strolling around in his underwear was because most people knew better than to laugh at him. Still, he was certainly a fan of his own voice. 'Most mermaid venoms offer just a sting,' he said. 'A sharp sting, but not much worse...mine's a little more potent. Probably won't kill you, but the pain...? Oh, you'll have never felt anything like it. It'll make your death feel like a birthday party. I've heard it can get to the brain, too. If I get enough in you. Let's see if I can manage that today.'

Trying not to panic and run out of the tent as fast as possible, I scanned the exhibition space. I needed a weapon. But there was nothing like that in here. Just the sculptures and the stands they stood on.

'Come on Ms Evergreen,' he goaded me. 'I'd expected a fighting spirit, and I have to say, I'm disappointed.'

'You really want to do this?' I said, hoping that maybe there was still going to be some way out of this that didn't end up in me having to fight. 'You won't just admit that you've been caught and come in?'

'Caught?' He laughed, his top lip curling upward. 'By who exactly? Lois Lane with no pulse? No, I'm afraid you're the one who walked into this situation, Ms Evergreen. And you're not going to walk out again.'

My jaw clicked side to side as I considered my response. I could still run. That was still a possibility. I could bolt for the door, grab Alex on route and race to town to find Whip. But then Macoy would get away, and I couldn't let that happen.

'First,' I said in a very slow and considered manner. 'I want you to be aware that this is entirely of your doing. You brought this on yourself. And second...' I contemplated what my next move was as I scanned the array of sculptures around me. 'I hope you're fast.'

I didn't wait for him to respond. Instead, I spun on my heel and grabbed the nearest sculpture to me. The artwork was balanced on a plinth, and was about the size of a rucksack, not to mention far heavier than I'd anticipated, but in this particular scenario, that was a good thing. Before a normal person would have a chance to blink, I lifted the sculpture above my head and hurled it at Macoy.

I watched in what was close to awe as it flew through the air. My aim was spot-on. My strength, incredible. Had I been up against a human, they would have been floored. But Macoy wasn't human, and as it turned out, he was fast. Not vampire fast, but fast enough that I had underestimated him. His shoulders dropped as he twisted his body to the side to move out the way of the incoming projectile. The sculpture missed him by a whisker, rushed past his ear, and smashed into another one of similar size.

'That was my wife's work,' he growled from the shadows as he took a side step around the outside of the tent like it was a freaking boxing ring. It looked like he genuinely cared. He took another step, and I did the same, keeping distance between us. Though I wasn't going to let him get to the doorway. Not a chance.

'If you want to save your wife's work, then just give up, Macoy. I don't have to break any more of these. But I can...'

'Don't you dare.' He clenched his fist. Before he moved, a sound from the other side of the tent stole both of our attentions. A low hissing which echoed back where the broken sculptures lay.

Something was slithering out of the broken shards. Something scaled, with a low reverberating hiss. Its slender body coiled back and forth as it wove its way across the ground. I hadn't read much of Chloe's book, and I hadn't even glanced at the page where this thing was written about. But I was well aware what it was, because less than a week ago I'd been terrified of one hatching while I was trapped on a plane with it.

'Seriously, Macoy?' My disbelief was almost enough to override the absolute fear I was feeling. 'How many basilisk eggs have you trafficked!'

CHAPTER
FORTY-EIGHT

It had been bad enough when I'd been worrying about the basilisk egg hatching before I'd got a chance to drop it off somewhere on the island, but now I'd gone and smashed open another. Well, at least I knew what all the buzzing noises I'd heard in here were: heartbeats of animals in eggs. And now one of them was out in the open.

'Just let me walk out of here with the Lidérc egg, and you don't have to get harmed,' Macoy said.

The fact that he had changed his tune so quickly didn't make me feel good. In fact, it made me certain that perhaps, right now, I needed to be more worried about the basilisk than Macoy. And if I'd needed any more confirmation of that, it came in the form of Macoy's heartbeat. It was so elevated, I didn't even need to concentrate to hear it. I could practically hear it battering against his ribcage. The man was terrified. And that was when I remembered Donna's warning: the moment a basilisk hatches, it hunts.

Sure, it didn't look that big – certainly no thicker than my wrist – and had this been the normal world, I wouldn't have been worried about it making a snack out of me. But this wasn't the normal world. This was para life, where a newly hatched hydra could bash the chest in of the woman who had trafficked it, and yet the same creature could be called from the depth of the sea with a freaking ocarina.

Yup, there was a lot about this world I didn't know.

The serpent had slowed its movements as its tongue flickered in and out of its mouth, and its head was very much facing in Macoy's direction, not mine. Whether it was its sense of smell or thermal sensing, something about the merman was more attractive than my dead body – and I wasn't complaining. But I hardly wanted a fourth death in Ravens Hollow by illegally trafficked animals, even if the victims had brought it on themselves.

No wonder Macoy looked ready to faint. For the first time since I'd seen him, I had the upper hand, and I fully intended to use it.

'How do we kill a basilisk, Macoy?' I said. 'Tell me how to kill it, and I won't let it kill you. Provided you give yourself over to the police, that is.'

The snake's head swivelled in my direction, its tongue flicking the air a few times like it was testing the scent. I froze, trying to work out whether it would be feasible for me to jump out of its reach if it came to that, but before I'd even figured out where I was going to jump to, it had turned back to face Macoy. Though I wouldn't have thought it possible, the mermaid paled further.

'It's blind right now. Attracted by heat and sound. Vibration,' he whispered so quietly that without my vampiric hearing, I wouldn't have caught it. 'You have to break its neck.'

Its neck? If you'd asked me yesterday, I'd have bet good money snakes didn't have necks. Was Macoy just messing with me?

The beads of perspiration weaving down Macoy's forehead and the look of blanched terror on his face said otherwise.

Right. So, pick up the basilisk, snap its snakey neck. Easy. Although there were also the fangs to think about.

'What about its venom?' I whispered back, only Macoy didn't respond. Mermaids clearly didn't have super hearing. And if I was to speak at normal volume, I would draw its attention back to me.

'If you're going to do something, now would be a great time,' Macoy hissed, as the snake slithered closer to him. The guy was trembling, and it wasn't helping his situation. All those vibrations were more than enough for the blind basilisk to pinpoint him.

I contemplated my options one more time: let the basilisk go for Macoy, hope the snake didn't want a meal immediately after its appetiser, and get out of there as quickly as possible. Or help the egg-smuggling, underwear-wearing, claws-on-a-goddamn-mermaid villain. God damn it, sometimes I hated having morals.

I wouldn't be able to live with myself if I let a man die.

The basilisk had its back to me, meaning all I needed to do was run at it full speed, grab it behind the neck, and twist, right? That was the plan. Though as I lifted my foot, a sound from outside the tent caused me to freeze mid-step.

And not just me. The snake, now only a matter of feet away from Macoy, had stopped, too. Its head was turning in a slow curve back towards the doorway, its tongue tasting the air with its constant flicking.

Panic rose through me as I homed in on the sound. Fast footsteps. I could tell that much. Was it Whip? It didn't sound like a human running, but then he wasn't human. And whoever it was, I needed to warn them that they were attracting the attention of a newly hatched basilisk, hungry for its first meal. But how could I do that without attracting the basilisk's attention myself?

Macoy was as rigid as one of the sculptures, and from the way his eyes were moving back and forth, I could tell he was trying to figure out how to get out of the tent and away from the basilisk. But the only way to do that was to go past me to the doors. Either that, or try to get under the fabric edges of the marquee, which would cause too much noise and attract the serpent. He needed to stay where he was. That was non-negotiable.

I had to protect Whip.

'Whip, there's a basilisk in here!' I yelled at the top of my lungs. 'Don't come in!' The snake swivelled so that its milky eyes were looking directly at me, its tongue flicking out between its fangs. Fear surged through me. It knew where I was, but at least Whip wouldn't come in. At least he would figure something else out. That was what I thought, until the snake's head twisted again, this time towards the rustling doorway.

My heart lodged itself all the way up in the top of my throat as the flap opened. What the hell was Whip doing? Had he not heard me?

My gaze dropped. Air rushed from my lungs.

'Pongo?! What are you doing here?' I gasped, staring at my four-legged bestie. Yet before I could recover from the shock, he lifted his paw and barked twice. Loudly.

The basilisk's head swivelled straight toward him.

FORTY-NINE

I didn't care how much noise I made. I leapt across the space to Pongo, scooped him up in my arms, and dropped him onto the plinth that the egg had been upon before. He barely fit, with his wide, furry paws squished up together, but it was the only place I could think of to keep him safe for a couple of moments, anyway. Which was all I was intending on it taking for me to kill this damn basilisk.

Pongo continued to shuffle, trying not to fall off the plinth, so the serpent knew exactly where he was, and moved accordingly. Thankfully, that meant it didn't notice as I grabbed it with both hands. I tried to squeeze tightly, only my hand slipped in the gooey slime from the egg that still clung to its body. So much so, that it nearly got out of my grip. Still, I squeezed tighter with my right, feeling the sandy smoothness of its scales as it writhed.

I'm holding a freaking basilisk.

I'm holding a mythological creature, and the only way that my dog would get out of this alive was if I kill it. It wasn't exactly doing my bit for animal welfare, but hey, I'd helped one of these hatch less than a week ago. I guess I was just setting myself back to zero.

Had I thought for even a moment that it was a normal snake and not a paranormal creature, that thought evaporated as it fought against me. I'd not fought a non-mythical snake since I'd turned vampire – or ever, for that matter – but I was sure as hell they weren't as strong as this. My shoulders burned as I'd tried to secure my grip on it, but it wasn't going to work.

The only way I was going to snap its neck was if I had my hands firmly around it, but now that it realised Pongo was currently off the menu, it redirected its attention. To me.

Its body squeezed around my arm so hard I felt the bones crack. I gasped in pain. Pongo barked, leaping from the plinth onto the ground and rushing towards me, as if he was going to help. And I admired his resilience – seriously – but there was no chance I was going to let him near this thing. He'd be dead before he'd even lifted an adorable paw.

'Shush! Please, Pongo, be quiet.' I didn't bother lowering my voice. Not when I wanted to keep the basilisk's attention focussed solely on me. 'You need to stop barking. I need to work out how I'm supposed to kill this thing...'

I glance across the tent to where Macoy had been standing a moment ago, only to see that he was using this distraction to get away.

'Pongo! Get him!' I yelled, nodding my head towards Macoy. I was wrestling a mythological snake, trying to stop it from eating my dog, or possibly me. The least said dog could do was to ensure the trafficker didn't get away. Pongo tilted his head to the side and offered me his paw. Although this time, he managed to do so without the two barks. Still, I was holding a mythical, venomous murder noodle.

'You and I are going to dog training school as soon as we get out of here,' I told him, only to feel a rush of air close to my upper arm. The damn basilisk almost got a bite in. I had to end it now. But I needed two hands to wring its neck, and that meant letting go of it – just for a microsecond – so that I could get my left hand in and use all the strength I'd got left.

It's no different to the hearing.

I had no idea if that was true or not, I just need to focus.

Pongo was still barking, and Macoy was only inches away from the tent doors. I needed to kill it now. And I couldn't mess it up. If I did, Macoy would get away, Pongo would become basilisk chow, and I had no idea what happened to a vampire if a basilisk got its fangs or gaze on one.

Rather than focusing my attention on the sounds, the way I had done before to isolate a source, I focussed on me. I was the one who needed to move. Who needed to do this. Who needed to be fast enough to killed the damn thing. I drew in a breath, locked my sight on the place just below the basilisk's head, and let go with the only hand that held it.

Time didn't have a bearing as I released my hands from around the scales, and before the creature even registered the loss of pressure on it, I was back with a proper grip. Without a heartbeat's consideration, I twisted. Seriously twisted. The type of twist you do when you're determined to wring every drop of water out of a swimsuit so it doesn't drench your bag. I felt it beneath the scales. The pop of the bones.

One last hiss sounded out into the night as the animal went limp in my hands. The relief and feeling of victory lasted just as long as it took to turn and see the tent flap wafting as Macoy raced for his escape.

'Over my dead body,' I muttered before glancing back at Pongo. 'Just don't get in the way, okay?'

FIFTY

I hadn't realised how stuffy it had been inside the marquee until my first lungful of fresh air, free from the mucousy stench of broken eggs, though a fair amount of it still coated my hands. There was no point wiping it on my jeans. No, I was going to wipe it on Macoy's tighty-whities when I got hold of him.

On second thought, stopping him from getting away without touching the Calvin Kleins was going to be the priority.

He was several feet away from me, and, surprise, surprise, he was heading straight towards the sea. I might not have known about mermaid claws, but I was sure the whole tail thing was going to be spot on, meaning that if he got in the water, I had no chance. Thankfully, vamp-speed running was one thing I could actually control. So I had a very clear, albeit very loose, plan. Catch him, avoid the claws, and then work out what to do next.

My feet barely touched the ground as I raced in his direction. The soft grass gave way to shell-littered sand beneath my feet as I reached out to grab hold of him. Unfortunately, there wasn't much other than his undies to grip, but my fingers tucked into the elastic waistband, and I yanked him backwards. The effect was an almost comical deceleration on Macoy's part before he toppled backwards towards me. I darted around him, avoiding a collision as his back slammed into the sand, and blocking the route between him and the water.

The air rushed from his lungs, though whether the pained expression on his face was from the way his back hit the sand and shells, or from the massive front wedgie he got when I pulled him back by his underwear, it was impossible to know.

'Bitch,' he spat, glaring at me as he scrambled to his feet. 'You're not going to get away with this.'

'I'm pretty sure I have,' I said confidently. There was no sign of the Lidérc egg, which I assumed meant it wouldn't survive underwater. And if Macoy was willing to leave without it, then he must have realised he had no other choice. Still, the last thing I wanted was to go one-on-one against those mermaid claws. Not without an extra weapon to support myself.

The only things around were waves, sand, and shells? Sharp shells?

I crouched down, picked up the largest I could reach without moving my feet or taking my eyes of Macoy, and snapped it in half. In terms of blades, it was only a couple of inches long—but it was going to have to do.

'You could just turn around, hand yourself in to the police station, and be done,' I told him. 'We don't need to fight.'

A smirk flickered up at the corner of his lip.

'You know, I think the Guardians are going to be ever so pleased that I've rid the world of you for them,' he sneered. 'And I do so love making powerful connections.'

'So that's a no to turning yourself in then?' I said. 'Fair enough.'

I didn't waste any time. Instead, I lunged straight for his side, slicing the sharp edge of the shell beneath his ribs.

A hiss of pain seethed from between his teeth, though the cut had been a shallow one. Enough to slow him? Maybe. Enough to stop him? No chance. I moved to go again, only for Macoy to kick up his foot and spray sand into my eyes.

'Crap!' It was my turn to seethe at the grainy sting in my eyes, although after a few powerful blinks, my sight was perfectly clear. Another tick for vampire powers, although when extra strong blinking would be needed again, I wasn't sure. Not that I was giving it much thought. I was ready to finish this. This time, when I went for Macoy, I didn't hold back. With the shell clenched between my fists, I struck at the top of his thigh.

'Bitch!' he screamed, though I had already removed it and was going for my second strike on the top of his arm. This time, I struck so hard, the shell embedded itself in his flesh.

With half my attention on Macoy and half looking for another weapon, I stepped back.

Deep green blood oozed from his body. One more strike between the ribs and he'd be properly down. But could I do that? Could I kill him? I had already killed two vampires. Why would this be any different? He was already weakened. And it wasn't like he hadn't killed. So why shouldn't I give him the ending he deserved?

This was different because I didn't have to do it. That was why. I could beat him without killing him. He wouldn't get far with a wound like that. And there was a way to make sure he didn't go anywhere at all.

'Elodie!' I could hear the voice calling my name, but I couldn't let it distract me. Macoy was still trying to make it to the water. With one hand, I grabbed him around the waist, pulling him back into me, as I picked up another shard of shell.

All I had to do was hold him there. Whip was coming. Whip would finish it off.

'Macoy Belkin! Stay where you are!'

It was Whip's voice, and the phrase *better late than never* was about to cross my lips, but before I could, Macoy reached his hand upwards. One quick swipe. That was all he got, but that was all he needed. The pain seared down my arm.

Jesus. He wasn't joking. Mermaid venom hurt like hell. The pain was blinding me. But I couldn't let him go. I swung my arm in the air again and again, not knowing if I was hitting Macoy or just empty air.

'Elodie! Elodie!' I heard the voice drifting somewhere in the ether and felt a pair of powerful hands grip my shoulders as they tried to hold me firm. But I couldn't stop. I couldn't let Macoy get away. And so I kept on swinging and swinging, my knees and arms growing weaker and weaker, until the pain grew too much and the world went black.

FIFTY-ONE

I t felt like the worst hangover of my life. Every part of my head throbbed. But how the hell was that possible? I hadn't had a drink last night, had I?

Had I?

I was having difficulty remembering what had happened the night before.

I cracked the case. I remembered that. A hydra. That had killed Wren...not to mention Thor and Esmeralda. One by one, images flashed through my mind.

Macoy in the tent. The egg in his hand. His claws, that venom... I had got him, hadn't I? I couldn't remember that part. I could remember stabbing him and then the pain and then... and then the voice. Whip?

That had been Whip's voice calling to me, I was sure of it. Had he come? Had he got Macoy? If he hadn't, then he needed to hurry. He needed to catch him before he could heal and get away.

I tried to sit up, but a searing pain ripped through my arm.

'What the hell?' I gasped. 'I thought vampires weren't supposed to feel pain.'

'Common mistake.'

I blinked my eyes open, though it took me a fair few attempts to open them properly and actually see something. When my sight had finally adjusted, I turned slowly to look at the figure beside me.

'Chloe?' I said.

She was in a seat beside my bed, and her eyes were red-rimmed. She'd been crying.

'Elodie,' she said. 'Finally, you're awake.' She reached forward as if she was going to embrace me in a sudden hug. Then, likely remembering our first encounter, she backed away. 'You had us so worried,' she said. 'You've been in and out of consciousness for four days.'

'I have?' I said, hearing the disbelief in my voice, although from the way my head throbbed, I thoroughly believed her. Four days? I'd doubled my time at Ravens Hollow and not seen a second of it. 'My God. Have you been here the whole time?' I asked.

Chloe shook her head. 'We've been taking shifts,' she said. 'Well, most of us have. This one's been here every second of the day. He hasn't left your side. He even insisted on taking his meals in here.'

Pongo. Pongo was lying right next to me, although in only four days he'd grown even more.

'You're such a good boy, aren't you?' I said, stretching slowly across to him to rub his head. With the most excited wag of his tail I'd ever seen, he lifted his paw and placed in on my lap.

'Yes, you're a good, smart boy. You're my best boy.'

I was still fussing over Pongo when I remembered Chloe was still there, though when I turned back she was staring at me, as though she had just witnessed a miracle.

'I can't believe you did it,' she said. 'I can't believe you worked it all out. Macoy. The trafficker. How did you do it?'

'What happened to Macoy?' I said, a sudden panic hitching my voice. 'Did Whip catch him? There are eggs. The sculptures, they're not just sculptures. They're eggs. And Alex? What about Alex? Is he okay?'

'Don't worry,' Chloe smiled. 'It's all sorted now. Alex is fine. Well, a bit beaten up, but he's healing up well. Well enough to get you that, anyway.' She nodded across the bedroom to where a large plastic crate was filling the corner.

'Is that...'

'Twenty-four bottles of mango hooch,' she said. 'Should keep you going for a while. And in answer to your other question, Whip got there while Macoy was still on the ground, thanks to you. He's been taken off the island now. There were seven other eggs in the exhibition. Can you believe that? And you still haven't explained how you worked it out.'

My whole body drooped as I let out a sigh of relief. They had caught him. His trafficking days were over. For now, anyway.

'I knew it all stemmed from the money. She was making deposits far bigger than the price of her paintings, so she had to be selling something else. Something illegal, most likely. And using her art exhibitions around the world were an obvious means of whatever it was. I also remembered the Mayor saying how Wren's people didn't want the sculptures moved. How they were susceptible to the environment. If eggs aren't incubated at the right temperature it can stop the hatching. It all just clicked into place.'

'That's incredible.' The way Chloe beamed at me, you would have thought I solved the mystery of the Mary Celeste.

'Well, you helped,' I said, flashing her a smile.

'I did?' she said.

'Yeah. If you hadn't given me that book of yours, I would never have worked out what had killed Wren and the others.'

Chloe's expression narrowed. 'Speaking of which,' she said. 'I saw the book downstairs. Did you rip a page out of it?'

A flush of heat coloured my cheeks.

'Sorry. I wasn't really thinking straight. Story blindness type thing.'

Her frown deepened as she shuffled closer. 'If you ever do that to any of my books again, we will have problems. But, considering you're alive and everything, I guess I'll forgive you.' Her frown broke into a wide grin as she took my hand and squeezed it tightly.

'I need to call the paper,' she said. 'Let them know you're awake. Nyrah too. She's been checking in daily. Bobby's even had June covering some shifts with you when the rest of us couldn't make it.'

June, Bobby's wife who I hadn't even met? A surge of gratitude flooded me. This town took community to a whole new level.

'Well, what shifts Whip would let us take, that is,' Chloe added.

'Whip?'

'He's been here every day,' Chloe said. 'Most nights, too. He'll be so happy you're awake. Speaking of the devil.' Her smile slanted to the side, and I moved my eyes to the doorway. There, leaning against the doorframe, was Whip.

'I'll leave you to it,' Chloe said with a smirk.

As I struggled into a better seated position, Whip held the door open for Chloe, then closed it behind her and walked over to the bed. So much for Chloe saying he'd be happy to see me.

His face was thunder.

'Elodie Evergreen,' he said. 'I'm pretty sure I gave you a very specific instruction. You were not to tackle things on your own.'

'You did,' I said. 'And I tried to contact you. I did, but if I hadn't gone when I did, Macoy would have got away.'

'I know.' He dropped his head into his hands. 'I know, you have no idea how horrific... Josephina, she tried, but—'

'Whip, it's fine,' I said. 'It's all okay. I'm okay.'

'But I shouldn't have let you go on your own. I knew how reckless you were. I should have done more to stop you.'

I would have loved to have seen him try, although I didn't say as much. Instead, I took his hand and met his gaze.

'The thing is, Chief Inspector, I don't have to agree with everything you say to me.'

'Yes, you've made that very apparent.'

'You're not listening to me. I don't have to agree with everything you say to me. Or anything at all. What you think has no bearing on me.' A smile lifted on my lips, though his brow remained furrowed.

And then, just like that, I saw the penny drop.

'The ward?' his eyes widened. 'It works.'

'One hundred percent.'

His expression shifted. 'Which means...'

'It means a few things. Like you can't be overprotective and stop me doing things, like tracking down the Guardians.'

A fresh wave of horror washed over his face. 'Elodie, you can't be serious!'

'I can. And I am,' I said firmly. 'I need to be. Every person here knew who I was, when I came, right? You all knew me as the person who killed the Guardian.' He nodded in agreement. 'Meaning it's not going to take long until one of the Guardians has found out this is where I've moved. If they don't already know. And something tells me they're not going to let a nobody like me get away with killing one of their head honchos.'

'We'll protect you. I'll protect you,' Whip said. The

certainty in his voice was enough to make my unbeating heart ache.

'That's sweet of you to say. It is, but I don't plan on putting anyone else, including you, in danger because of me. One way or another, I'm going to end up facing them. I'd rather go into that situation armed.'

He pressed his lips tightly together, as if he was biting his tongue. But the fact that I wasn't having conflicting thoughts about whether tracking the Guardians down was a good idea or a terrible one was another sign that Whip was no longer able to influence my thoughts.

'We need to think about this from the positive angle,' I said, adjusting my position and wincing at the pain.

'There's a positive angle to you telling me you're planning on taking down a ring of ruthless killers?' He said, with his most withering look.

'Well, there's a positive angle now that we know that the ward is working. Because now if you ask me for a drink and I say yes, it'll be because I want to say yes, and not because you want me to.'

The fear was still there, but there was a twinkle in those green eyes, too.

'And if you feel like you want to kiss me again?' he said.

'Well, that would be very presumptuous of you,' I said, unable to suppress a grin. 'I think you should probably ask me for the drink first.'

'Right. Of course. But if I really, really wanted that kiss...' Our eyes were locked, and I could feel the grin stretching my cheeks. Did I want to kiss him?

Yes, but I was only a week into my life in Ravens Hollow and time was one thing the two of us had plenty of. I could take this slow. And there was also Alex to think of. Kind, sweet Alex who made me smile in an entirely different way. And yet, my body moved involuntarily towards Whip's, closer and closer until...

'Ow! Pongo!'

Whip and I sprang apart as my dog bounded on to my lap and ran a slobbery lick up my cheek. I struggled to stop his wagging tail from knocking me sideways. Whip and I sprung apart.

'I guess he wants us to go on a date first,' Whip grinned as he leaned forward and ruffled the dog's fur as he planting a gentle kiss on the top of my forehead, causing a thousand butterflies to erupt inside me.

'Sounds good to me, just as long as you know he'll probably want to come along.'

EPILOGUE

From up above came the rustling of wings in the rafters, though not a single pair of eyes moved to see whether the sound was made by a bird or bat, or something more sinister. Perhaps because all the people gathered there already knew the truth; there was little more sinister in all existence than those assembled around the table.

Twelve bodies, all cloaked, with their hoods raised, looked to the thirteenth person. The one who sat at the head of the table. Like most of those gathered, the only part visible of them was their hands, the fingers of which were wrapped around a tall stemmed wineglass. Their red nails glinted.

'Numbers?' she said. Though she only spoke a single word, it lilted with venom.

'Expanding,' a man to her left responded. His voice was higher in pitch than hers. Unnaturally squeaky. 'But... but it is slower than anticipated. Marginally. Fluctuations are to be expected, Mistress. In any business.' He spoke rapidly, as if he expected a reprimand.

Apparently, she didn't consider his comment worthy of a response.

'It was London, Mistress,' another male took over, though the tremble in his voice was only marginally less than the first. 'The Guardians are fearful.'

'Fearful?!' Outright laughter. Tighter and melodic, yet somehow shrill enough to cause a shudder down each and every one of their spines. 'What happened in London is laughable. And anyone who is fearful of such an occurrence does not deserve the gifts that have been bestowed on them. You would do well to remind your Guardians of that.'

A second shudder ran through the other participants. It wasn't just a warning to the Guardians. They knew that. It was also to them. Slip up, and you would pay the price. Immortality was great, until you came across a stronger or more cunning immortal. As the situation in London had proved. Not that it was an immortal who caused the trouble then. No, just a nosy journalist with impressive throwing skills who had turned a standard transformation and relocation into the biggest mess they'd had to deal with in over a decade.

'Talking of Elodie Evergreen,' the woman spoke again, 'has it been confirmed that she is now living in Ravens Hollow?'

'Yes,' the squeaky voice spoke again. 'She has taken a position at The Oracle there. The paper.'

'And is she being monitored?'

A slight pause filled the room. So quiet that those few heartbeats that still drummed did so at a volume loud enough to rattle the room. One or two shuffled in their seats until another voice spoke. Another woman, who, unlike the men who had spoken so far, pushed back her chair and stood up.

'She is being monitored, Mistress,' she said without a hint of trepidation. 'I have seen to it. I have someone on the island. Someone who will ensure that she does not get in our way.'

Another silence took hold. A collective breath remained

held as all the silent participants waited for the mistress's response.

'And how, exactly, is your person doing that, without drawing attention to our little enterprise?'

'They have been keeping their distance, but it is their intention to get closer to her every day. To ensure that what needs to be done can be done, if it comes to that. Though for now, they do not believe there is any imminent risk. According to my source, she knows nothing.'

'And you trust them?'

Though it couldn't be seen in the darkness of the cloak, or the dimness of the room within which they sat, a small smile twisted at the corner of the woman's lips.

'I trust them with my life. Believe me, Elodie Evergreen will never see it coming...'

THIS ELODIE ADVENTURE might be over, but how about a fresh perspective with a bonus chapter? Send me my exclusive bonus chapter.

HEXES AND HEADLINES PREVIEW

Bunny Bandit.
Jewellery thief turns out to be the
family pet.

I stared at the title of my current article, not sure if I should laugh or cry. Over the course of the day, I had interviewed the family in question, watched on as Diego took photographs of said rabbit, and written a four hundred word piece on the light-fingered floof, who'd been stealing things from its owner and taking them back to their hutch. To be fair, it wasn't a bad article. It was heartfelt and humorous, not to mention packed full of details, from the dates the owners had first reported items going missing to the police, to the neighbours they'd fallen out with over the suspected thievery. Neighbours who were all too happy to pose for photos and insist that it was all water under the bridge.

In terms of the type of easy-reading fluff piece people wanted to find in a small island paper, it was bang on the mark. Only I hadn't spent years working up the career ladder to write fluff pieces. I was an investigative journalist. Or at least I had been, before one of those investigations led to me losing my pulse and being thrown into the paranormal world. Now I was a vampire, living on the other side of the world, writing stories about thieving rabbits.

In fairness, my move to Ravens Hollow had meant to be a chance to slow down. To get used to this new version of me. Not to mention the island and town that I had moved to. But that plan of a quiet pace had been derailed when, on my very first night here just under two months ago, there'd been a murder at the annual art festival. As the police struggled to work out who was responsible for the gruesome death, it had been all hands on deck. Well, that's what I'd decided, anyway. I'm sure my new boss, Bobby, the editor-in-chief of the Ravens Hollow Oracle would've liked it if I'd slowed down a bit and taken my time settling into the paranormal community, rather than turning up on their doorsteps with a series of probing questions. Especially given how new a vampire I was – still am, for that matter – and how little I knew about the para world by then.

However, if I *had* slowed down and taken a backseat to the story, I wouldn't have uncovered the illegal egg smuggling operation happening right under our noses. And it wasn't chicken eggs we were talking about. No, these were paranormal creatures. Basilisks, Hydras. The report we got from the police even said there was a hippogryph egg in the mix. So... yeah. That had been one heck of an introduction into paranormal life. Thankfully, the people involved had been arrested – those who weren't killed by the creatures, that is – and operations shut down. After that, it was time to start enjoying normal life as a Ravens Hollow resident. Or as normal as it could be when your neighbours were a pixie and a poltergeist.

Three months ago, I would have thought anyone who said something like that was clearly taking something, but I genuinely was neighbours with a pixie, who loved gardening almost as much as they loved playing the piccolo, and a poltergeist who threw things at said pixie whenever they'd had enough of the music. I had to admit I was grateful for the interventions, given that it meant I didn't have to complain myself and would normally get a few nights' peace and quiet afterwards. Not that my house was completely quiet. Not with all the training I was doing with Pongo.

Still, other than the nighttime serenades and time spent walking and training Pongo, life was incredibly slow. Which I loved. But I was missing the rush that came with a decent story to investigate.

The bunny bandit fluff piece was pretty much on par with everything else I'd written over the last eight weeks, which included a write-up on a group of non-shifter seagulls that got drunk on an open bottle of mango hooch – the island's favourite tipple – and an extended piece on a red-panda-shifter who was using her own fur to make clothes. I never thought being a vampire could be dull. And yet, here I was, wishing something would happen.

The only thing that was worth any of my time were the hunting restrictions that had been placed on the island. Despite there being a total of five werewolf packs and various carnivorous shifters who called Ravens Hollow and the surrounding land home, they had been reduced to hunting in only sixty percent of the forests. While the mayor and the council maintained it was in the best interests of all the inhabitants, many residents disagreed, insisting it was actually putting the biodiversity of the landscape at risk. Two such residents were Ines Ortega and her sister Sofia.

I was working with Ines to get the story the attention it deserved, but it was difficult. The matter had been brought to the attention of the council almost a month ago, and they had yet to come back with any solutions.

As I stared at the computer, I let out a long sigh, then opened up an email, ready to ping the article across to Theodora, the copy editor.

Snack. Snack. Snack.

The single word echoed up from the floor by my feet.

I looked down. Pongo – the stray puppy I'd found when I first moved to Ravens Hollow – was aggressively hitting one of his multiple buttons sprawled out beneath my desk. Button-training Pongo was a work in process, and though we were now up to over a dozen individual words, occasionally he'd hit the wrong one and had to correct himself. But the way he continued to thump on the piece of plastic, he knew exactly what he wanted.

Snack. Snack.

'Don't worry, Pongo. I've got some,' Chloe said. My work bestie focused mainly on sports and events on the island and had a desk opposite from mine. 'Come here, boy.'

When I first arrived, the fae's hair had been a delicate lilac, but now it was a hot pink. She looked equally great in both.

'You should probably give him a couple,' I said as Pongo trotted over to her. She grabbed the jar of dog treats – which were even more expensive than the ones I got him – and unscrewed the lid. 'He always wants more than one.'

'I'm not surprised,' Chloe replied, dropping a few by his feet. 'I can't believe how much he's grown in the last few weeks. Do you know what breed he is yet?'

I bit down on my bottom lip, not really wanting to answer.

When I'd first found Pongo, he'd been a skinny ball of matted fur, and obviously I'd expected him to fill out and get bigger, just not at the rate he'd been doing so.

He was now at least double the size he had been. And with his mix of dark and light brown markings, my research had been annoyingly conclusive. As much as I didn't want to admit it, I was fairly sure I'd gotten myself a Leonberger.

Before Pongo I'd never even heard of the breed. Now though, I knew more than I wanted to. Like the fact they could grow up to 170lbs. Which meant that even though he was already bigger than the average springer spaniel, he had a lot of growing left to do. He was already decimating my food budget, which I could deal with, but a more major issue was that I drove a Mini. A vintage Mini. The type where anyone over five foot seven struggled to even get inside. If he kept growing, the only way he'd fit in the car would be with the window wound down and his head hanging out. Fingers crossed we had a long time until he got there.

'Oh, I'm sure he's just some kind of mixed breed,' I said, flashing Chloe a hopeful smile.

A moment later, the speaker buzzed again.

Thank you, it said. Chloe beamed.

'You're welcome, Pongo,' she said, her smile growing wider still. 'You're such a polite boy, aren't you?'

She slipped another biscuit out of the jar and handed it to him, carefully avoiding my gaze, as if I wouldn't notice.

'Those buttons are such a good idea,' she said. 'I can't believe how easily he can communicate with them.'

'I agree,' I said. 'The only problem is, now he wants to bring them everywhere with us.'

'Well, that's a good thing, isn't it? Means you can always know what he's thinking.'

'True, I suppose.'

Dog training had started in earnest after I'd recovered from a nasty mermaid venom sting. Mermaid venom. I wouldn't have believed it was an actual thing if I hadn't experienced the agony myself. But hey, I had the scar to prove it. A very thin hairline scar that ran along my forearm. Considering I'm immortal, I assumed it would have disappeared, but it had turned a soft silver, and I had the feeling it was going to be with me for life. However long that was.

Pongo wasn't to blame for me getting cut. The venomous scratch came courtesy of the former head of the mermaid mafia. But Pongo had turned up at the scene, desperate to help and protect me and that was something he just couldn't do. Firstly, because he was a pup, but also because he wasn't the best at listening or follow instructions. Even getting him to sit had been a trial. So, we'd started button training. So he could tell me exactly what he wanted.

It had its advantages. But I wouldn't say it was without problems either.

Bored. The word buzzed up from the floor. *Walk. Bored. Walk. Bored. Bored.*

'You and me both, buddy,' Diego said, strolling across from his desk on the other side of the office. 'It's a bit slow here, isn't it? Don't worry – you'll get used to it.'

'Believe it or not,' came another voice from across the office, 'some of us do still have plenty of work to do. So it'd be great if you could keep the noise down. I need to get these copy edits done before we go to print.'

'Sorry, Theodora,' the three of us chorused.

The Ravens Hollow Oracle was a lot smaller than the paper I'd worked at in London. Just six of us in total. Initially, I'd assumed I'd find it claustrophobic, working so closely with such a small team, but the truth was, they were great. Even Theodora, when she wasn't on deadline.

'Speaking of work...' Dylan said, coming over to join the three of us. 'I need to speak to some advertisers. Thought I might as well make the most of the sun and take the call at the beach bar. Fancy coming, Chloe?'

Whilst I knew what type of paras both Chloe and Diego were, I had yet to figure out what sect Dylan and Theodora belonged to. One thing I had figured, however, was that Dylan was hopelessly in love with Chloe. But she was engaged to Mick, a man I had never met, but who was known island wide, first for running the only auto shop on the island, and secondly for being co-brewer of the famous mango hooch.

'Sounds great,' Chloe said. 'Only there's the wolf pack lacrosse tournament in Wraith Woods this afternoon. I'm going to head over there in five.'

'Next time then.'

'Of course,' she said, flashing him a smile that I, and everyone else in the office, could see made him melt.

'I'll hold you to that,' He grinned as he picked up his satchel and headed over to the door, before pressing his foot down on Pongo's button.

Bye, the speaker chirped.

'Bye, Dylan,' we replied in unison.

As the door clicked shut behind him, Diego leaned closer to me.

'Have you been listening in to what's going on in there?' he said, nodding his head towards Bobby's office.

I'd more or less got to grips with my vampire senses now, including tuning in and out of different noises at will, instead of just whenever my body decided I should. Like me, Diego's hearing was well beyond that of a tip, and most paras too, meaning we could both listen into conversations going on behind closed doors if we wanted to.

But Bobby was my boss, and a good one. That wasn't something I was okay doing.

'No,' I shook my head. 'Have you?'

'No,' Diego replied, his eyes still trained on the door. 'It's weird, though. Bobby never has his door shut like that. But this is the third time this week. Maybe we should, just to see if he's okay?'

'What are you whispering about?' Chloe said, her eyes narrowing on us. 'You know, it's really rude.'

'Sorry, you're right,' I said, not even sure why Diego and I had been whispering, anyway. It wasn't like Bobby would be able to hear us from inside of his office. 'We were just talking about Bobby.'

'Bobby?' Theodora said as she swivelled to face us. Apparently, she'd not been quite as focused on her work as she'd pretended. 'What were you saying?'

Diego and I looked at each other, mostly to decide which one of us was going to speak. There was no point hiding the truth from Theodora. As far as I was aware, she'd been working at The Oracle almost as long as Bobby, and if anyone was likely to know what was up with him, it would be her. But before either of us could say another word, Bobby's voice bellowed from his office.

'Just give it up! No, you listen to me. You call me one more time, and I'm calling the police. This ends now.'

Hexes and Headlines
RAVENS HOLLOW INVESTIGATIONS BOOK 2

When the bark definitely IS worse than the bite

A **deadly hex** is turning my newspaper colleagues' skin to bark – and it's up to me to find the magical killer before they strike again.

I thought moving to Ravens Hollow would be simple. One month into my new **supernatural life**, I figured my biggest challenges would be housebreaking my oversized puppy and writing fluff pieces for the local paper.

Then **dark magic** hits *The Oracle*, pulling me straight into an investigation tangled with vindictive sea witches, feuding werewolf packs, and ancient tree sprite magic even the coven can't crack.

Now I'm chasing clues with Police Chief Whip – **an immortal siren** cursed with secrets – and Alex, a too-**charming lion shifter** who knows how to get under my skin. But in a town where everyone hides something and magic always comes at a price, finding the truth could cost me more than I'm ready to lose.

And the vampire trafficking ring that turned me? They haven't forgotten about me either.

Note from Ella

First off, thank you for taking the time to read **Fangs and Front Pages**, the first book in the *Ravens Hollow Investigations Series*. If you enjoyed the book, I'd love for you to let your friends know so they can also experience this action-packed adventure. I have enabled the lending feature where possible, so it is easy to share with a friend.

If you leave a review **Fangs and Front Pages** on Amazon, Goodreads, Bookbub, or even your own blog or social media, I would love to read it. You can email me the link at ella@ellastoneauthor.com

Don't forget, you can stay up-to-date on upcoming releases and sales by joining my newsletter, following my social media pages or visiting my website www.ellastoneauthor.com

ABOUT ELLA STONE

Lover of all things magical, mysterious, and mildly chaotic, Ella Stone writes fast-paced urban fantasy with a generous pinch of paranormal drama, a splash of slow-burn romance, and enough supernatural shenanigans to keep your heart pounding and your tea cold.

When not plotting vampire betrayals or helping were-wolves find some clothes (and occasionally their dignity), she's usually curled up with a book, surrounded by cats who believe they own the place—and, frankly, they do.

Her books include the *Dark Creatures* saga, the *Bloodsucker's Blog* trilogy, the *Witchlight Magical Mysteries* (co-written with the brilliant Heather G. Harris), and the brand new *Ravens Hollow Investigations*—a series full of magical crimes, dangerous alliances, and secrets that refuse to stay buried.

Expect charm, danger, and just enough mayhem to make things interesting. Welcome to her world. It's weird, it's wicked, and you're going to love it here.